D1808508

THE JOURNEY
THEY NEVER
EXPECTED

THE JOURNEY THEY NEVER EXPECTED

EVELYN CARTER

COPYRIGHT © 2019 BY EVELYN CARTER.

LIBRARY OF CONGRESS CONTROL NUMBER: 2019901161
ISBN: HARDCOVER   978-1-7960-1361-0
             SOFTCOVER   978-1-7960-1363-4
             EBOOK   978-1-7960-1362-7

All rights reserved. No part of this book may be reproduced or transmitted in any form or by any means, electronic or mechanical, including photocopying, recording, or by any information storage and retrieval system, without permission in writing from the copyright owner.

This is a work of fiction. All of the characters, names, incidents, organizations, and dialogue in this novel are either the products of the author's imagination or are used fictitiously.

Any people depicted in stock imagery provided by Getty Images are models, and such images are being used for illustrative purposes only.
Certain stock imagery © Getty Images.

Print information available on the last page.

Rev. date: 01/30/2019

To order additional copies of this book, contact:
Xlibris
1-888-795-4274
www.Xlibris.com
Orders@Xlibris.com
789503

THE TRAVELER'S SURVIVAL INSTINCTS

Chapter One

Threngrin Stoneaxe stomped his boots on the ground, an attempt to warm his cold, numb toes. The snow hadn't melted completely yet even though it was an early spring.

In the valley below, the lights of the village beamed around the blackened, dark mountain, showing warmth among the dark meadows.

Threngrin was short, much like a small human. His face was round and broad. He had curly hair, and the tops of his feet were covered with coarse hair. He rarely wore shoes, except during winter. He preferred to be barefoot. He was not a forward type of person but was observant and conversational. When it came to fights, he ran and hid, but he loved to adventure.

He was one of his kind that lived at ground level. Most of his kind lived underground. His home was in a mountain hillside just on the edge of town, which was where he had lived all his life.

The town was small, but more and more people were settling here, making this their home. All different kinds, shapes, and sizes—people from all over came to start a new life. People came here to sell, trade, or buy as they passed through, and many just came to check the place out. The town started with only a few people. Threngrin and his family were one of the first settlers here. He had seen the town grow over the past years.

The place became a town when the town founder came here to settle and with her power and wealth began to make the town grow and give them what they needed, but the town founder also had a dark side, and if you double-crossed her, you would disappear without a trace. She could give, and she could take it away. Although no one had ever seen her dark side, they could only imagine what she would do. Many people had heard rumors of what she had done, but no one had ever seen or witnessed such an event. No one knew if the stories were true. They could only believe they were.

Many people were once adventurers and decided to settle and set up shop. Others stayed and worked for the town founder, mining stones, mining granite, or building homes for new settlers.

The small town was protected by a palisade built around it, with two guards positioned at the entrance and four guards walking around inside at all times. Even with the few guards they had, the townspeople considered themselves safe in their mountain forest. The people came to respect the town guards and learn to live with each other.

Threngrin leaned against the palisade at the north gate. His facial expression was thoughtful and relaxed. The day was calm and peaceful, full of life. Behind him was the great mass of the mountain, the palisade was the entry and exit, and the granite of the mountain kept unwanted guests out.

Threngrin was flushed from the heat of the sun beaming down on him. He just stood there staring into the woods, and he saw peace, adventure, but also danger. Sirra the Jewel Maker spotted Threngrin staring off into the distance. She slowly sneaked up to him and placed her hand on his arm.

"There you are."

Threngrin looked down at the small young girl's hand on his arm. They had been friends for many years, and the touch of her hand reminded him of their childhood and all the adventures they had done together in the past.

Sirra was short, stocky, and three feet tall. She had a big nose, ruddy cheeks, dark eyes, and black hair. She was strong and brave. She had no fear when it came to fighting. She was always cheerful, very social, and an outgoing person, and when it came to fights, she used her size to her advantage.

Although Sirra's father lived to be 301 years, he was a well-respected man, and he taught her how to fight and keep her ground. Her father loved being an adventurer and traveling, but his health got to the point where he couldn't anymore, and they settled here. Sirra wanted to carry on her father's dream, to be an adventurer just like him.

Sirra and Threngrin were just like most people. They loved to go out on wild adventures, with no idea where to go. Every summer they would set out to see what they could find. Some people would call it curiosity, some would say it's a death wish, and some would say someday it would get them killed, but despite what others said, they continued on for fun and adventure, to return with great stories to tell.

"Here I am." Threngrin giggled.

"So are we heading out on our fun adventure, to explore the land, to see what is out there?"

"Yep, we are, but—"

He was cut off quickly. "Where are we going? What direction should we go first? I think we go east—no, maybe west. No, I think north—yep, we should go

2

north, I like north. What you think? North?" Sirra said, talking really fast, moving her arms back and forth.

"I was thinking—"

"North, right? I knew it, you like north. So north it is. See you tomorrow." She gave him a hug and walked away.

Threngrin stood there watching her as she walked away. He had learned that he never gets a word in when talking with her. He also knew she didn't know north from south. As long they were out on their adventure, they could head east, and she would think they were heading north. She had no sense of direction. She would get lost in a brown sack.

The early sun barely started to rise, and Threngrin stood in the doorway, watching the leaves swirling on the ground. Threngrin lifted his mug and swallowed the last of his slop. It wasn't bad, it wasn't great, but it was gone.

With a slight sigh, Threngrin took his well-worn boots that was by the door and jammed them on his feet. He had some things to do before his long journey.

The day was cool but not cold, the sun began to cut through the thick trees, and Threngrin could feel the warmth on his head. The trade post was in the center of the western edge of town. Threngrin set out for the path leading to the bridge that crossed over a small stream. By the time his short legs carried him to the bridge, he had broken out into a sweat. This was a long hike for someone with short legs, but straight ahead he saw the trading post, not much farther to go.

Threngrin's mood changed when he reached the trade post. He noticed a group of travelers standing in the doorway. This group was rude and had no care in the world, demanding everything they wanted. Threngrin could feel their eyes on him as he made his way through the crowd and into the trade post.

Threngrin made his way to the counter. He gave a young man standing there his list. "I'll rustle up your goods," the young man cackled as he turned away.

"What are you staring at?" a demanding voice came from behind him.

Threngrin's eyes widened, and he shook his head and gave a snort to answer the question.

A little bony finger poked him in the middle of his back, enough pressure for Threngrin to notice. "I asked you a question." A little laughed slipped out from the voice behind him.

Threngrin never moved a muscle. He stood very still and stayed very calm. "I believe I gave you an answer."

"No, you never gave me an answer."

Threngrin took a small step sideways and turned. He was nose to nose with her. She wore a chain mail shirt that was very worn-out, along with a worn cap that was made from leather. Her boots were light, showing wear and strain from all the traveling. She rubbed her hands together as she looked at the shelves of food.

"You must be traveling?" Threngrin said with a slight grin.

"It looks like you are leaving town. Going somewhere special?" Sirra said, tapping her chin in thought.

"I've never met anyone who could be so observant as you are." Threngrin giggled.

"Well, I try my best." She laughed. "I try to keep an open mind."

"I know," Threngrin agreed.

Threngrin felt a soft squeeze on his arm. "So where are we going?"

At the sound of a burlap sack being slammed onto the counter, Threngrin jumped, knocking a jar of pickled veggies onto the floor. "Wow, little man, you can jump, and you jumped really high." Sirra laughed.

"A bag of apples, two pounds of bacon, hardtack bread, and a chunk of cheese. Is there anything else you need for your long journey?" he finished with a snicker.

"Yep, my jar of pickled veggies you made me drop on the ground."

"No can do. That was my last one."

"You forgot olives. You must have olives." Sirra laughed.

Threngrin glanced at Sirra as he reached into his pocket and said distractedly, "You've got to be kidding."

"No can do. I have none to give you," he said as he took the money for Threngrin's purchases and nodded his head good-bye.

Threngrin and Sirra headed out with their bags filled with food and supplies. They had everything they needed for their long adventure. After what seemed like hours of walking, they came to a place that didn't look right. Tall pine trees, with needles green, almost yellow, covered the forest ground. Thick vines and green moss covering the tree trunks were preventing the sunbeam from coming through. The forest was huge. Threngrin knew that shelter would be hard to find if danger should occur.

That feeling of danger, Sirra could sense it even as her mind wandered. Focusing real hard on the trail twisted around trees, ferns, and other fungus, she pushed away any fear she had. The air smelled of heavy decay, overwhelmed with thick fog that made it hard to see. Some parts of their surroundings were still covered with snow, and with the warm air, snow was beginning to melt, causing the air to become dense and making it hard to breathe.

The odor to Threngrin wasn't unpleasant. There was something joyful— adventure. It was like refreshment to his spirit, which brought excitement and delight to Threngrin's soul.

It seemed like many hours had passed, and they made very slow progress. It's not because they felt exhausted but because of the excitement within them. He kept his ears and eyes open, focusing on the woods, their surroundings, hoping for a sign of something good.

The trail came to a fork, and they paused, then stood there listening, thinking. Threngrin could feel the earth talking to him, the twists and turns of the land,

4

just as his father could. He could sense and feel the vibes from the surroundings of the land, and within minutes he knew which direction to go.

Threngrin decided to go north even though Sirra wanted to go south. They had no map and no compass, just a feeling and the surroundings of the land talking to him, and that led them deeper into the forest.

They pushed through the dark, thick forest, the air dense as they continued to follow the path, keeping a steady pace in hopes of getting through before nightfall.

Sirra glanced up into the tall trees and soon realized that they had to hurry. The sun would be setting soon, and this was not a good place to camp for the night. Sirra quickly picked up the pace. Threngrin grabbed the back of Sirra's cloak, holding on as tight as he could. The deeper into the woods they went, the darker it got. They knew it was yet early in the evening, but they also knew they didn't have much time before the darkness was upon them.

Threngrin noticed in the distance, even though it was very faint, a bright light. Not knowing for sure what it was, Threngrin took off running. "It's the end of the forest."

"Threngrin, wait! Come back, it might be something else."

Threngrin couldn't wait. He had to see what it was. Running as fast as his little legs could go, he quickly came to the edge of the forest. He stopped fast in his track. Sirra soon caught up to him, out of breath. Breathing heavily, they stood there looking over what looked like a river. There was a suspension bridge that crossed over the river, but it was falling apart and did not look safe. Threngrin had to see where the bright light was coming from. The bridge appeared to be missing boards. Some of the boards that were left were rotten through and barely hanging together. The ropes holding the boards together were also rotten. Some of the ropes were hanging down, and in some parts, the ropes were very loose. The bridge appeared to have been there for over fifty years with no one ever attempting to cross it.

Threngrin was very determined to get on the other side. He carefully placed one foot on the board in front of him. The bridge began to sway from side to side. Threngrin froze in place, waiting for the bridge to stop moving.

"Don't do this. Get back here!" Sirra yelled. "It's not safe, and it's a long way down."

"I must get to the other side. I have to go over there. Stop yelling at me!"

"Whatever you do, don't look down," she signed.

Threngrin couldn't resist. He slowly looked down. He gasped for air. He quickly held his breath, and his eyes got really wide when he realized he was 150 feet up in the air.

"Threngrin!" Sirra called out.

"It doesn't matter," he said to himself quietly. "I am going to get to the other side even if it kills me."

Threngrin lifted up his right foot slowly and placed it on the next board in front of him. The bridge moved again.

"Threngrin, this is really stupid. Come—"

"I am doing this with or without you," he said, cutting her off. "So shut up and follow me."

The next few steps were really tough. Boards were missing, and parts of the ropes were really loose. Threngrin managed to walk on the edge of the rope, keeping his balance straight. He finally made it to the next board. Sirra slowly lifted her left foot and placed it on the rope. Trying to keep her balance, she slowly moved toward Threngrin. She was inches away from him when the bridge began to sway. She froze in place, afraid to move, and fear quickly overtook her. Feeling nervous, she tried to stop shaking her legs and feet and focus more on her balance, but she was failing. Parts of the rope began to tatter slowly, the bridge started to shake, she could feel the ropes snapping under her feet, and she could no longer keep her footing. Before she fell, Sirra managed to grab a piece of rope hanging down. "Help!" she cried out.

Threngrin moved slowly toward the edge of the board and saw Sirra hanging just below him. He got down on his hands and knees. He reached his hand out as close as he could toward Sirra. "Grab my hand!" he yelled.

"I can't! I—"

"If you don't, we both will fall to our deaths. Grab my hand now."

Sirra slowly reached her hand out to his, but the rope broke. Threngrin caught her hand midfall. He slowly pulled her back up onto the bridge. The bridge began to rip apart, causing it to sway with more momentum. They had to move quickly before the bridge completely fell apart. There was no time to take it step by step. They took off hopping, jumping over missing boards. Just as they reached the last board, the bridge fell apart, falling down into the river below them. They barely made it. They both were hanging over the edge, holding on to a rock. Threngrin pulled himself up and then helped Sirra.

Sirra pulled herself together, and without a word, she punched him right in the face, knocking him to the ground, landing facedown.

Threngrin slowly sat up. "What was that for?" he said, rubbing his nose.

"You idiot! You could have gotten us killed!"

"But I didn't, and we made it," he said so proudly.

Since they took so much time crossing the river, the light had disappeared, and what little sun was there began to go down. Sirra noticed the sun began to turn yellow, trees began to disappear, the grass turned to sand, and the air thickened with dense fog, making it hard to see. They did make it though the dark forest, but they had no clue as to where they were now. They had no choice but to camp there for the night, next to what looked like two oak trees.

Chapter Two

The next day, Sirra decided to follow the riverbank, until they reached the end of the river. There were very few trees, and they noticed there was nothing but sand and dirt. Threngrin noticed this bright light again off in the distance. He stopped and pointed toward the light.

"No!" Sirra yelled. "You following that stupid light is how we got here, wherever here is," she stated, looking around.

But to Threngrin, it didn't matter. It had been one uneventful week of nearly perfect yellow skies. What could really go wrong?

Threngrin nodded and pointed in the direction of the light. They followed what seemed to be a dirt road. After what seemed like hours of walking, they finally reached what seemed to be a bridge. It was small and narrow. It was barely wide enough for a person to cross it.

"No, not another bridge!" Sirra yelled as she backed away.

"I am just going to check it out." His eyes were still focused on the light ahead of him.

As Threngrin walked slowly up, he saw a glass bottle lying next to the bridge. The glass bottle had something glowing inside. It was so bright, you could barely look at it. Without thinking, Threngrin bent down and picked it up. Threngrin rolled the bottle from side to side, even held it upside down, and with every move he made, the glowing inside the bottle got brighter and brighter. Then an awful sound came from inside the bottle, a sound they had never heard before. Threngrin finally learned how he could open the bottle. He placed his fingers on the little cap and pulled. He wanted whatever it was inside.

"Don't you—" But before Sirra could finish, Threngrin had already opened the bottle.

Green vapors encompassed the area, making it hard to see and very hard to breathe. The vapors were so strong, it started to burn his eyes. Threngrin threw the bottle to the ground. Sirra ran up to Threngrin, grabbed his arm, and pulled him across the bridge. About halfway across the bridge, the vapors began to disappear, and their vision became clear enough for them to see again. The bridge seemed long. It was like there was no ending, and just as they were about to give up, the bridge led through hill country, with a thick forest and foothills all around them. Here the vast dark fir trees surrounding them and chunks of rocks and granite were all they could see.

"Now what?" Sirra commented.

"Look!" Threngrin pointed. "The bright light."

"I think we should go this way. No more bright light or shining things."

"Don't you want to see what it is?" Threngrin asked with a grin.

"No! I don't care what it is."

"Come." And Threngrin grabbed her by the arm.

Sirra suddenly noticed some kind of fog rolling in. It was very dense and thick and had a horrible smell. She couldn't even see her feet in front of her. It was so thick, it was like they were wading through water. The air was so thick, it made it almost impossible for them to breathe. Feeling their way around trees, bushes, and vines, they quickly came to a small stream. Threngrin stopped dead in his tracks. He rubbed his head, then his chin, looking up and down the stream. Pacing back and forth, he rubbed his head again. Threngrin didn't like to wade in water. He was so afraid of getting wet. To him water was way too cold. It could swallow him up, and it made him itchy all over. It was like having a lot of spiders crawling all over him.

Sirra noticed how restless he was becoming. She reached for his arm, not saying a word, and pointed toward the right. There they decided to head toward the rock mountain.

After what seemed like miles of walking, they finally made it to the rocky mountain. There seemed to be no easy way up to the top. Looking around, she got this feeling that something wasn't right. It was way too quiet, and she felt as if someone or something was watching them. It brought chills down her spine.

Just as Sirra was going to take a step forward, a crackling sound put them on their toes. The ground began to tremble. Stones began to fall around them. The earth started to move from under their feet. Then it stopped. It was quiet.

"What was that?" Threngrin asked, holding on to Sirra's cloak really tight.

"I don't know, and I don't want to stick around to find out. Keep going." Sirra pushed Threngrin ahead of her.

They took a few more steps, and the crackling sound began again. The ground trembled, shaking around them. Rocks and larger stones fell, knocking them off the edge of the mountain.

Once the debris had settled, Sirra slowly sat up. All she could see was dust from the stones that fell around her. She started moving the stones one by one to find Threngrin, but he was nowhere to be found. She started to look around, not sure where she was. Then she noticed there was no way out.

After moving the last stone in hopes of finding a way out, she heard a moaning sound coming from the other side of the wall.

"Threngrin!" she yelled. "Threngrin!" Not hearing a response, she cried out again, "Threngrin, answer me!"

"I am here!" he cried out.

"You're alive." Sirra sighed and took in a deep breath, a sigh of relief. "But where is here?"

"Where are you?" Threngrin asked as he slowly rose to his feet.

"In what looks like some sort of room, and don't ask how I got here. But there has to be a way out. Start looking," Sirra stated as she ran her hands along the wall.

As she walked along the wall, pushing and punching, it seemed that there was no hope in finding a way out. Threngrin sat on the ground with his back up against the wall. "There is no way—" And he fell through the wall to the other side.

"Hello." Threngrin grinned while lying flat on his back.

A crackling sound came from underneath them, causing the ground and walls to vibrate around them. Waving one arm, Sirra motioned Threngrin over next to her. As he moved slowly along the wall on the opposite side of the room, the floor gave way, and they fell into a larger section of what they believed to be a cave. The room was filled with dust and debris, making it hard to see or to breathe. Sirra slowly rose to her feet and made her way to Threngrin. Once the dust settled, they noticed a strange deep cut in the rock. From the short distance, they saw two red glowing eyes staring straight at them. Sirra froze. Threngrin crouched low to the ground, covering his head with his hands.

They watched as this ugly, smelly giant creature moved gracefully toward them, as though it was daring them to make the first move. The creature stood straight up, standing seven feet tall and eight feet in length. The creature's head was large and black as tar. Its body was shining and a deep tan. Its feet looked like a horse's hooves, and its tail was tufted and white like a tiger's.

It opened his mouth wide, drooling, showing its ridged and dark-stained teeth like they were his next meal. Standing from a distance, they could smell its bad breath. The breath of the creature was as bad as it was ugly.

As the creature stood in front of them, watching them very closely, Threngrin moved slowly behind Sirra. Threngrin held on to Sirra's arm so nervously. He had the notion to lie on his stomach and wiggle his way out of the cave through the small hole in the wall.

The creature appeared to be observing them closely. He made no move to charge at them. He could bounce anytime and take them out quickly, but instead he stood there waiting for them to move first.

In a swift moment, Sirra saw an arrow pass her head and hit the creature on its side. A short stocky man appeared around the bend of the cave wall, which they didn't notice was there, a way out.

"Don't you move a muscle! You were inside the creature's mouth. Now you are inside its home, and he is pissed," he said in a low voice.

The man rushed toward the creature to toss a rope over its head. But he was a second too late. With the sudden movement, the creature leaped up and caught the man as he was tossing the rope up into the air. With the rope barely over its head, the creature opened its huge mouth, biting the rope and the man's head off with a snap. The body gushed blood everywhere, hitting Sirra and Threngrin as the creature shook his head from side to side, then tossed the body as though it was a rag doll.

Sirra and Threngrin froze, not moving as the creature's eyes turned toward them, as they were next in line.

Suddenly the creature opened its mouth and made a horrible loud sound. The sound was so high-pitched, it made their ears ring. They both dropped to the ground, covering their ears, trying to block as much of the sound as they could.

"What in the world is it doing?" Threngrin whispered.

"It's taunting us, calling a mate, I think," Sirra said in a low voice.

"So you understand the creature?" Threngrin giggled, squeezing her hand.

Sirra's eyes opened wide. "No! I don't even know what this thing is." Sirra let out a small chuckle. "I was just guessing."

The creature opened it mouth again, letting out another long, high-pitched screech. This time the sound was so high and so loud that the rocks above their head started falling around them.

"I think he might be saying, 'You are my next meal,'" Sirra whispered to Threngrin as she gave a crooked smile at him. Threngrin chuckled back.

Suddenly to their surprise, from the top of the cave, loud screeches echoed throughout the cave.

Eyes widened, Sirra noticed that there was a way out, but there stood another creature. This must be his companion coming for dinner. The creature paused and raised its head, sniffing the air, trying to find them.

The creature quickly turned his focus on them, and before they could collect their wits to move, the creature leaped right in front of them, surprisingly quick. The creature's claw struck Threngrin across the chest, sending him back, landing on the cold ground. Confused, Threngrin struggled to get to his feet, leaning up against the cave wall.

Again the creature let out a loud screeching sound. The sound rumbled inside the cave, causing large stones to fall around them, and they quickly scrambled trying to find cover. After pushing all the debris out of his way, Threngrin scrambled to his feet. He saw the creature lying on the ground a few feet away from them, twitching and wiggling. Odorous purple blood was gushing from the creature's head. Large stones struck the creature, surrounding it. Sirra slumped against the wall, dazed but unhurt. With some effort she waved at Threngrin with an assurance that she was all right.

Sirra slowly walked over to the creature. The creature was barely moving, and she stood there for a moment, then picked up a spear that was lying on the floor and stabbed it through the top of its head. Almost instantly, the creature took in its final breath.

Threngrin slowly walked over to the creature. It was as ugly dead as it was alive. With relief that it was over, Threngrin leaned up against the cave wall, and Sirra sat down, covering her face with her hands.

"Would you stop breathing on me?" Sirra shouted at him.

"I-I'm not," Threngrin stuttered.

Sirra and Threngrin held each other close, holding their breaths, afraid to make a sound. The other creature lingered around, watching, waiting for something to move. They both lay on the ground and covered themselves with branches and whatever was around them, avoiding making any sudden movement or sound.

The creature finally gave up, Threngrin watched as the creature made its way back into the cave. Not knowing for sure if the creature actually gave up or was playing games, they stayed put.

Sirra slowly turned around, her eyes opened wide. The other creature was nose to nose with her. Sirra scrambled to get to her feet, and the creature latched onto her leg. Threngrin leaped up and grabbed Sirra's arm.

"Don't let me go!" Sirra cried out.

The creature was way too strong for Threngrin to hold on to her arm. With one big pull, Sirra slipped through his fingers. He watched helplessly as the creature flung Sirra from side to side while screeching as loud as it could.

"Help!" Sirra called out.

Not knowing what he could do, he spotted a big boulder on the other side of the cave. Threngrin ran as fast as he could, picked it up, and threw it at the creature's head. The boulder bounced off the creature's head and came back toward it, knocking it down to the ground. Stunned and dazed, the creature released Sirra, dropping her to the ground. Threngrin grasped for air and managed to get to his feet and ran over to Sirra. He then grabbed her by the arm and dragged her out of the cave.

Limping and in a lot of pain, they scrambled down the hillside and hid in the first brush they saw. The creature came out of the cave screeching, standing straight up, and looking around, its nose up in the air, trying to get a scent to know where they could be. Sirra and Threngrin held each other close, afraid to move.

Hours later and not a sight of the creature, Threngrin stumbled on his feet. "We made it out alive," he said with a grin.

"No thanks to you. The next time you want to explore something shining, make certain we know what it is first, or the next time I will leave you on your own," Sirra snapped back at him.

"I-I saved us." Threngrin chuckled.

"You are as dumb as a wheel of cheese," Sirra commented.

"Wheel of cheese." Threngrin smirked.

Chapter Three

Everything became quiet, the sky became an orange yellow, and the air became cool. Sirra looked around. "Where are we now?" she asked with a worried look on her face.

"We haven't moved, we are in the same place, so what is happening?" Threngrin said with fear in his voice.

"Come, we have to move," Sirra whispered, grabbing Threngrin's arm.

They proceeded along the dirt road, hoping it would lead them to a better place than here. Suddenly Threngrin felt a tingling feeling throughout his body. It was a feeling like something or someone just went right through him.

They were not alone.

There wasn't anything around them, but Threngrin heard a sound, something approaching them. It almost sounded like wooden wheels from a wagon. Then just ahead of them, he saw a wagon. A broad-wheeled wagon, it looked more like a square box. Who was driving the wagon, and where did it come from?

Threngrin stepped off the road. It looked like it was heading right toward them. He saw the driver snap a whip, hitting the horse that was pulling the wagon. Threngrin couldn't tell what or who the driver was, or if it was something worse. Threngrin rubbed his eyes, thinking that maybe he was seeing things. He slowly opened them, and now he saw two more horses standing behind the wagon. As they moved closer and closer, he saw a set of unnaturally red glowing eyes.

Threngrin shook his head, feeling a little strange inside, not sure if what he was seeing was real or not. Threngrin thought about dashing behind a bush, but there was no bush to hide behind.

"What is it, Threngrin? You look like you have seen a ghost."

Threngrin raised his hand up slowly, pointing straight ahead of them. "You don't see them?" He watched the wagon and horses slowly disappear and reappear. But this time it seemed to be getting closer. He saw that their hair was a yellowish brown, their skin had a bluish tone, and their eyes were red and huge.

Sirra looked ahead of them, looking in all directions, but saw nothing. "Nothing is out there, chump. Come, let's move on, and time is wasting." Sirra grabbed Threngrin's hand, tugging him to move. They only moved a few feet, and the wagon appeared to be getting closer and closer to them, and with a quick glance from the corner of his eye, Threngrin noticed a stream of water on his far left. Threngrin stopped in his tracks, pulling Sirra back toward him, and took off running toward the stream of water.

Sirra stopped suddenly. "I am not feeling so well."

"What is it?" Threngrin's eyebrows shot up and down, feeling the same way.

Threngrin stumbled over his feet, and the color of his cheeks turned pale. He looked down at his feet. He was seeing double. "Well?"

Sirra quivered, leaning closer to Threngrin. "Nothing, keep going."

Threngrin paused, seeing something that was flying in front of him. Abruptly he shook his head, trying to clear his mind.

They finally reached a path that crossed another stream. Their moods had started to change. Sirra became fidgety, and Threngrin's temper had become very fretful.

The wind rushed across them, flinging up leaves and twigs. Above their heads, the clouds began to spin yellow and brownish. There was something there, something in the wind. Something gentle tugged at their clothes, something very gentle, and carefully tugged Sirra's hair. Then it disappeared into the trees and bushes. Sirra thought she heard voices softly murmuring, calling her. It was faint and at a distance. Sirra strained to listen, turning her head, slowly moving around to catch the sound and see where it was coming from.

Threngrin moved closer to Sirra, his breath coming out slowly as he grabbed Sirra's bag strap, trying to get her attention. Threngrin saw yellow and golden flowers that lined a path surrounding them. Tall trees and grass surrounding the stream looked different than before. Gazing at the stream, Threngrin felt alive. Something strange was going on, but he couldn't figure out what it was.

Threngrin spotted a large flat rock overlooking the stream ahead of them. He couldn't help himself. He had to check it out. Threngrin saw a green bottle with a long neck from deep within the stream of water. Threngrin bent down to take a closer look at the bottle. As he picked up the bottle, it made a chuckling sound. Inside the bottle, it looked like there was a small reddish box. Sirra ran up to Threngrin. "It's just a bottle."

Threngrin shot her a glaring look, like he was saying that it was more than just a bottle. Something else was inside, and he had to find out what it was. Sirra placed her hand on Threngrin's shoulder. "Wait!" she said tensely. "This is not a good idea."

He pulled out the cork on top of the bottle. The bottle fell apart, and the box landed on the ground. There was a slight hissing sound, and a yellow aroma filled the air around them. As they watched, the box began to glow very brightly. The top of the box flew off, and a light began to swirl within, forming different shapes. Then another blast of bright light—it was so bright, it blinded them. While rubbing their eyes, trying to regain their vision, Threngrin heard a sound, a low growling sound in the distance. It took only a few minutes for their vision to be restored, although they were still a little hazy. They were surprised to see everything had changed again. The flowers were gone, the stream was wider, and blue crystals were all over the place. The path behind them was gone, and large purple birds were flying above them like they were their next meal.

"Threngrin, you just had to open the bottle! What are you thinking?" Sirra yelled.

Threngrin's attention wasn't on Sirra or on the flying birds. He turned and headed toward what sounded like water running.

"Come, this way," Threngrin said as he took off heading in that direction.

As soon as they got within earshot of the running water, Sirra slowed down to a steady walk, while Threngrin broke into a run. Threngrin's legs pumped frantically as he sped past Sirra and almost went into the water before he could stop himself. It hadn't occurred to him that with his silly action, he could have fallen into the water, and with all that armor . . .

As Sirra approached Threngrin, she saw him holding what looked like a small jasper. It was deep green and had a tint glowing around it. It was something that they had never seen before. Not paying attention to what he was doing or where he was going, Threngrin walked right into the stream of water. At first he jumped as the waves covered his feet, but his attention was more on the shiny green jaspers.

"Threngrin! No, don't!" was all she got to say before he cut her off.

"Look, another and another!" Threngrin yelled as he was picking them up and putting them in his bag.

Little waves hit her feet with every step she made. The jaspers guided them farther downstream. She became more nervous as they continued on. The river was too close to the cliff side. The underbrush grew really thick along the bank, making it really hard to see anything.

The flow of the water began to move more rapidly. Something didn't feel right, something was wrong, though Sirra didn't think about it too long. She focused most of her attention on Threngrin, keeping a close eye on him. It was getting really hard to see as the overgrowth of bushes grew bigger and bigger, covering the stream, but in the shadows under the brush, the water started to form something black. It looked like parts of it seemed to be curving away from the cliff and was heading straight toward the middle of the river. There was a bright yellow haze that was so bright, it dazzled her eyes. It was hard for her to pay attention to Threngrin. She was more concerned and focused on what was ahead of them. Then she spotted it, but she didn't have enough time to tell Threngrin to look out.

The ground started to vibrate. The rocks around them began to rumble. A few minutes later, the ground shook harder and harder. Then the ground began to move—to the left, to the right, and back to the left, making it hard to stay standing. It took all their effort to keep their balance. Sirra became worried, her heart pounding hard, deep down in her chest. Her hands started to sweat, and she rubbed her fingers together. She tried to hold her breath, breathing as slow as she could, not moving an inch, waiting for something horrible to happen.

"What is that?" Threngrin asked.

"Someone or something you pissed off," Sirra snapped back.

"What? Me?" Threngrin sounded so innocent.

"You have to pick up everything you see. Can't wait. You can't just walk away and leave things alone, and you just have to have it," she said with disgust in her voice.

"Yeah, you know it. I have to keep up with my great collection." Threngrin grinned.

"Your collection!" Sirra snarled at him.

"My great collection. All things so—," was all he got to say.

Without warning, the river bottom dropped away. What was a sandy floor changed to a slope of rocks and black mud that fell off into a black hole. The water grew colder and colder as they continued to fall.

As they were falling down into the black hole, Sirra became frightened, fearing what would be at the bottom. She thought of an ugly creature with its mouth opened wide waiting for them. The thought of killing Threngrin also came across her mind. Once they had reached the bottom, it was nothing they had expected. Sirra flopped forward onto her stomach, landing on a pool of mud, and Threngrin landed on a pool of water.

A group of green glowing jaspers formed around them. They had a strange low-toned voice, a tone that could barely be heard, but there was something with more of a growling sound that caught their attention, a sound they'd never heard before. It was impossible to tell what it was. Not knowing its source, they had no way of knowing if it came from behind them or farther down the path.

Threngrin finally managed to get out of the pool of water. With a waterfall running down on his head, he had some difficulty getting his footing. Sirra was trying to get to her feet when Threngrin touched her shoulder and pointed. Still stuck in a pool of mud, she saw there was movement up ahead. It appeared to be vast in size, in the shape of a human being, but more of a huge creature coated with millions of shiny green jaspers.

Threngrin was fascinated with the creature. His eyes widened as he saw all the shiny green jaspers. He was so drawn to them, he forgot about Sirra and the trouble she was in. Threngrin watched as the shiny green jasper moved closer and closer to them. Still struggling to get out of the mud, Sirra felt something pulling on her foot. She immediately started to sink back into the pool of mud. Threngrin quickly noticed Sirra struggling to stay up above the mud. Keeping a close eye on the shiny green jasper, he reached out his hand but was unable to reach her, as he kept slipping and sliding in the mud. Sirra started to panic. The more she tried to move, the more she started to sink. Sirra then saw what looked like a log floating next to her. She was just at arm's length from it. She wiggled and kicked her feet, although whatever was holding her foot kept her from moving forward. She managed to free her left foot, and as hard as she could, she kicked whatever it was holding her, and soon she was free. She managed to pull herself through the thick mud to the log and pulled herself out. She wrapped her arms around the log, afraid to move. She was finally safe. Threngrin wiggled his way to Sirra and reached his arm out to help pull her to him. Just as Sirra was at arm's length away from him, the log moved. Sirra held on to the log tight, not letting it go. The log slowly started to rise, moving from side to side. She grabbed the log tighter. The log then moved faster and faster. She was losing her grip, and finally it threw her up into the air, her back hitting a stone wall with great force, and she landed on what seemed to be black goop. She slowly pulled herself together, rubbing the back of her head. She sat there out of breath. Then she glanced up at Threngrin. "What the hell is that?"

"Don't you know? I thought you knew everything." Threngrin chuckled.

Sirra scooped up a handful of goop and threw it at Threngrin, hitting him in the back of the head. "You think you are so funny," she snapped.

He did not even twitch, being amazed at the glow of the room. "Where are we? What is this place?" he asked in a calm voice.

Sirra looked around carefully. It appeared they were either in a cave or what looked like a small chamber of some kind. What appeared to be small arches supporting the low ceiling made the room seem like a cave. There were stone walls, water flowing through the cracks. The chamber smelled like mildew. It was very damp and cold. The air was very difficult to breathe. They had already encountered one trap. What lay ahead of them, and how many more are there? Her chest felt tight, and her lungs filled with mist in the air. There was anxiety in both of them that had never been there before till now.

Sirra's heart skipped a beat. She straightened very slowly, rising up to her feet, her mouth dry with terror. Her legs felt like rubber. She could take only a few steps before she had stopped.

Sirra had to learn the hard way not to trust anyone or anything she saw, and in this dark hour, she thought of her father. He had set out on one of his adventures but never came home. Since that time, long ago, she had to learn to survive on the pain of losing her father. Threngrin, she thought of him as her only family, yet she knew he was not much of a fighter. Although he did save her life a few times, fighting was not his specialty.

Chapter Four

Sirra and Threngrin focused on the surroundings, totally confused and lost. They had no idea where they were. The area seemed to be underground. Just how far underground, they couldn't tell.

Threngrin stayed close behind her, holding the back of her cloak tight, not letting go. Sirra ran her hand up against the stone wall, knowing that there had to be an exit somewhere. Keeping her hand on the wall, she kept her sword up, knowing that something could be hiding somewhere behind the solid stone, and this time she was ready. Water was steadily dripping, and the sound echoed throughout the chamber, making it hard to tell which way to go. She turned her head to look up, examining the stones above their heads. It seemed solid. There was no way of breaking through or telling what might be above them. Quickly she forced her attention ahead of her. Something caught her attention. There was something in the distance, something strange. There was something uneasy rolling in her stomach, and a feeling she couldn't explain.

Looking around this place, she thought it felt more like a trap. It felt like they had been in this position once before. They took their time watching every step and surveying the chamber. The ground was uneven. There was a puddle of water all over the ground from water leaking from the walls. As they went around the bend, Threngrin placed his hand over a stone. He barely missed the movement beneath his palm. Blinking, he tried to see what it was. Threngrin pulled his hand away quickly and tapped Sirra on her shoulder. Something was there, waiting for the right time to attack, something small, yellow, and shiny, and it was very deadly. Threngrin couldn't help himself. It was shiny and very pretty. He had to get a better look at it. With their every step and movement, it sparkled. It shone really bright. It even changed different colors of yellow, which made him attracted to it more. Threngrin had to touch it. He had to get a better look at it. Threngrin just had to see what it was. He reached out his hand and started to take a step forward, when Sirra motioned Threngrin to slowly back away from the damp stone wall, not making any sudden moves. Standing there, they kept a close eye watching the small object. She felt something was wrong. The ground beneath them started to sink. They sank ankle deep in some kind of slimy green mud. The slimy mud clung to their ankles and sucked at their feet, tightening around their skin like a rope. Their hearts jumped a beat. Their breaths leaving their lungs in a rush, Sirra forced her mind to remain calm, trying to keep from panicking.

Rather than fight the green ichors, they tried to shimmy their way out, but with every movement they made, there was some kind of mist glowing, moving around them. The mist spun around, and bright drops of water formed together over the large damp spot where the water dripped constantly. Suddenly the mist came to something unknown, penetrated all the wet soil, and disappeared into the darkness. Sirra starched her head, waving her sword in the air, not knowing for sure if it was still there. She still couldn't believe what just happened. They were free from the slimy green ichors, but they were afraid to move. Where did it go, and what was it?

Sirra took a deep breath and took one step slowly forward. Nothing happened. Moving slowly, they continued to follow this path. Sirra and Threngrin found themselves deeper underground than they thought they were. Sirra noticed this awful smell. The smell was nearly overpowering as they got deeper underground. The air was becoming thick and very hot. Dangerous gases seeped from green pools. Yellow vapor lingered throughout the air. Sirra carefully checked their surroundings before continuing on, but the deeper they went, it became harder to breathe. Threngrin's knees bent. His body was ready to jump into action or take off running. Sirra had this strange feeling that something was going to happen. It had been too quiet.

Sirra took her time looking the area over, not moving too fast, walking very slowly, and trying not to breathe or disturb the vapors in the air. Threngrin slowly pointed to the three openings ahead of them, which all appeared to go deeper underground. The passages looked like they went on for miles.

"I can't see," Threngrin cried out.

"Would you keep your voice down," Sirra whispered.

Cautiously Sirra moved very slowly. She felt deep down inside that they weren't alone. She pushed her nervous hand through her hair, and they chose to take the center passage, not sure where it would lead them.

Despite the strong scent, the vapors remained heavy, yet through the thickness, Sirra caught glimpses of something. Not knowing what lay up ahead of them, Sirra prepared herself for anything, her sword up and ready to fight the first thing that would jump at them and Threngrin walking behind her as close as he could, holding her arm. They continued moving forward, walking very slowly. Their eyes started to burn, and tears welled up. Threngrin wanted so bad to rub his eyes, but he knew that the thick vapors that was filling the air was very dangerous. They got on their hands and knees, and slowly they managed to crawl their way through the vapors, to avoid the gases in the air. Crawling on the floor, Sirra found it much easier to see and breathe again.

After hours of going down this long passage, they finally reached a large chamber. Sirra snooped around the room very carefully. She noticed the position of each stone in place, the dark green gleaming pools of steam coming from them. She then noticed holes that had formed in the ground, causing the ground to become uneven. She focused on the room. The room felt alive. Something was in here, but what?

Very carefully she moved one step toward the left. She motioned Threngrin to stay close to the wall, although the walls made her feel uncomfortable. The holes in the ground made her feel uneasy. She knew the wall was still the safest place.

Sirra heard a squishing sound coming from under their feet. She slowly turned toward Threngrin. Threngrin was standing in a pool of purple and yellow slime. He looked down at his feet, slowly picked up his right foot, and moved backward. Something moved. They couldn't tell what it was. Sirra felt something in the air. A swirl of vapors appeared as it rose from the pool in front of Threngrin.

Something brushed Threngrin's leg. It tugged at his pant leg. Not even looking down, he jumped upward, kicking out with his foot. He felt the impact, sending whatever it was into a purple bubbling pool. He landed in a crouched position on the other side of the room. His hands were up, ready for round two.

Sirra slowly made her way over to Threngrin. She spotted a slow movement above their heads. The ceiling was alive, and there's what appeared to be light. Maybe it was light coming from outside.

Without hesitation, Sirra grabbed Threngrin's arm. She launched forward, running along the wall, her hands barely touching the wall's surface as they raced around the green pools, climbing higher with every step until they reached the top. There she spotted a small light breaking its way through the cracks of the wall.

Sirra and Threngrin used their feet and started kicking the wall in hopes that they would break through to the other side.

Just ahead of them, there was a hideous screaming sound, echoing through the chamber. Something then fell to the ground, causing the chamber to rumble. The creature's cry sounded like a command as its wing spread and began flapping angrily. Its beak opened wide, and yellow vapors spread throughout the room as its wings fanned the air.

The bird in size was much like a vulture, but its wings were shorter than a vulture's. The bird was purple, and its head was larger, larger than any bird they had ever seen. Eye to eye, the bird flew toward Threngrin, snapping at him with its fierce beak.

Threngrin dodged the bird, landing near a green pool that was bubbling. Carefully he moved close to the wall, knowing he would be dinner for the screaming bird. The purple bird flew past him again. Threngrin ducked out of its path, and the bird quickly turned around and headed for him again. To Threngrin's surprise, with one good punch he knocked the bird out of the air as he took a big jump. Threngrin didn't realize that this was no ordinary bird. As he jumped up into the air, something hit his leg, knocking his feet from underneath him and landing him on his back. In that second, the bird changed directions and was looking at him face-to-face.

Sirra dashed toward Threngrin, her hand going for his waist. Threngrin was wounded. He had suffered a severe blow to his head. She was confident that she was strong enough for them both. She grabbed his waist and pulled him toward her, ducking to avoid the flying bird coming at them, and then in the blink of an eye, she drove her dagger into the chest of the bird.

The bird roared loudly. The echo was so loud that the chamber walls shook. Sirra sat on the ground, helping Threngrin. She found herself face-to-face with another creature staring her down. A large monstrous lizard was appearing out of one of the green pools. Green slime dripped from its mouth, its tail was long, and it had spikes coming out of his back. Sirra slowly stood up. It swung its tail at Sirra, hitting her in the leg, knocking her back down on the ground. Sirra thought that this creature might be a baby dragon. She had never seen one before, and this was something new to her.

The creature had clawed feet. He had speed like no other creature they had seen before. Sirra had no time to panic. They had to find a way out before it's too late.

"How-how are we going to escape? There is no way out," Threngrin stuttered. He was trying not to draw attention to himself, but the question lingered on his mind.

As Threngrin stared, Sirra reached out her hand and touched his hand. "Escape, yes! You are right, we have to escape," she whispered, drawing herself closer to Threngrin.

"But there's only two ways out of here. One is we die, and that's a sure way, and the other . . ." Threngrin hesitated. "The other is worse."

Sirra glanced at Threngrin. "Worse? What can be worse than death?" she whispered.

"I don't know, so-so we die, good plan," Threngrin nervously commented.

"Escape, this is a problem, and we shall solve it." She lowered her voice.

"We are hiding behind this thing, trapped, and we have to solve this, how?" Threngrin said sarcastically.

"I don't know. How about you come up with something," Sirra snapped back.

"We could jump on its back and fly our way out of here." Threngrin grinned.

"And do you know the way out, or how are we supposed to capture this baby dragon?" Sirra question him.

"I don't know. That's where you come in, you figure it out, and I'll hide here, waiting."

"You are such a coward." Sirra snickered. "And what is the other option you mentioned?"

"We stay here forever." Threngrin giggled.

The vapors were getting heavier, filling the chamber quickly. They had to find a way out fast, for time was wasting. They were so occupied and finding a way to escape, but they never heard the dragon creeping up behind them. Sirra felt the hair on the back of her neck stand straight up. She felt something warm and moist, something very wet, sticky. The smell was unbearable. She could feel every breath the dragon made on the back of her neck. The dragon breathed in and out of his nose, leaving a sticky feeling. Threngrin watched the dragon lingering over her, and he moved his head from side to side. His drool was covering Sirra all over, and panic flared in them. They knew they had to get out now. The dragon seemed to be getting stronger and more dangerous as the vapors grew thicker and thicker. Sirra's mind was working overtime trying to find a way to escape. She had grown to trust Threngrin. She had no choice if they wanted to get out alive. Threngrin was never the one to fight, but now he had to. Sirra could not move. She had to remain still and quiet. Any movement could cause the dragon to attack. It was all up to Threngrin to get them out, and all Sirra could think about was how much trouble they were in and their fate lay in his hands. He hid from fights.

According to her figures, the only way out of there was to go through the dragon or die trying to. If they were lucky enough, they might find a secret passage.

Chapter Five

Sirra's eyes made a slow, careful circuit of the large chamber. Her mouth went dry, her heart pounding so hard against her chest, she was unable to move or speak, frozen with terror. She felt the dragon's breath on her face. Sirra blinked, turned her head toward Threngrin, and nodded.

The dragon stood straight up facing them. It had a hungry look in his eyes, and Threngrin, so filled with fear, took a step backward and fell to the ground. He wanted to scream, as loud as he could, but when he opened his mouth to do so, his throat closed, letting no air in or out.

"We are going to die," he stated, trying to push the words out of his mouth as hard as he could. Threngrin slowly rose to his feet.

"No, we are not!" Sirra yelled.

Face-to-face, Sirra didn't expect to see what she was seeing. She wiped her eyes several times, blinking a few times, but there in front of them was this dragon, and it grew. The dragon was huge and had six legs and two heads. Sirra had doubts herself if they were going to survive this at all.

The dragon had changed in shape as well as in size. The vapors in the room were beginning to change the dragon, and it appeared to be very quickly. Right before her own eyes, the dragon started to change again. It was growing a third head. Sirra had no choice. She took one last look at Threngrin and jerked her hand away from him, and her only thoughts were for them to get out alive. The dragon standing tall, on all six legs, let out an awful roaring sound from one of its head, which caused a chain reaction, making the other two heads roar. The sound was so loud and had such a high-pitched volume, it echoed throughout the chamber, causing the room to vibrate. The dragon started to wiggle its body from side to side, wiping its tail back and forth, getting ready to make its move. Sirra turned, and as short as she was, she used that as her advantage. She curled up into a small ball and rolled underneath the dragon right between its legs, uncaring of the curious look she was getting from Threngrin.

Sirra bit her lower lip as she planned for her attack. The pain from her lip was real, and it enabled her to focus on what needed to be done. The dragon started to move slowly toward Threngrin, running on all six of his legs. The movement from the ground made the stone from the walls and ceiling start to crumble around them. She managed to get underneath the dragon. Lying there, she slowly and quietly removed a dagger from her belt and drove the dagger through its body and muscle and into its chest. She jerked the knife as hard as she could into the dragon as she rolled away to the other side of the room, avoiding the poisonous gases coming from it. The dragon's head spun quickly, throwing Threngrin into the air, hitting the wall with great force. The other two heads let out a roaring sound, causing the room to vibrate more. The wall and ceiling started to crumble again. The dragon spun around quickly, and its tail caught Sirra in the leg, sending her into the air, landing her onto a large boulder.

Sirra's leg where the dragon hit her was beginning to throb and burn. She was having a real hard time moving around. The dragon slowly moved toward Sirra. The dragon was weak from the loss of blood, but to him it was dinnertime.

A strange tingling feeling had begun in Sirra's calf muscle. Pain was radiating up her leg toward her thigh and down to her foot. She tilted her head toward Threngrin, afraid of what was going to happen. The dragon's mouth slowly opened wide, she could smell its bad breath, and its teeth were yellow and green. All three heads were looking at her, and their eyes were bright red, filled with fire.

Threngrin took a gliding step toward Sirra, his back against the wall. He had to get close to the dragon without it noticing him. Sirra slowly rose to her feet, but her leg went out from under her. She went down, hitting the ground hard. The tingling in her leg made it impossible for her to stand. Her foot was rigid and beginning to swell, unable to move.

Threngrin finally reached Sirra's side, and he pushed her back against the wall, lunging forward. He launched his sword straight into the dragon's chest, trying to hit the dragon's heart. The dragons howled, their heads went from side to side, and blood was spraying from their mouths, hitting the walls, ceiling, and even Threngrin and Sirra. Then finally it collapsed onto the floor.

"How badly are you hurt?" Threngrin whispered.

"This place is a death trap. We have to get out of here." Sirra's voice was full of fear.

Threngrin reached down to help Sirra up on her feet, but in the blink of an eye, Sirra felt something around her waist, a viselike grip, pinning her against his skin. Something caught her from behind, pulling her backward against its chest. The dragon was strong, unable to break free. Sirra threw her head back, hoping to make contact with the dragon's face. The back of her head hit the dragon so hard in the chest that pain exploded behind her eyes and in her temple.

Threngrin managed to get up and balance himself on one leg. He picked up a heavy rock, waited for the right time, and smashed it over the dragon's head. The dragon stumbled as it fell to the ground. Threngrin slowly, with great caution, reached for the dagger lying on the ground next to Sirra and sliced the dragon's throat in the blink of an eye. The dragon released Sirra, and as she was falling to the ground, she heard the dragon take its last breath. She managed her way over to Threngrin and sat on the ground next to him. She soon became aware of Threngrin's hand at the nape of her neck, massaging her gently. She closed her eyes to shut out what was happening to them, feeling completely helpless. But in that moment, not realizing what was happening, the dragon managed to creep up behind them again. Sirra felt mist on her back. Threngrin smelled the scent of death. Slowly they turned. The last head was staring at them with fury in its eyes. It was still alive. The dragon's body began to shake and tremble, and its head swung back and forth. Right in front of them as they watched, the dragon formed another head.

"It's not dead. How could that be?" Threngrin cried out as he tried to hide behind a huge boulder.

"It doesn't die," Sirra whispered as she followed him, crawling on her hands and knees.

"What do we do now? I know we die. We sit here and die, that's all there is. We stay here and die. Die I tell ya," Threngrin rambled on.

"Wait I—," was all she got to say.

"Die, die, die, di—"

Sirra grabbed him by the arm. "Shut up. I know what to do."

Threngrin froze, looking at her with disbelief in his eyes. "What?"

"Give me your sword," she demanded as she reached for it.

"No! That's my sword, and you are not taking it. Over my dead body will I let you have it." Threngrin jerked his sword away from her.

"All right have it your way." She grabbed Threngrin by the arm.

"Wait, what are you doing?" he snapped, pulling his arm back.

"I am going to feed you to the dragon so I can get out alive." She grinned.

"Cute, I tell ya, cute." He chuckled.

"I need your sword to kill the dragon. You have to stab it in the heart," she gradually explained.

"Why didn't you just say so?" He smirked.

Sirra had enough. She ripped the sword out of Threngrin's hands. With all the might and strength she had, she climbed on top of the boulder, waiting patiently, nervously, as the dragon moved closer and closer to her. At the right height and the right time, she launched forward, stabbing the dragon deep in it chest, hitting the heart. The dragon shook for a brief moment, knocking her off the boulder with its head, landing her up against the wall. As the dragon slowly fell to the ground, Sirra watched closely as the dragon took its last breath once again.

Threngrin came out from behind the boulder, slowly walked up to the dragon, and kicked it, making sure it was dead. "I want my sword back." He chuckled as he pulled the sword out of the dragon.

"I should have the sword, and you have the dagger," she demanded.

"Nope, nope, little person, it is mine." He grinned.

"Little, how—" She stopped in the middle of her sentence. "We will talk later," was all she could say.

Sirra fell to the ground, her legs burning like it was on fire. The pain she had forgotten came back. She glanced down at her leg. It was red, with white spots, and swollen. There were purple lines going all over, which looked more like veins. They started at the bottom of her foot, up her leg, and now reaching her hip, but that was not the worst thing. From the hard landing of the dragon, the ground beneath them shivered, cracking, a forewarning this was not a safe place and it's not over.

A part of her was working furiously, testing the ability of her strength, so determined to find a way out of there, finding a way to survive. Another part of her wanted to give up, to stay right there, relaxing up against the wall.

"We have to move, now." The voice came from behind her. "I know you are unable to move, but the walls and ceiling are collapsing."

Sirra knew that Threngrin was right. If they don't move out of here, they would be trapped and lost in there forever.

With all her effort, she fought through the pain and fear, looking for the energy and the power within herself to move.

"Hurry, we must go now. I will carry you as far as I can." Threngrin reached down, slowly picking up Sirra in his arms. She wrapped her arms around his neck, holding on as tight as she could.

She became aware of the warning signs that were around them. She could sense that they would not be getting out of there alive. The feeling ran deep in the pit of her stomach, twisting and turning like a knife went right through her.

Threngrin finally found a small passage. Just as they entered the passage, they heard a loud noise from the chamber they were in. There was a loud crashing sound, and they felt the ground rumbling beneath them. The walls and ceiling collapsed, and the room they were in was now gone.

"Could you put me down? I am fine now." Threngrin slowly put her down, making sure both her feet were on the ground. He glanced at her and smiled. They had to keep moving quickly. Sirra decided to take the lead. She was able to spot danger better than Threngrin. Sirra was very weak, and with every step, the pain was unbearable. She had to use the wall to support her balance. Threngrin took up behind her, staying as close as he could. They had to move fast and quickly. They had no time to waste. Another wall collapsed behind them, and then another. As hard and difficult as it was, Sirra started to pick up the pace. They soon came to a new area in the chamber. It was smaller than the one they were in before. Looking around, Sirra noticed there was a small hole in the ceiling. It wasn't too small for them to get through. Finding good footing and with a sore leg, Sirra managed to climb her way up to the hole. Threngrin followed Sirra up through the narrow opening to the next room.

The room was small and very dark. There was a faint smell, a smell of something decaying. Not sticking around to find out what it was, they felt along the chamber walls, covering as much surface as they could with the little time they had.

"Over here!" Threngrin yelled.

Sirra watched as Threngrin ran his hands along the wall, not knowing for sure what they had found. Threngrin felt a soft spot in the wall. As he slammed his fist through it, stones around them crumbled.

The ground trembled, the walls started to crack, and chunks of rocks fell from above their heads. Threngrin turned and grabbed Sirra into his arms, trying to protect her from the falling rocks. He slammed his fist again, making the hole bigger. The ground trembled again, throwing them against the wall on the other side of the room.

Threngrin jumped to his feet, grabbed Sirra around her waist, and pushed her through the hole. She landed on the other side, knocking her to the ground. As she scrambled to get to her feet, she heard a sound coming from behind her. The wall had collapsed, and dust and debris began to fill the room.

Sirra jumped toward the wall, digging at the stones, throwing them behind her. "You're trapped!" she cried out, clawing at the stones.

The stones were heavy, damp, and cold to the touch. Her hands began to tingle, feeling numb. "Threngrin, are you all right?" she called out, unable to stop, her heart pounding so hard, she could feel every beat within her. He couldn't be dead. "Speak to me! Say something."

Sirra finally heard something, it was faint, and it sounded like a moaning sound. It was so faint, she could barely hear it. "Threngrin!" she cried out.

"Go," he ordered. "Do not stay here. Get out while you can. I will find another way out."

She couldn't leave him. He sounded hurt. She had to get him out. With all her strength and willpower, she tried to move the big boulder that was blocking the exit. She wasn't going to give up.

Moving the stones as fast as she could, racing against time, the ground began to tremble, and the chamber started to buckle, collapsing in on itself.

"Go! Go now!" Threngrin yelled.

The sound in his voice was easy, unconcerned, without worry, but deep down inside he was afraid. "I'll be back," she promised.

With tears in her eyes, she spun around quickly and raced toward an opening that led to the next chamber. With every step she took, moving farther and farther away from him felt like weight of stones hitting against her chest. She could barely breathe. She had a deep desire to turn back to help him. But it was done, too late. Everything behind her had collapsed.

She raced away from the falling debris, running through chamber to chamber, climbing her way up to the surface. She felt a light mist of water throughout the chamber walls as she ran past. She knew she was getting closer to the surface. Deep down inside she felt that part of her was left behind, with Threngrin in the collapsed chamber.

Sirra finally busted her way into an opening in the surface, feeling the cool, refreshing air on her face. She normally would feel grateful, but her mind was wandering, worrying if Threngrin was alive and well. It was all she could think about. Nothing else mattered.

Sirra collapsed to the ground once she got outside. Her wounds throbbing, her leg felt like it was on fire, reminding her that her leg was getting worse, but there was no time to stop. She had to block out the pain and focus on saving Threngrin.

With every achy bone and muscle in her body burning, she made every effort to continue on her way. She knew Threngrin, and he knew how skillful she was and that she could continue on without him. Her father had given her access to all his knowledge, and he had centuries and centuries of experiences in adventures and how to survive.

Sirra doubled back several times, making sure she marked the trail back to Threngrin. She knew he had to be alive, and she wasn't giving up.

Weary as she was, she settled in a small group of trees halfway down the mountain, not wanting to be too far away from Threngrin. She had to rest, to give herself time to heal. She had to find a way to put herself back together in order to find Threngrin. She glanced at her leg again. It was getting worse. Not only was her leg swollen, so was her foot. There were more purple lines covering most of her, and now they were all the way to her hip. She could feel her leg trying to split open as if something was working its way out. Her body quickly broke out into a sweat, and she realized then that she was running a high fever, and this was not good. She had no idea what she had, but she knew she was in danger, and there was no help for miles. She managed to find water and berries to eat. With food and a good night's rest, things would be better in the morning, she could just hope.

The wind was blowing hard, and the bitter cold intensified deep in her body all the way to her bones. Shivering, she managed to bury herself deep among the trees and bushes for cover. Shaking from the cold winds, afraid, being alone, she thought about what Threngrin had done. He had saved her life, pushing her clear of the collapsing wall.

Threngrin had never shown this side of him. It's not his character, not even in battles. Threngrin mostly ran and hid during fights and waited them out till they're over, or he would stab the creature once and take off running. But not this fight. Sirra had felt something rise in him. She sighed softly with grief as she closed her eyes. She had to find him. She could admit to herself that he was gone and she was never going to see him again, but she wouldn't.

So many times while she was learning how to be an adventurer from her father, it was Threngrin who was there for emotional support. Even through the most dangerous, frightening times, Threngrin had always been with her. Sheltering her in the only way he knew how, keeping her alive.

Sirra settled deeper into the bushes, hiding herself from whatever might still be out there. Her father had often told her stories of his adventures, evil things that he had encountered at night, things that only happened at night. She had always believed that the stories were made up. Later she realized they were stories to make her strong, to be as good an adventurer as he was, but in order to do that, she had to live through the night.

Sirra closed her eyes. As she settled in for the night, she felt her breath slowly leaving her body and her heart relaxing its beat. Her last thoughts were to find Threngrin and not to give up. He had to be alive.

Chapter Six

Sirra opened her eyes, and instantly she felt the rush of pain sweeping through her body. The pain was so unbearable that every time she moved, breathing was very difficult. It was then that Threngrin managed to come back into her mind. She needed to focus on him.

Suddenly Sirra's body tensed. She felt something was lingering around her and that she was no longer alone. There was a sound of something approaching her. A sound of wooden wheels turning, sounds like a wagon crunching over gravel.

Sirra heard the snap of a whip hitting a horse that was pulling a wagon. The horse snorted and strained. Obviously the wagon was heavy. She couldn't see the driver, and she had no idea if the person was friendly or not. She hid farther into the bushes, waiting for the wagon to pass in hopes she wouldn't be noticed. But it was too late. She was spotted along the roadside. The driver's eyes spotted Sirra from about twenty feet away.

Sirra watched as the wagon slowly passed by her. Holding her breath, feeling her heart beat as it pounded so hard and so fast in her chest, trying not to move a muscle, she lay there as still as possible.

The wagon passed by, and everything was quiet. Sirra thought the danger had passed and everything was clear. But the driver stopped at the edge of the trees with a hard tug on the reins. "What are you doing in there?" The voice was raspy, and he spoke slowly.

The driver dropped to the ground and circled around her. "Come out, I say! Come out of there," he said, waving his arms around.

Frightened as she was, she watched as the driver took a step closer to her, and she slowly crawled out from under the bush. His eyes focused on the dagger hanging from her belt. He was old and wore a dark metal breastplate that was so worn-out, it had seen many battles, along with heavy leather boots that had seen many years of traveling.

"You, little woman, you look hurt. What is your place here?" He took another step forward.

"I-I am an adventurer." She paused for a minute. "And my friend is trapped up there in that stone cave," she continued as she pointed up toward the mountain.

Sirra didn't realize it at first until she turned around, but everything had changed again. The stone mountain that was there had disappeared. It was now nothing but a mountain hill with grass and trees.

The old man laughed. "There is no stone mountain, little woman. Did you hit your head? No matter, I can help you with your wounds. I have something that will help you. Come here, let me see," he said, reaching out his hand.

Sirra slowly made her way to the old man. She wasn't sure if he was trustworthy, but her leg was on fire, and the pain was unbearable. She needed something. The old man rolled up her pant leg. He took one look and shook his head. "It's a douser," he said, shaking his head again.

"What is it?" she asked frantically.

The old man scratched his head. "It is purple snarls infection." He chuckled.

"Purple what?" she cried out.

"Purple snarl infection it is. It lives and grows inside you. It is deadly. Good thing I ran into you." He chuckled again.

"Ya," she said with a slight sigh. "Just how deadly is it?"

"Oh, it will consume your body. You maybe had two—maybe three days, but no worries."

The old man turned back toward his wagon. He rumbled through a few of his saddlebags. He finally reached for his last bag, and there he found four potions and a knife. Without saying a word, he stuck a small piece of stick into her mouth, grabbed her leg, and did a small slice in her leg, just an inch above her ankle. The slice was about an inch long. Blood and what appeared to be small purple bugs came flying out of her leg. The old man squeezed her leg as tight as he could, and more bugs flew out. Sirra bit down on the stick, trying not to scream, and at the sight of bugs flying out of her leg, she tried to get up off the ground as fast as she could. The old man held her down with all his strength as he squeezed her leg again. Most of the bugs were out, but there were still some eggs that hadn't hatched yet. The old man poured one of the bottles of potion on her leg and wrapped it up.

"Here are some potions. This one will help with your wounds and will kill the rest of the bugs." He slowly handed her the potions. "Now get yourself to the village. No little woman should be out here," the old man growled deep in his throat.

"Why should I do that? I have to find Threngrin," she declared.

The old man nodded his head. "You will see, little woman." And he climbed back onto the wagon.

Little woman? Who does he think he is, calling me little woman? she thought to herself.

The horse pranced on the dirt road, snorting its breath into the chilly air. The old man took a sudden jerk on the reins. "I'm just warning you!" the old man yelled back.

Sirra had no idea what the old man meant. But what was even worse, where did Threngrin go? What happened to the stone mountain where the cave was?

Sirra shook her head in disbelief that Threngrin could ever be gone. He wasn't even supposed to leave her, and the thought, unbidden, sneaking in, tugging at her conscience, was something she had to control.

"Threngrin!" she said it loud as she looked up to the sky with tears in her eyes. "Where are you? Where did you go?"

Sirra circled around and saw everything had changed. All the land markers she had placed were gone, trees were different, the layout of the land was different, and there was no trace of them ever being there. Now feeling alone, scared, she had no clue or idea where to start looking for Threngrin.

How could she survive without him, live without him? They had been friends for years, lived in the same village. They had shared their every waking moment together since they were youngsters. They shared their minds and thoughts together. She realized she needed him to be alive.

Sirra had to find him, and time was wasting, but she had no idea where to even start. She closed her eyes and took a deep breath, and when she opened them, everything had changed again. The only thing that remained the same was the bush she was standing next to. She noticed a faint path that was covered with grass, and there were some marks she left that led up to this small mountain. It looked smaller than the one they were at, and she wasn't even sure if it was the same one she left Threngrin in.

Sirra's knees were drawn up, and her chin was propped in her hands. She had always had Threngrin by her side, always ahead of her, and his relentless pursuit was always getting them into trouble. Sirra sighed and straightened very slowly, rising to her feet. It was time for her to move on.

She knew she had a long journey ahead of her. She took one of the potions, and within minutes of drinking it, she felt different. Her pain was gone, and her wounds were healing. The old man never told her what the other two potions were, so she thought they were extra healing potions. She put them in her bag for safekeeping.

Sirra was torn on what to do and which way to go. There were only two markers she had found, and the path was no longer visible. She needed to find a village. She needed help.

It had been hours, and she had not seen any other road, path, or a village. "That old man doesn't know what he is talking about, a village," she mumbled to herself. "I bet it's a trap and he's planning on eating me for dinner. A village, ha."

The sun began to sink behind the green hills. It was going to be dark soon. She continued on her journey in hopes she would reach a village before nightfall, if there was indeed a village.

The road finally changed, and it stretched out, going down a slope, winding through huge boulders, and then disappearing back into the thick forest. She found herself in a small clearing, a thinning space of trees. Sirra followed what appeared to be a path with her eyes, weary, afraid, and scared. She had never adventured alone. Threngrin was always there, with her.

As the sun began to set, there was a slight chill in the air. Sirra clutched her cloak close to her. The journey ahead of her was nothing but forest and rolling hills, and the darkness of the tall oaks and hickories reached as high as the sky.

The sun had set, leaving only bright blue stars. The huge trees had blocked most of them, leaving Sirra alone in the darkness as she moved along the rough gravel path.

Sirra noticed something very unusual, the stillness in the air. There was no buzzing and chirping, which were normal at this time of night. Birds were normally out with the setting of the sun, looking for food. There was nothing but silence. Sirra listened closely for any life sound, but she could detect nothing. The silence was disturbing, and the feeling of being alone was even worse.

She forced herself to kick the stones on the path and to turn her thoughts back on Threngrin—all the adventures they went on, the times they spent together, laughing, telling stories to each other. If Threngrin was here, he would know what to do. Then again he would run and hide, she thought to herself. The more she thought of him, the more she started missing him.

She was in such deep thought about Threngrin, she didn't notice the low branch. It brushed against her arm, causing her to jump to one side. She pulled out her dagger from its belt and glanced back to a leafy branch. She sighed, then continued on, and she sped up to a quicker pace. She was deep in the forest, and only the moonlight was able to peer through the thick trees. It was so dark that Sirra had trouble seeing the path or what lay up ahead. She was still curious about the silence. It was as if all life had disappeared. She felt a bit anxious and glanced around her, but there was nothing on the path or moving around the trees.

Pausing for a brief moment, she gazed at the clear night sky, taking deep breaths before passing the trees beyond.

She walked slowly as the winding path had become narrowed, leading to what appeared to be open land. She took a few steps, and the open land disappeared into a forest of trees and bushes. She rubbed her eyes, blinking a few times, feeling uneasy as her mind was playing tricks on her. A few steps later, she was on a wider trail, and bits of sky began to show through the thick forest. She could see the bottom of the valley in the distance. She had to be getting close to a village, but to her it could be at least two more days of journey.

Feeling tired and hungry, she felt relief that she was heading in the right direction, or so she hoped. She quickly picked up the pace, humming her favorite tune as she continued on her way. She was so focused on the path, kicking pebbles and thinking about the village up ahead, that she didn't noticed the huge shadow that was rising rapidly, detaching itself from the bushes behind her. It was moving quickly toward the path in front of her. The shadow was almost in front of her when she sensed something was above her. She felt a cold mist lingering in the air above, threatening to crush her little being. With a startled cry, she jumped aside, dropping her bag on the ground, and whipped out the dagger from her belt.

Sirra turned around, but she couldn't see anything. Everything was dark, and there was barely enough moonlight to see the path. She turned her head from side to side, looking up and down the path, but saw nothing. A gust of strong wind went right past her. She swung her dagger, but nothing was there. She swung her dagger again. She swung so hard, she fell to the ground. The shadow flew past her so fast and the wind was so strong, the dirt from the road swirled up around her, making it hard for her to see or breathe.

Sirra rubbed her eyes. Slowly she got up to her feet as she waited for the dust to settle back down. She tried to peer into the darkness in an effort to see what was out there. She could see nothing. She slowly moved with caution in an attempt to catch something in the moonlight.

She could feel the shadow lingering around her. She could feel its eyes following her every move but could not see it. Slowly she bent down to pick up her bag and wrapped it around her neck. It was all she had left of Threngrin.

Everything was still, quiet. For a long moment there was nothing. Then suddenly the shadow lunged with great force and swiftness. Its powerful being seized her, lifting her abruptly off the ground and holding her high.

"Well, little one, what are you going to do now? So brave, so strong, yet so small?" The voice was deep.

Sirra tried so hard not to drop her dagger from her nerveless fingers. She struggled to free herself. Fear rambled through her mind as she swung her dagger in midair.

She had no idea what creature had her. It was more powerful than any creature she had met before. Then the creature held her out to its side, avoiding the dagger she was swinging.

"I could cut you up in little pieces and feed you to the wild animals or keep you for myself, if I choose, although you are small," the voice continued.

"Not if I kill you first!" Sirra yelled, struggling to get free.

"How? You tell me, little one. You can't kill what you can't see." The voice laughed, mocking her.

"If I get my hands on you—"

"Enough." The voice became cold. The creature turned its head quickly toward Sirra, its eyes glowing bright ruby red. There was no body, just these creepy eyes.

Right before her eyes, the creature slowly formed itself into what appeared to be human but not quite human. She then realized this was her chance to free herself. With all her effort, she reached her arm out as far as she could, trying not to drop her dagger. She swung as hard and as fast as possible, not knowing for sure if she would even come close to hitting it.

To her surprise, the creature let out a loud screeching sound. She did not notice herself that she was high in the air, and when the creature released its grip, it sent her to her death.

Sirra was now descending to her death as she fell to the ground. She struggled, and she raised her arms in the air, trying to grab on to something that was not there to prevent her from falling.

After what seemed like a lifetime of falling, she finally hit a few trees on her way down, slowing her fall, and she landed on a big bush. As she lay there looking up at the sky, her only thought was she was alive.

The shadow appeared again, looking down at her. "How was your trip?" The voice laughed.

Sirra lay there frozen in fear. She could hear the voice but couldn't see anything or anyone.

"I'm bored now. You are no fun to me." And with a gust of wind, the shadow disappeared.

Still dazed from the fall, she straightened herself out of the bushes, rubbing her arms and legs, trying to restore circulation throughout her body.

Sirra wasn't sure if the shadow had left. She slowly picked up her dagger and her bag and headed down the path. She made it through the forest and to hills covered with grass and red daisies. She remained on the path until she reached the end of the valley.

Coming out of the darkness, she saw there was a big difference. The moon was full and clear, and she could see it hanging in the sky just above her head. Its glow brightened the valley and the path she was following. The path took her over hills, and there were times she would come across ruts where heavy rain washed away part of the path. The wind had picked up rapidly, whipping at her cloak as she walked. She was forced to look down, shielding her eyes from the flying dust from the path.

Sirra still felt uneasy by the night's silence. Besides the rushing sound of the wind, it was too quiet. At one point she thought she heard a crying voice, but it was gone, and she never heard it again.

Finally as she reached the slopes of the valley, the hills began to level, covering the lands in grass where it dipped downward at a slight incline. She had to be getting close.

Sirra noticed that she was on the outer edge of the valley, where the path went around large bushes and grass that was as tall as she was. She suddenly stopped, stood still, listened, and waited. Then she heard something but was unable to detect what it was. She quickly ran to the bushes ahead of her. Diving into the bushes, the branches whipped against her face, knocking her back, but she managed to move herself to the center. She remained quiet, looking at the night sky, straining her ear to hear something. But she heard nothing. She waited for a moment, making sure it was safe, and then crawled out of the bushes. She was afraid of nothing, scaring herself to death.

As she continued on her way, she heard the sound again, coming from the tall grass. She turned to look and saw something moving. Sirra took off running, but in the middle of her run, something hit her from behind, knocking her face-first to the ground. She reached for her dagger and slowly rolled onto her back. Just as she rolled over, in the blink of an eye she was face-to-face with a sheep. She shook her head and looked again. A sheep, she was afraid of a sheep.

The morning sun slowly began to rise. Sirra noticed the bushes began to thin out as the path got wider, and from a distance, she saw a yellow light flickering. Excited, she picked up her pace, reaching a fork in the road. One was leading toward the flickering light. As she got closer and closer, she saw what appeared to be a building. The road got wider as it led her into the village.

Chapter Seven

Sirra was tired and hungry, and she hurt all over, from the top of her head to her small feet. All she wanted was food and a bath.

Sirra walked slowly into the village. She could see torches burning through small-framed windows. The houses were low structures and had sloped roofs. The buildings were made with wood and had some stone foundation.

Sirra spotted an inn. It was a large structure with two wings. The building was made with huge logs and a high stone foundation. The center of the inn was lit well with torches that brightened the room. She could hear voices from within, and there was laughter and shouting. Half of the wing was the sleeping quarters for guests that stayed only for a few nights. The other half was for guests that stayed for longer periods of time. Sirra could smell roasting meat lingering in the air, which made her really hungry. She had no food for the past two days. She quickly made her way up the steps to the big double doors.

The big door swung open into a large room filled with tables and chairs. Each table had tall candles that were lit, making the room so bright that she had to adjust her eyes to see. At the back of the room, there was a long serving bar that ran the length of the wall. There's a few men gathering around the bar, noticing her as she walked in. Their faces showed amazement, and they quickly returned to their drinks, glancing back a few times to see what she was up to. Sirra stood in the door for a few moments more as she glanced around the small crowd of people. She walked over to the table on the far left.

The old man from behind the bar noticed her as she sat down. His clothes were worn-out from everyday use. He had white hair, his beard was as white as snow and came down to his chest, and he had a big belly that wiggled as he walked. Sirra couldn't help but notice as he approached her.

"Hey, ol' friend, what brings you here?" The old man grinned.

"I would like a room, some of that meat that smells so good, and a warm bath."

The old man laughed. "I can give you a room. The meat is for tomorrow night's meal. But I could get you a plate of slop. The bath will cost you extra." He chuckled.

"Fine, I will pay extra for the bath. What is slop?"

"Eggs and rice and a slice of bread."

That's slop? she commented to herself. "Fine, bring me a plate of your slop."

Sirra couldn't help noticing the doors in the back of the room. She watched as the old man opened them into the kitchen. She saw two cooks arguing. One of them had a wooden spoon, waving it around in the other's man face. She saw the old man saying something to them, and then he returned to the bar. "What strange people," she said under her breath.

Sirra glanced around the room and couldn't help but stare at the men sitting at the bar. She was so used to having a bar full of people pushing and shoving, rushing to get their morning food. Streets would be crowded with people walking, running, arguing about something. But here it was quiet. The only people she had seen were the six men and the innkeeper.

"Here you are, my lass. Chow down, and when you are ready, I'll show you to your room." He chuckled.

"Are you and those men the only people here?" Sirra asked, with curiosity in her voice.

"No, my lass. There's about forty or fifty, I would say. We used to be small, but we have some travelers that pass by and stay a few days, or some like the old lad over there"—he turned and pointed—"that has stayed forever. He has been here, oh, 150 years, I would say."

"Then where is everyone?"

"Oh, most are in fields working, in mines digging, and some even hunt. Those men have nothing better to do than come in here, argue amongst themselves, and tell stories. But we do have a general store down the road, a blacksmith, and of course the inn. If you are looking for some fruits and veggies, there are carts at the end of the village. Now eat up before it gets cold," he said, waving his hands.

Sirra looked down at her food. She was hungry but no longer felt like eating. She was more tired and sore than hungry. She knew deep down inside she needed to eat to keep up her strength. But looking at the plate of food reminded her of Threngrin. How he was when he would eat. He would talk and eat at the same time, and food would come flying out of his mouth, hitting her right in the face. She would get so mad at him. Now she would give anything to have him back here.

Sirra was sitting with her back to the main entrance of the inn, when she heard the doors swung open, and a voice appeared from behind her. She couldn't move. *It couldn't be*, she said to herself, as her heart pounded so fast in her chest. She shifted slightly to catch who it was that entered. With disappointment in her eyes, she saw it wasn't Threngrin. The stranger was of medium height, was slightly built, and had grizzled black hair. The stranger hesitated in the doorway, looking around. The old man pointed toward the back, to the bar.

"Your room is ready, my lass." The old man chuckled.

Sirra jumped, jerking her head to look up at him. She never heard him walking up to her. "Yes," she quickly responded.

"Room, food, and a bath, that would be two gold."

"Right." Sirra took her bag off from around her neck. She went through it to see what Threngrin had.

"Here, this is all I have." She handed him a small green jasper the size of a pebble.

"My, my lass, you should take this to the man at the general store down the road. I can't take this. When you get back, your room will be waiting." And he handed back the jasper to her.

Sirra pushed her plate back and gathered her things. She walked out to the porch and saw that a young woman was standing at the back of an old cart parked out front of the building. She was lifting two half-full sacks onto her shoulder. The door was being held open by a heavy-built middle-aged dwarf. Sirra finally made her way through the crowd of people lingering in the streets, amid carts coming and going. She entered the general store. Her eyes rapidly adjusted to the darkness of the room. Although it was early morning, there wasn't much sunlight coming in. The only light was the lit candles and an old lantern hanging from the ceiling.

Sirra saw an old man standing behind the lower part of the counter. He had white beard and was short, stocky, and slightly showing his age.

"How can I help you, lass?" the old man asked, leaning over the counter with a big grin on his face.

Sirra walked over to the counter and handed him the jasper. "The innkeeper told me you could help me. I would like to sell this."

"Sure, I can help ya." He nodded, and he took the jasper and held it up toward the candle next to him. Not believing what he was seeing, he reached for his eyepiece to take a closer look at the jasper.

The old man's eyes widened. "I will give you thirty gold," he stated quickly as he turned back toward her. "I haven't seen a jasper for years." The old man was still rolling the jasper between his fingers, being amazed at her find.

"That will be fine," she said with excitement in her voice.

She was so fascinated on how jolly he was over the jasper. She didn't care how much gold he gave her. To her it was just a small green jasper.

The old man reached for a small brown bag that was wrapped around his waist and gave her thirty gold. He was still rolling the jasper around in his hand.

"You know that it's just a jasper." She giggled.

"No, my lass, this is not just a jasper." And he held it up to her face. "Jaspers are rare. You normally don't find them or even see them."

"How much would a large-size jasper be?" Sirra had this twinkle in her eyes, a twinkle of curiosity. She just wanted to see how the old man would react.

"This is a large jasper!" he shouted. "You won't find any large ones. They only come in the size of a pebble to the size of a gold piece."

"Really, so you have never seen one bigger than a gold piece?"

"Of course not. Anyone that I know never had!"

"I will keep that in mind, and thanks for the gold," she said with a warm smile.

"No, thank you, come again." The old man was holding the jasper up in the air. He never looked back at her as she was walking out the door.

Sirra just stood there outside of the general store. She couldn't believe that the old man went nuts over the small green jasper. To her it was just a small green rock that Threngrin had collected on their adventure, and the large jasper she had was worth even more.

Making sure she didn't lose her bag, she wrapped it around her neck. Her eyes were getting heavy from the lack of sleep. She blinked her eyes a few times, and she thought she saw Threngrin walking right past her.

She knew it was time for a warm bath and a good night's sleep. She was seeing things that weren't there. She pushed her way through the crowd of people, making her way back to the inn.

Sirra slowly made her way to the inn, and as she opened the door, the old man was standing right there. She was startled by his quick appearance. "Your room is ready."

Sirra jumped. "Thank you," was all she could say.

The old man showed Sirra to her room, where her warm bath and bed were waiting. She couldn't wait to hit the bed.

Sirra was awake the next morning from the warmth of the sun beaming through her window. She had risen so early that no one else was awake yet. The inn was silent as she moved from her small room to the center of the inn. Her body began to shake. Her fingers became cold from the morning chill in the air.

The village was always cold in the early morning. The mountains and hills surrounding them kept the sun from getting in. The village won't feel the warmth of the sun till midmorning, when it reached the top of the hill and chased away the chill.

Sirra sat down at the table in the corner. She leaned back and folded her arms, trying to keep warm. She sat there in the darkness, her shoulders slumped, and her heart felt heavy with dread. All at once she felt him standing next to her—Threngrin. He stirred in her mind once again—his touch, his laughter, his jokes. She finally felt such deep sorrow.

The connection she felt surprised her, the sense of him being here, and the way she could feel his presence alarmed her. Sirra had to close her mind, shut him out. She couldn't afford finding out the truth about what really happened to him. Nothing she did would stop her stomach from knotting and twisting. She had to face it. Threngrin was gone, and he was never coming back.

At the sound of a noise coming from the back room and the smell of food, Sirra turned her mind away from Threngrin. She thought she was alone. Then at the startling sound of a door being slammed open, she reached for her dagger. She held her breath and waited. It was the innkeeper entering the room. Sirra sighed and relaxed back in her chair. The innkeeper was laughing at something the man next to him said. She watched them as they were going around lighting the candles on the tables for the morning rush coming in for their meals. Their eyes met as she glanced around the room. The innkeeper was startled, not realizing she was even in the room.

"My, my, aren't we early," he said with a cheerful sound in his voice.

Sirra glanced up at him and nodded. "Yes."

"Well, my lass, food will be ready soon. Ham, eggs, and bread. I'll bring you a plate when it's ready," he said as he placed his hand on her shoulder.

"That would be fine." She smiled back at him.

Moments went by, and Sirra heard voices. People were coming into the inn for their morning food. Soon the room was full of people, and before she knew it, her plate of food was right in front of her.

Sirra couldn't help but overhear the conversation the two men were having next to her. They were laughing and going on about this young man who stumbled into the village a few days ago, yelling and shouting that something was after him and was trying to eat him. She did think it was silly and strange. She tried not to laugh as she finished her meal.

Sirra pushed back her plate and waved her arm at the innkeeper. Without saying a word, she gave him one gold for her meal, got up, and walked out.

She pushed her way through the crowd, making her way to the blacksmith. She needed a different weapon if she was going to find her way back home.

She walked into this huge room where she saw a sword, a few daggers, a spear, and some axes hanging on the wall. There were a few people buying, selling, and trading their goods, and in the far corner, she noticed a man making a weapon. Sirra gradually made her way to the young man standing behind the forge. The young man was slim and slightly built, had little hair on his head, and was of medium height.

"What can I do for you, lady?" he said, walking out from behind the forge.

"I am looking to buy a sword."

"A sword? You're kind of small, don't you think, to be holding a big sword." He smirked.

Sirra was so used to comments people would make about her being small, she paid no attention to him. "I might be small, but I know how to use a sword. I am actually looking for a short sword."

"I have the perfect sword for you." He turned and grabbed the sword that was hanging on the wall. "A young man just sold it . . . oh, let's see, a few days ago, I believe."

Sirra took the sword and looked it over. It looked so familiar to her. She had seen it somewhere. "How much would it be for the sword?"

The young man rubbed his chin with his fingers, then tilted his head to one side. "For you, little lady, fifteen gold."

Sirra reached into her bag without any hesitation and gave him fifteen gold. The young man nodded and walked away.

She stood outside the blacksmith, looking over the sword. The hilt and crosspiece had two snakes entwined. She knew she saw it somewhere but couldn't remember where.

It was getting late in the afternoon. Sirra finished all the errands she needed to do. She got supplies and stocked up on food. She was ready for her journey. She headed back toward the inn before the lunch rush was over. It was a nice little village, but it wasn't home. Tomorrow she was leaving to find her way back to her home. This adventure was more than she expected.

She managed to get through the crowd of people. She finally reached the inn and slowly opened the door. There was still a crowd of people eating their lunch, drinking, and telling stories, and she even noticed six men arguing in the corner. Sirra walked around the crowd of people until she found an empty table and sat down.

"You must be the newcomer in town?" a young man asked, grabbing the chair from the other table and sitting down. "So what brought you to the village?" He leaned over the table, his eyes bulging, his head slightly tilted to one side.

"I came here looking for a friend, but he's not here." Sirra felt her body shaking, her hands trembling. The young man really made her feel uncomfortable. "He's a halfling, He g—"

Cutting her off so quickly, he said, "A halfling?" He laughed. "I heard talks about a halfling. There is always a halfling around here."

"He's a friend," Sirra stated, being puzzled at his laugh.

"This halfling, what is—?"

Suddenly the sound of shattering mugs hitting the floor lingered through the air, startling Sirra, and she turned toward the end of the bar, where she saw a young man who was holding the door for an old man. This person was staring back at her, his face a face of terror. "Threngrin." Sirra's mug of ale froze in her mouth. Her eyes focused on the young man that was standing there, not sure if what she was seeing was real.

Sirra turned her head slightly to get a better look at the young man. Joy lit her face, and disbelief vanished from her eyes. She jumped from her chair, leaving the man there in midsentence, and rushed to the young man standing by the door.

She seemed weary, yet she ran wildly through the crowd toward him. She was stunned. The man at the table just sat there, watching Sirra as she hurtled her way through the crowd like a horse.

"I thought you were dead. You're alive. I looked for you everywhere." Sirra stood there, staring at him, and couldn't believe what she was seeing. Her mind felt numb, and she was at a loss for words. She could only stare at him, and then she finally cleared her throat. "I thought you were dead. How did you get out?" she screamed, struggling to get the words out, and then she stopped, in frustration. She covered her eyes with her hands and sobbed.

"Sirra!" Threngrin called out, slowly reaching her hands to uncover her eyes. "It's okay, I am alive,"

"But how?" She was so confused.

"I don't know. All I heard was a strange sound and a faint voice. Then I woke up just outside this village in those tall grass, with a bunch of sheep nibbling at me."

Sirra couldn't help it. She started laughing, and she laughed so hard that she knocked a mug of ale onto the floor. She quickly stopped, then stared at him, still in shock and seething with anger.

"You are happy to see me?" Threngrin said, grabbing her hand.

"Of course I am. I was so worried about you. I looked for you that day, all the places around there, but I couldn't find you. I sat there till morning, afraid to leave you behind. Don't you ever scare me again!" Sirra shouted out. "I thought I lost you!"

"I know you were worried. But after I pushed you out, everything went black." Threngrin looked deep into her eyes. "I wanted to save you."

Sirra could hardly stand the conversation. She knew Threngrin was telling the truth. Threngrin could see the worried look in her eyes, the confusion she was feeling, the fear she was having, and this angered her.

"I saw you were hurt. I wanted to help you." Tears rolled down her face.

Threngrin took her hands. "And we both could have died."

She turned away from him, tears rolling down her face, tears of joy and fear. She couldn't look into his eyes, knowing he was right. There was silence between them. Then her stomach churned and knotted.

Threngrin glanced around the room and spotted an empty table and steered Sirra toward it. "Sit, let's eat." He grinned. "And tomorrow we start out on our adventure again."

Sirra glared at him, shaking her head. Would he ever fear anything?

Chapter Eight

The early morning sun was trying to peek its way through the clouds that were rolling in. Thunder rumbled throughout the valley, alerting the people of a storm that was brawling. Sirra and Threngrin were planning on leaving for their adventure, but the storm was preventing them from leaving.

They made their way to the center room of the inn, where they saw everyone scattering around, preparing for the storm. Huge black clouds rolled in from the north, suddenly settling over the entire village, blotting out what little sun there was, and soon heavy rain reached them. All workers in the fields came to a halt and returned to the village. People rushed to secure their carts, to gather everything they could, and brought them inside the buildings. The rain pouring down was tremendous. A blinding streak of lightning brightened the dark clouds for miles, and deep rolling thunder echoed over the village, shaking the ground. They continued one after another. The people began to fear that the hills all around them would wash down, destroying their homes and fields, and some of the people worried that the hills surrounding them would become a waterfall with the heavy rain and would come crashing down on them.

The people gathered in the inn and talked worriedly over their mugs of ale as they watched the rain falling from the doorway. The streets became flooded, some of the road started to wash away, the wind began to pick up, and you could hear the wind howling through the cracks in the inn. Leaks began to form in the roof and the walls of the inn, and the men scrambled around trying to find what they could do to repair it.

Sirra and Threngrin stood in silence, listening to what people were saying, seeing the worry in their faces as they all huddled in small groups. Many were afraid of losing their homes and having to start over. They all were hoping that the storm wouldn't last long, but there was no sign that the storm was going to clear up anytime soon.

By midday the rain was still at a steady downpour, heavy fog began to roll in, and the temperature began to rise from the rain, making everyone uncomfortable.

The door swung open quickly, and an unusually large man, about four feet tall—not one bit of him was muscle, and his belly poked out above his belt line—came storming into the inn.

He was out of breath trying to speak. "Hel-hel-help, most of my sheep are gone! There is something out there!" he shouted. "Come now!"

The innkeeper walked up to the young man and put his hand on his shoulder. "What are you rambling about? Your sheep more likely just ran off because of the storm."

"No! I put them all in their pen. When I went to check on them, most of them were gone. Something ate them, I tell ya! Something ate them!"

Garth was the village's handyman, and he would repair and fix things around the village, but to some of the people, he was the village idiot. He would get excited and worked up over nothing. Some didn't believe half of what he would say.

"Come, come, Garth, sit down and rest. It's been a long day. Rest for a while, and later when the storm blows over, we will find your sheep." The innkeeper helped Garth to the table.

"I know something is wrong. I know what I am talking about," he stated, scratching the top of his head.

Suddenly the ground began to tremble, the inn started to shake, candles were falling off the tables and onto the floor, and the lantern that was hanging from the ceiling fell right in front of Sirra.

"See, I told you that there was something out there, something just right outside our village, and it is going to eat us!" Garth jumped up out of his chair and ran to the doorway, looking out.

An old man appeared out from a dark corner. He was short, stocky, and heavy built. His arms showed off muscles and strength. To some, he was mean. He usually kept to himself, except when the village was in danger. He made sure everyone got to safety. People called him the village protector. Not everyone had met the man. The village referred to him as a sheriff.

"All right, just settle it down. We will go check it out. We need some more men to go with. Anyone?" the sheriff stated as he walked to the middle of the room.

"We will help." Threngrin stepped forward, followed by Sirra and a few more men.

They all headed out into the storm, and from what they could see, most of the village had been destroyed by the storm. Continuing on their way past the entrance, they saw the earth beneath them had changed. The pouring rain and the trembling of the ground was slowly wracking the village around them. They followed a narrow path leading them to the pens where the sheep were being kept.

The sheriff took the lead, and the men all followed behind. He wore heavy armor that was black, his boots was leather to protect his feet and legs, and his breastplate was chain mail to protect his torso. He focused entirely on what was ahead of them, pushing his way through the rain and strong winds.

Threngrin reached down toward his belt and realized that he was missing something. He stopped dead in his tracks and turned toward Sirra. "Wait, we can't fight. I have no weapon."

Sirra laughed as she handed him her dagger with a slight grin.

Threngrin snatched the dagger out of her hand. "Wait, what am I going to do with this?" he yelled as he held it up close to her face.

"Do like you always do. Poke the creature and run." She chuckled.

"Seriously?" he yelled as he waved the dagger in front of her.

"Seriously," she snapped back as she turned to walk away.

"Wait! Stop right there!" He turned her back around, facing him. He spotted something hanging from her belt. "That is my sword!" he shouted out.

"No, it's not." She smiled.

"Yes, it is. I know that's my sword!"

"It's mine. I bought it fair and square." She grinned.

"With what? You have no gold."

"The small jasper that was in the bag." She smirked.

"You mean you sold one of my jaspers to buy my sword?" Threngrin yelled.

"You mean our jaspers, and yes, I did. Now take the dagger, and do what you do best. Run up to the creature, poke it, and take off running and hide." She was trying so hard not to laugh.

"Really? I want my sword, and I want it now! Give me my sword!" he shouted, jumping up and down.

Sirra just grinned and walked away, leaving Threngrin standing there. Threngrin took the dagger and placed it in his belt. With anger in his eyes, he watched her walk away. He was going to get his sword back if that's the last thing he did.

The innkeeper saw Sirra and Threngrin arguing and then Threngrin standing there alone. He slowly walked up to him and put his hand on Threngrin's shoulder. "What's going on?" he asked.

"Sirra has my sword, and she won't give it back to me. Instead she gave me this." He took out the dagger and held it up in the air.

"You two are arguing over a sword while something is trying to eat us?" he commented and walked away.

They all came to a complete stop, as their eyes gazed around the surrounding area. A sudden rumbling, crackling sound echoed throughout the valley, like a roaring thunder from a distance, yet it was so close. They watched as huge boulders of rocks crashed down the mountainside, landing near the village. The ground beneath their feet started to shake, moving up and down, and to their left, they saw something unusual appearing from the ground.

The creature looked like a huge many-legged worm. It had six legs with sharp hooks suitable for grasping, and its strength could snap small trees in half with one hit. Its shell was tough and yellow, and it covered its entire body but its belly. It had big black eyes. Its mouth was lined with tiny teeth, and it had two antennae that could sense movement.

Threngrin froze for a moment as he saw the creature moving toward him. He threw back his dagger. He found himself face-to-face with the creature. His skin turned pale and his eyes were wide as he saw the creature opening its mouth. Threngrin squinted from the bright lightning that shot across the sky as he tried to attack the creature, but he missed. One of the men raced toward Threngrin, pushing him out of the way just as the creature was about to snag him. Both men landed on the ground.

Suddenly Threngrin felt something hit him hard on the left side of his head, knocking him to the ground. He cried out in pain as he struggled to get to his feet. He rubbed his cheek, feeling a large welt developing. He searched the surrounding area, and there was nothing around that could have hit him.

Then the ground began to tremble, moving right under his feet. Threngrin took off running, not sticking around to see what it was. Sirra stood there watching another creature appear out from the ground, and in the blink of an eye, the creature grabbed the young man standing there with its mandibles, crushing and grinding him. Sirra watched as the creature dissolved the young man in its mouth.

Another young man ran past Sirra with his sword drawn, and the creature turned quickly toward him and struck him with a stream of acidic enzymes. The young man fell quickly to the ground, screaming in pain. Sirra ran up to the man and pulled him back toward the village, leaning him up against a tree. Threngrin ran behind the creature with his dagger drawn, and he stabbed the creature in its back. Quickly the creature turned and hit Threngrin with one of its legs, sending him flying into the air. Sirra noticed that Threngrin didn't even break the skin on the creature.

The ground began to rumble, moving where Sirra was standing, and another creature burrowed up beneath Sirra and attempted to grab her. Sirra moved quickly out of the creature's way. Threngrin saw Sirra in danger and ran toward the creature. It squirted a stream of acidic enzymes at Threngrin, and in a quick response, he hit the ground. Threngrin quickly struggled to get to his feet, grabbed Sirra by her hand, and they both ran for cover behind a tree.

Now there were three creatures lingering about, and Sirra had no idea how to fight them. Their backs had some kind of protection, and they squirted acidic enzymes. Defeating them would be impossible.

The sheriff sent a few men toward one of the creatures, but the creature grabbed one of the men with its mandibles, crushing and grinding him till the man was dissolved in the creature's mouth. Sirra and Threngrin watched as the creature took three of its legs and one by one the men went flying into the air. Then a stream of acidic enzymes came flowing out of its mouth, hitting one of the men.

The sheriff sent out four men this time, and they slowly walked around the creature, sneaking up behind it. At the same time, each man swung their sword, hitting the creature on its back, but not one of them was making any damage. The creature turned around looking at them, face-to-face for only a moment, and then the creature hit the men with its legs, sending them into the air.

Sirra then realized how she could defeat the creature. She drew out her sword. She got close enough to the creature and put herself into a ball. She slowly rolled underneath the creature. She took her sword, stabbed the creature in the belly, and sliced it open. She watched as the entrails of the creature fell to the ground. The creature reared up, then collapsed to the ground. Sirra barely escaped the dying creature's fall.

Sirra managed to get to her feet and took off running toward Threngrin. She sat down on the ground next to him, catching her breath. She heard from the distance the men cheering that she got one. Threngrin looked at her, shaking his head as if he were saying, "You are nuts."

Sirra had studied the other two creatures that were left. One had eaten but hadn't spit, and the other one spit but hadn't eaten. Although she knew she couldn't convince Threngrin to go be eaten by one of the creatures, she had another idea.

Sirra turned, looking at Threngrin with a grin on her face. Threngrin didn't like the look she was giving him or how her eyes glowed when she got an idea.

"What? Why are you staring at me like that? I really don't like the look you have," Threngrin said as he slowly moved away from her.

"I have a job for you," she said with a smirk on her face.

"Why don't I like the sound of that?"

"I need you to run out toward that creature." She pointed out. "Get the creature to spit at you. All you have to do is poke the creature and run."

"What? No! No! No! I am staying right here where it is safe. Besides, I hurt my leg, see," Threngrin said as he lifted his leg in the air.

"You look fine to me. I will give you my sword." She smiled gracefully at him.

"You mean my sword? And no, you go. Have the creature spit at you. I will sit right here."

"You know we could have the other creature just eat you." She smiled at him as she got up off the ground.

"You are so funny, Sirra, funny."

Suddenly from the distance, Sirra heard someone screaming, and she turned quickly and saw two men dragging one of the men back to the village. Sirra took off running toward the few men that were left standing. They made another attempt to attack the creature, but none of them got close enough. The creature turned on them, sending out a stream of acidic enzymes toward them. Sirra knew now this was her chance to attack.

She waited only a moment for the creature to turn away from them. She pulled out the sword from her belt and slowly walked up to the creature. She lowered herself to the ground, wiggling her way toward the creature on her stomach. She took her sword and stabbed the creature in the belly, slicing it open. She rolled quickly from underneath the creature as its entrails hit the ground, and the creature collapsed.

Threngrin and the men came running to her, and the men cheered as they stood over the creature lying dead on the ground. They had one creature left, and Sirra knew this one was going to be more difficult to defeat.

Threngrin climbed on top of the dead creature and held his little dagger up in the air, jumping up and down as if he were the one who defeated the creature. Sirra shook her head at him, then turned to walk away.

The wind picked up rapidly, making it difficult to see with the pouring rain hitting them in the face. Sirra noticed that the creature had gone back underground, but how long until it would appear again? The pouring rain and the bright lightning that scattered across the sky made it even harder to spot the creature. The creature that was left had not eaten yet. Sirra was more worried on who was going to be the next meal, so she thought about how to kill it.

Everyone stood outside the village waiting, wondering where the creature was going to appear. The ground beneath them began to tremble, and the earth started to move. Sirra felt something beneath her feet moving. Then suddenly she heard someone from inside the village screaming. Sirra and Threngrin took off running toward the village, and to their surprise, they saw the creature burrowing up underneath the ground and grabbing one of the villagers with its mandibles, crushing him and then dissolving him in its mouth.

"Now what?" Threngrin said, looking at Sirra. "You have all the answers."

"I am not sure," Sirra stated as she watched the creature closely. "This one is smarter than the others."

One of the men out of anger took off running toward the creature. When he was just within reach, the creature hit the young man with one of it legs, sending him into the air, landing on top of one of the buildings.

Sirra tried to get close enough to the creature, but strong winds came gushing through the village. The wind was so strong, it ripped shutters from some of the buildings, and pieces of wooden roofs went flying past her. Sirra ducked, trying to avoid the flying debris, not realizing just how close she was to the creature. She felt the creature hitting her with its legs, knocking her to the ground.

Sirra scrambled quickly to get to her feet just as the creature spit its acidic enzymes, barely missing her. She then heard a crackling sound just off to her right, a sound that she had never heard before. Sirra slowly backed away from the creature just as a strong force of wind uprooted a tree, landing it in front of her and flattening one of the buildings.

With the storm getting worse and the creature in the village, there was no safe place for the villagers to go. Sirra knew that there was only one chance to defeat the creature. Sirra looked back at Threngrin and nodded.

Threngrin ran up to Sirra and grabbed her arm. "No! Don't do this."

Sirra squeezed Threngrin's hand and turned away from him. She climbed the tree that was lying on the ground and stared down at the creature. Threngrin saw that Sirra was within reach of the creature, so he dashed around the tree, took out his dagger, and with all the force he had, he stabbed the creature in the back and took off running. But Threngrin didn't move fast enough. The creature quickly turned toward him, hitting him with one of its legs, sending him flying into one of the buildings. Without the creature seeing her, she quickly jumped off the tree, took out her sword, and rolled herself under the creature, slicing its belly open. The creature reared itself up, trying to get its last hit, and it collapsed onto the ground.

Threngrin slowly got himself up off the floor, being grateful that the door was opened, and walked outside. He saw Sirra lying on the ground, not sure if she was hurt, so he took off running. He reached down and touched her hand. Sirra did not move. Threngrin jumped up and cried out for help. All the men that were standing by the inn came running toward Threngrin. The innkeeper slowly reached down and picked Sirra up and carried her inside the inn.

Chapter Nine

By morning the storm had blown over. People left the inn and returned to their jobs, and some started doing repairs around the village. The storm had taken off shutters and tore off roofs, scattering them around the village. Trees uprooted by the strong winds had flattened a few buildings.

The rain finally had stopped, the huge dark clouds cleared, and a clear blue sky brightened the villagers. Everyone was relieved that the rain had finally stopped. The warm sun began to dry up the roads and the fields, leaving just small puddles here and there.

Threngrin made his way to the center of the inn, where he saw a group of people sitting at the bar. They were talking about the battle and how brave Sirra was in defeating the three creatures, and some were talking about the men that lost their lives. The men had been raising their mugs of ale all night to their friends' memory. "It's a disgrace that my friend is dead, in a battle, and we don't even know how to fight. I can't believe we are mourning like this," one of the men said as he held up his mug.

"It's called grieving," the other man said as he fell off the barstool.

Threngrin noticed all the ale on the floor and one of the men sleeping in a corner. It looked like the men had been here all night. He slowly shuffled his feet across the room and sat down at a table. He turned up his nose at the mug of ale that was set in front of him. He tried so hard not to let his emotions show, fighting back the tears that he felt coming. He was worried about Sirra. She had not woken up yet.

Threngrin kept seeing in his mind Sirra lying there on the ground, not moving. If only he was there, he could have saved her, pushed her out of the way. Sirra was lying there with one of the creatures' spikes in her leg. With every swing, the creature got her leg. Of course the creature got his last hit as it was falling toward the ground, knocking her to the ground as well. She had cuts all over her body by one leg, and there was a gash on her head from the creature's other leg. He couldn't block out the image of what she looked like when he ran up to her.

Sitting here wasn't helping. He had to be doing something. He stood up, pushing his chair back up against the wall, and walked outside the inn. He saw the village was destroyed by the storm. Shutters from some of the buildings were ripped off, and shingles were torn off roofs and scattered across the village. Many of the homes were flattened by trees. Some of them had minor damage. Threngrin stood there watching as people were trying to repair what they could and clean up to restart building again. Threngrin decided to give the villagers a helping hand in patching up roofs and rebuilding the village. It was going to be tedious work for everyone.

Three days went by, and the village was finally back to its normal life. The storm and the creatures were only a dim memory, except for Threngrin. Threngrin was just finishing up repairing the toolshed. He had finished repairing some of the building and homes when he noticed it was almost evening. Threngrin was going to call it a day when he heard someone mention something about Sirra. Not waiting to hear what he or she was talking about, Threngrin took off running toward the inn. He swung open the door and saw the innkeeper walking around the corner.

"She's awake and asking for you," he said, waving his arms.

Threngrin's heart stopped beating for a moment. She finally woke up when no one knew for sure if she ever would. He took off running to her room and pushed open her door. He couldn't believe that Sirra was sitting up and smiling. He slowly walked to her side and sat down on the bed and grabbed her hand.

"How long have I been out?"

"Three days. I was worried about you," Threngrin said as he reached out and touched her face.

"Three days!" she yelled. "What happened?"

"The creature hit you as it was falling, knocking you to the ground. But you did kill it, and it almost killed you. I am sorry I wasn't there to protect you." Threngrin got up off the bed and walked to the window.

"It wasn't your fault. I didn't get away fast enough." Sirra climbed out of bed and walked over to Threngrin.

Sirra grabbed him by the arm. "Look at me," she said, pulling at him to face her. "There was nothing you could have done. Don't go blaming yourself."

"So you remember."

"Yes, I remember everything, so stop worrying. I will be fine."

"Wait a minute, why are you out of bed? You shouldn't be up yet!" he shouted.

"I am fine. Three days in bed, I want food," she stated as she walked toward the door. "You are joining me?" She giggled.

Sirra and Threngrin slowly walked to the center of the inn. Everyone in the village heard about Sirra, and to their surprise, all the villagers were there in the inn, waiting to join them. One by one they ran up to Sirra, shaking her hand and hugging her. They were grateful that she was alive and the fact that she saved their village.

The innkeeper had a special table set up for Sirra, and he prepared a meal for everyone to celebrate.

Sirra sat down at the table. The innkeeper brought her a mug of ale and a plate of food—roasted pig, rice, and a slice of bread. It was more food than she had seen in a long time. Three days without food, she would eat anything at this point.

One of the men stood up, knocking his chair to the floor, and held up his mug in the air. "To Sirra, who helped save our village," the man called out.

"Ya, to our new friends, who will always be welcomed here," another one called out as he was spilling his mug of ale onto the floor.

"You both will always have a home here. We will never forget what you both have done for us." The innkeeper smiled and shook their hands.

One of the villagers approached her slowly. He was short, stocky, and heavyweight, with a long nose, long black hair, and deep blue eyes. He stood there in front of her with a dreary look on his face. He reached down, gently grabbed her hand, and slowly placed a small piece of mantel in her palm. He fought hard to keep the tears back as he looked into her eyes. "I want to thank you for saving my son. They say he might never walk again, but he is alive because of you. Take this metal. It's our way of honoring you in a battle that you defeated." He squeezed her hand tight and nodded his head as he turned and walked away.

Sirra looked down at her hand and then back up. She had tears in her eyes as she watched the old man walking out the door. She slowly opened her hand again. It was a small piece of metal shaped as a shield. Tears rolled down her face as she stared down at this piece of metal. In the center of the shield was a small jasper. It was the same jasper she sold at the general store a few weeks ago. It was his son she saved.

It was getting late in the night, and the villagers continued drinking and eating, but Sirra no longer wanted to drink. She felt empty inside. She wasn't fully herself yet. Threngrin helped Sirra to her room and called it a night.

Four days had passed, and Sirra and Threngrin were getting ready to leave. It was time for them to move on. Most of the repairs on the village were completed, but the villagers still had months of work to do. They gathered their things and headed out. Just as they reached the door of the inn, it swung open, barely missing Threngrin.

"One of the miners is missing!" he yelled out.

The inn had a small group of men sitting at the bar, and they turned quickly around. One of the men ran up to the miner and grabbed him by the shirt. "Who was it?" he yelled. "Who!"

"I believe it was your brother. We can't find him."

Threngrin turned the young man around, facing him. "Tell us what happened."

"We were digging in the mine, and your brother, Oscar, fell through the wall to the other side, which looks like a cave. We heard him call out for help, but when we got there, he was gone."

Threngrin turned and looked at Sirra and nodded his head. Sirra shook her head but knew Threngrin couldn't refuse. He had to go check it out. They carried their things back up to the room, except for Threngrin's brown bag, and met a group of men in the inn.

Threngrin, Sirra, and a few men followed the young miner to the mine. They entered the mine. It was dark and cold. Sirra had a bad feeling about this. They finally reached where Oscar fell through. One of the miners gave Threngrin a lantern. Sirra nodded and quickly pulled Threngrin after her. They headed down the narrow passage, barely wide enough for them to fit. They hurried to a wide open area in the cave and halted, breathless.

Cautiously they pushed their way through another crack, which was a small passage, just enough space for one person to fit through, and Threngrin slowly peeked in and saw a larger room. For a moment Threngrin saw nothing, but he heard a distinctive sound. He slowly started backing up, hitting Sirra.

"Something is definitely in there," he mumbled. "I can't see anything, but I heard something. It's standing in the far corner. I can't tell who or what it is," Threngrin said, shaking.

"We've got to get closer. It might be Oscar."

"In there? Have you lost your mind? You're just back on your feet."

"Then you go, and I will wait here." She laughed.

"Me? Why me? No, that's all right. I will sit this one out."

"Just go!" she said in a strong voice.

Threngrin's eyes went wide. He tried to get past Sirra, but she pushed him, shoving him through the crack and into a large area. As fast as he could, Threngrin quickly scrambled to get to his feet and hid behind a boulder. He couldn't believe she pushed him. A moment later, Sirra peeked through the crack to see what was happening. She didn't hear anything from him. She saw Threngrin moving uncertainly from one boulder to another, finally reaching the last boulder. He froze in his track. He couldn't bring himself to get close to see what it was.

Threngrin stayed focused on the corner as he started to walk backward. He was going to make his way back to Sirra, but with every step Threngrin made, it moved slightly toward him. Sirra slowly made her way to Threngrin in hopes it didn't spot her, but it did. It sensed both of them when they entered the room.

Threngrin looked toward Sirra and grabbed her arm. She turned toward him quickly, and his face was white with fear.

It got closer and closer until they finally got to see what it was. It stood about nine feet tall, and its body appeared thin. Its arms and legs were long and ungainly. It had three-toed feet, and its arms were wide, with hands that had sharp claws. It had hairlike mass growing out of its skull and had greenish black hair. Its eyes were sunk back in its head and black as black could be.

They watched as the creature continued to walk closer to them in an upright manner but hunched, with its shoulder sagging. The creature got a few yards from them and started throwing stones toward them.

"What is this? Throwing stones at us?" Threngrin said, hovering closer to the ground.

"I have no idea, but we can't stay here. We are going to have to make a run for it."

"What? Look at that creature," Threngrin said, lying very close to the ground. "It should be a piece of cake."

She giggled, as she patted him on the back. "I will stay right here waiting. You just let me know how that works out for you."

The creature continued to throw stones at them, trying to get them out of the corner. One of the stones hit the wall and bounced off, hitting Threngrin in the back of his head.

"That's it. It wants a stone war, so be it," Threngrin said as he gathered up some stones.

Threngrin gathered up what he could, and one by one he started throwing them at the creature. They continued throwing stones at each other for only a moment, and then the creature let out a screeching roar. It echoed so loud throughout the room, they covered their ears. The creature then moved closer to them and swung its hand at them, hitting the boulder they were hiding behind.

The echo was so loud, it brought attention to another creature. This other creature's nose twitched from not only the unfamiliar odor but the disturbing sound. One eye sunk deep in its socket opened, and the other eye partly closed. It blinked a few times, and then it fully opened. Once again its long nose twitched from a scent that lingered in the air.

The body slowly got up and sat in a sitting position. Its gangly arms were as long as a man's, and they hung from its shoulders. They were slender but showed muscles under green yellowish skin, revealing great strength. The creature's legs were long and thin, but they supported the creature's weight without any difficulty.

Its hands and feet had very sharp claws. Its skin was like some kind of moss, and it covered its whole body. In some places it was smooth, while in others it was rough and wrinkled. The creature's head had black hair, very stiff. It had very sharp and pointed teeth, and its nose was long and very pointy.

There was something in the air—not only a smell that had woken the creature up from its long sleep but a sound from another creature calling for help. It slowly turned its head around, sniffing the air. The creature was looking for clues to find where it was coming from. It followed the tunnel with its nose twitching till it came to a room and stood in the doorway.

"There are now two of them!" Sirra yelled.

"Time to go," Threngrin said as he ran to the next boulder.

The creature turned toward Threngrin, swinging its arms, trying to hit him. Sirra ran up to the creature. She jumped up and stabbed it with her sword, hitting it in the back. The creature quickly turned toward Sirra, and it swung its arms just as she ran underneath it. She jumped onto a boulder and waited until the creature was close enough to her. She then jumped in midair, slicing the creature across the chest. The creature quickly swung its arms, hitting the boulder Threngrin was hiding behind.

"Why isn't this thing dying? You hit it twice," Threngrin said, standing behind Sirra.

"I do not know! Like am I supposed to know?" Sirra shouted.

The creature took another swing at them, and Sirra lifted her sword and hit the creature in its leg. She took off running to the other side of the room. Threngrin then ran after Sirra, but he didn't get too far. The creature knocked him to the ground, sending him across the room, stopping in front of Sirra. Threngrin was lying on his back, having trouble breathing, afraid to move. The creature hit him hard, knocking the wind out of him.

"If we don't kill this thing, we are going to run out of boulders to hide behind," Threngrin said as he tried to get up.

The second creature walked into the room, moving toward Sirra. She took off running toward the creature. She stopped just within reach of it and waited. The creature looked down at her, then took a quick swing. She then took her sword, jumped up, and stabbed the creature in the chest as hard as she could. The creature slowly backed up, and the first creature swung around with both arms, hitting Sirra, throwing her to the ground. Sirra struggled to get to her feet as the first creature moved closer and closer to her. She didn't move fast enough, and the creature was right upon her. She wiggled her way underneath the creature, jumped up, and stabbed it in the belly. She managed to get to her feet and ran over to Threngrin.

"These creatures aren't falling or dying," Threngrin said as he grabbed Sirra's hand.

"I know." Sirra turned to look at him.

"So what are we going to do? They're going to kill us if we don't do something," he said, being very firm.

It wasn't long until both creatures were right there behind them. One of the creatures swung its arm, smashing the boulder they were hiding behind. The other creature went to swing at Threngrin, and Sirra raised her sword up, slicing the creature's hand off. The creature's hand landed on the ground right in front of Threngrin. He looked down at it, being a little hysterical for a moment. He then kicked it across the room. Sirra lifted up her sword and started swinging back and forth, hitting the creature with every swing, but the creature kept on swinging its arm and walking toward her. The other creature came after her with full force. It raised its hand, and Sirra raised her sword up, slicing its hand off.

Threngrin dashed toward the first creature with his dagger up in the air, not realizing the hand that was on the ground was just inches away from him. With the creature's back turned toward him, Threngrin slowly walked up behind the first creature and stabbed the creature in its back.

Threngrin then backed up just within reach of both hands. Both hands quickly jumped up, and they latched themselves onto his legs—one on his left leg and the other on his right leg.

Threngrin felt something crawling on his legs. He looked down at his legs and saw the hands attached to him. He froze for a moment, then panicked. He jumped up and down, kicking his legs up in the air, and started running around the room in circles, screaming.

"It's on me!" Threngrin yelled out. "It's on me! Get it off!"

Sirra was finally able to grab Threngrin by his arm to stop him, but she had trouble getting him to calm down, to stop kicking and jumping around. Once she got him calmed enough, she then reached down and tried to remove the hands. Threngrin was trying so hard to remain calm and not move, but he didn't know how much longer he could stand still. The urge for him to run was high. The hands had such a tight hold around Threngrin's legs, it was hard for Sirra to remove them. She took Threngrin's dagger from his belt, and she started prying the fingers from the first hand until it finally fell off. Threngrin then kicked it as hard as he could across the room. Then Sirra started on the other hand. Its grip was tighter. Sirra had to use all her strength to get this one off. Threngrin kicked it across the room.

"What is this thing, and why can't we kill it?" Threngrin asked, rubbing his leg.

"I have no idea. I have never seen a creature like this before. There is something strange about this creature, but I don't know what."

Sirra noticed by both creatures' shadows on the wall that they were right behind them. She tried to turn around as fast as she could, but it was too late. The first creature swung out his arm, and its claws grazed her back. Sirra fell to the ground. The graze was just enough that it scratched her. Her back soon felt like it was burning, like it was on fire. She then rolled around on the ground a few times. The pain was unbearable. Then she took her hand and felt her back, and she saw blood. Threngrin saw that Sirra's back was bleeding and that she was hurt. He ran up to her, grabbed her hand, and dragged her out of the creatures' way, but the second creature was upon them both. Threngrin took his dagger, and quickly he stabbed the creature in the chest.

The second creature swung at Threngrin, sending him flying across the room and landing him up against the wall. Threngrin placed his hands on the ground, trying to force himself up. He slowly struggled to get to his feet, dazed and disoriented. Threngrin then felt something underneath his hand moving. He slowly moved his hand and quickly wiggled away from it. He managed to get to his feet and slowly backed away, but the hands were following him. They were moving. Threngrin kicked at the hands, but they still kept on following him.

"Sirra," Threngrin said softly. But she didn't hear him. "Sirra!" Threngrin yelled louder. But still she did not respond. "Sirra!" he screamed at the top of his voice.

She turned toward Threngrin. "What is it?" she yelled back. Sirra was fighting both creatures, swinging her sword as fast and as hard as she could. Just as she went to give another swing, the first creature raised its arm, and she quickly brought her sword down, slicing the arm clear off its body.

"The hands, they're moving. They're chasing after me!" he cried out as he kicked the hands across the room again. But this time the hands quickly turned toward him. Threngrin kicked at both again and took off running, but the hands moved quickly, and when he turned back to look, the hands were right there.

"Take you dagger and stab them."

"You want me to do what?"

"Stab them!" she yelled. "Just stab them. I am kind of busy here."

Threngrin slowly backed up away from the hands, and the hands slowly crept across the floor toward him. He took out his dagger, and he hesitated for a moment. He then turned his head slightly, just enough where he barely saw the hands, and with a quick force, he stabbed one of the hand right in the center. He slowly reached for his dagger and removed it from the hand. He waited for only a brief second. The hand stopped moving, but the second hand latched itself across Threngrin's mouth. Threngrin turned and quickly took off running toward Sirra. But before Threngrin got to Sirra, the hand had moved up to Threngrin's eyes and covered them. Threngrin ran into a wall and knocked himself to the ground. He rolled around, prying at the hand until it finally came off his face, landing on the floor. Threngrin took his dagger and stabbed the hand in the center.

"I got it, I got it!" Threngrin shouted, jumping up and down. But then his eyes widened, and he was very surprised as he watched the hand with a dagger in it creeping its way toward him. "What?" he said as he watched his dagger move across the floor.

Threngrin tapped Sirra on the shoulder and pointed toward the hand with a dagger in it, moving toward them, and at the same time she noticed both creatures were regenerating. Both creatures were slowly growing back a new hand. They were healing themselves.

Sirra stepped back, leaning up against the wall. "Oh boy, we are so dead, so dead!" she cried out.

"What? What are you talking about?" he said, grabbing her arm.

"We can't kill these things. Look, they are regenerating their body parts, and if that hand reached the creature, it will reattach itself. So no matter how many times we stab or slice them, they will not die."

"Now you noticed?" Threngrin began to shake as he fell to the ground.

"I didn't know. I just now noticed the hand."

"So how do we kill them, or how do we get out of here."

"Not sure!" she yelled as both creatures took another swung at them and missed. They both ran past the creatures to the other side of the room.

"Oh no, the arm is moving toward the first creature," Threngrin pointed out.

Sirra then noticed the lantern that was still up against the wall. Not knowing for sure if it would work, Sirra ran and grabbed the lantern. She took the cover off of it and held it up toward the creatures. The creatures let out a loud roaring sound and slowly backed away. Sirra saw how the creatures were so afraid of fire. She turned back toward Threngrin, knowing that if she did this, they would be left in the dark. She nodded her head at him, and Threngrin slowly moved his way toward Sirra and squeezed her hand.

Sirra waited until the creatures were close enough to her, and she then threw the lantern onto them. The creatures became balls of fire and roared out as loud as they could, swinging their arms around, and soon fell to the ground. Moments later, a great blaze of fire brightened the room, blinding Sirra and Threngrin. Then something exploded in the center of the room, sending them flying across the room and hitting the wall.

Sirra and Threngrin got knocked out by the blast, and they both lay there lifeless.

Chapter Ten

Sirra and Threngrin lay on the ground lifeless. The blast from the explosion knocked them out. A cool breeze bearing down on them from the north sent a chill throughout Sirra's body, causing her to stir. Sirra being dazed and disoriented slowly came to. She reached over and shook Threngrin, trying to get him up. It took only a moment for Threngrin to get his thoughts together, and he slowly sat up. They sat there huddled together in the blackness, trying to get warm, not saying a word. Everything to them had changed. Their surroundings were totally different from what they remembered. They were no longer in the cave.

They could hear something move, the scraping sound growing louder and louder. They sat there, not saying a word or even breathing as they listened, not sure which direction it was coming from. Threngrin wanted to run but was afraid that what was out there would attack him if it found him, and he was more afraid that if he moved, it would hear him and attack him on the spot. Threngrin moved closer to Sirra. Shaking as the cool night breeze blew across them, Sirra motioned for Threngrin to move slowly behind the bushes that were close by. Sirra knew they were in trouble.

Suddenly again they heard a sharp bark, the sound of a dog barking, another bark, then another, and then very quickly it changed to a growl. Cautiously Sirra raised her head above the bushes, trying to see in the complete darkness where it was coming from. The creature was crouched down to the ground directly across from them. Some fifteen feet away was a huge yellowish brown canine. It was stocky and had more muscles than any other creature that Sirra had ever seen. Its white teeth showed and was gleaming as it watched them. Sirra and Threngrin sat there facing each other in complete stillness. The creature breathed at a low and steady pace. It was growling and snapping right in front of them. Then with a snarl of rage, the creature sprang up toward them, its mouth open wide, ready to attack. Quickly Sirra grabbed Threngrin and held him tight, and just as the dog leaped into the air to attack, it quickly disappeared.

Sirra and Threngrin shook their heads and rubbed their eyes a few times, looking around them for the dog.

"What happened, and where did the dog go?" Threngrin asked, glancing over his shoulder.

"For a moment I thought we were dinner," Sirra said, pulling herself away from Threngrin.

"Ya, me too, but I don't think I would taste so good," he said as he patted himself, making sure he wasn't missing any body parts. "By the way, the dog, where did it go?'

"I don't know. It just disappeared."

"Dogs don't just disappear," Threngrin snapped quickly with a sharp voice. "Where did it go?"

"I don't know," Sirra quickly responded.

Threngrin turned his head to take another look around, and he jumped so high, he hit Sirra, knocking her over. The dog was right up to his face. He could feel it breathing on him, its eyes glowed, and its mouth opened wide, showing all of its teeth. The dog slowly rose up its paw, ready to strike. Threngrin closed his eyes and covered his head with his arms, waiting for it to attack. Then in the blink of an eye, the dog disappeared again.

"What is going on here? What is this place? We have to get out of here!" Threngrin said as he scrambled to get to his feet.

Sirra grabbed his hand and jerked him back down to the ground as fast as she could. "Sit back down! Don't move," she whispered in a calm voice.

"What? Stay here? We can't. We must leave now. I really don't want be its dinner or its snack," Threngrin said, panicking, looking over his shoulder for the dog.

"If you make any sudden movement, you will be its dinner. I have no idea where we are or what is going on, but I do have this feeling that dog is still out there waiting. Just sit back, stay calm, and wait," she said, holding his hand.

"Stay calm? Stay calm? How can I stay calm? You're not the one that this dog tried biting the head off. It was me, and twice, may I remind you!" Threngrin pulled his hand away from Sirra and crossed his arms. "Stay calm, she said. Ya right," he said to himself as he stared into the darkness.

Sirra heard his comment, and she quickly turned toward him, gave him a hard stare, and shook her head. All they could do for now was to wait for the right moment to run for it.

Hours went by, and there was no sign of the dog anywhere. Sirra wasn't sure if the dog gave up, disappeared for good, or was waiting for them to make a move. Sirra slowly stood up. Checking out the surroundings, she could tell it was all clear. She tapped Threngrin on the back and gave him a slight nod, and they broke out in a slow jog. They went around trees, bushes. They were in the heaviest and deepest part of the forest. The night was clear and very quiet. The only sound they heard was their feet stepping on twigs that covered the ground. Low branches whipped their hands and faces as they ran, leaving marks on their skin. They ran as fast as they could, moving around oak and pine trees, jumping over fallen branches that had broken off the trees. They finally reached a slope, and they scrambled up as fast as their legs would go, not pausing to look back but only focusing on what was ahead of them. They watched the ground rush past them, not leaving a trail. Slipping and tripping over twigs that covered the ground, they finally reached the top of the slope, and all they could see was miles of open land and trees. What was really ahead of them, they had no clue.

They stood there. Sirra had a strange feeling, a feeling that made the hair on her arms stand up. Someone or something had been following them for a long time. She wasn't really all that surprised, but it was like whatever it might be, it was in no hurry to catch them. She even thought that maybe she saw something lingering between the trees, but she never saw it again. The feeling she had taunted her for the last couple of miles, telling her to keep her guard up.

After they rested for a brief moment, they took off running across the uneven ground, moving around bushes and boulders that lay in their path. Threngrin followed, dodging the low tree branches that she pushed out of her way to get through, forgetting that he was behind her. The muscles in his legs began to hurt as he tried to keep up with Sirra. Sirra glanced back a few times, still having this feeling that they were being followed. Threngrin watched Sirra as she jumped over branches, intent on getting through the forest. Sirra's legs began to burn, and she was beginning to get tired, but the fear of something that was out there kept her from stopping. They had no choice but to continue on.

Suddenly there was a movement in front of her, between two pine trees. It was enough to convince her that they were being followed. She stopped in her tracks and slowly drew her sword and waited for whatever it was to appear. Threngrin suddenly tensed as he finally saw something move just ahead of them. It was moving closer to them. Threngrin reached for his dagger and realized that he no longer had a weapon. He searched the ground around them and came upon some rocks about the size of his hand. He figured if nothing else, he would stone it to death. It slowly crept its way out from behind the pine trees, moving its way toward them, and to their surprise, they saw a large green thing. Its body covered in warts, this creature was standing right in front of them. They both froze in place. They had never seen such a creature like this before. The creature's wicked claws crunched against the ground beneath it as it slowly moved its way toward them, staring them down as if they were its next meal. Then without warning, the creature raised its claw to take its strike, but in the blink of an eye, it disappeared. Threngrin almost laughed out loud, feeling that he was beginning to lose his mind. They waited quietly and patiently, making sure the creature was gone before they made any sudden movement. Once Sirra felt that they were once again alone, she took off running again as fast as she could.

Moments had passed, and the few trees that were ahead of them grew closer. It was like they were coming to a whole new area of the forest. There was no sound. Nothing seemed to be moving around them. It was as if all the living creatures had disappeared and they were the only living things around. The sky became lighter as the night began to fade, and slowly the stars above them disappeared.

They finally reached an area where there were barely any trees. They both fell to the ground beneath a tall oak tree, their hearts pounding so hard and so fast from the strain of running. Sirra knew they couldn't stay there for long. Although their legs hurt, they had no choice but to continue on. They lay motionless, trying to catch their breaths. Sirra dragged herself to get to her feet, glancing in all directions. Nothing seemed to be moving around them, and it appeared that they made it out without being something's nightly dinner. But she knew deep down inside they were still not out of danger. Sirra slowly reached down and dragged Threngrin to get him on his feet, pulling him along as they made their way through the trees, and soon they came to a steep slope. Threngrin followed behind her, not caring where they were going. He had enough trouble trying to keep one foot in front of the other.

The slope became rugged, and the surface was covered in boulders. Trees had fallen, bushes were covered with thorns, and the ground was uneven, making climbing very hard. Sirra tried to keep a steady pace as she climbed over the obstacles, hurrying as fast as she could. Threngrin followed, trying to keep up. They scrambled and clawed, trying to keep their footing as they slowly made their way up the slope. The stars had disappeared, and the sun had slowly appeared above them. They could feel the warmth of the sun driving away the chill that was lingering in the air. Sirra was beginning to get tired, and her breathing was getting short as she continued on. Threngrin, still following her, fell to the ground and started crawling, dragging his body behind her. His arms and hands were cut, and he had scratches from the rocks and bushes as he tried to keep up with Sirra.

Suddenly just as they made it halfway up the slope, Threngrin cried out and fell, grasping a boulder. Sirra quickly turned around in fear. She caught in her sight something huge, something coppery with a little green tint that slowly rose from behind the mountain slope.

Threngrin was lying on top of a boulder and motioned Sirra to crawl quickly over to him, in hopes that the creature hadn't seen them, and as he tried to keep his balance, the boulder started to move underneath his feet.

"You are hurting me," a voice came from underneath him.

Threngrin quickly stood up, screaming, losing his footing, and fell down the mountain slope. Sirra watched Threngrin roll down the mountain slope until he came to a complete stop at the bottom. She quickly made her way down to him.

As she reached the bottom, she saw Threngrin lying facedown on the ground. She bent down and slowly rolled him over, being very careful not to hurt him. His eyes popped open, making Sirra jump about two inches off the ground. He just stared at her, not saying a word.

"Are you hurt?" Sirra said, grabbing his hand.

"That boulder talked to me."

"Boulders don't talk." She giggled.

"And dogs don't disappear." Threngrin turned his head, staring at her. "But it did."

"Threngrin."

"No, no, boulders don't talk, dogs and creatures don't disappear, and I bet you that thing up there will disappear too."

"You must have hit your head during your fall." Sirra reached over and patted his head.

Threngrin pushed her hand away. "I am telling you that boulder talked to me. And I didn't hit my head. I am perfectly fine."

"Sure you are. Can you stand up?"

"I can, but I am not going anywhere. I am going to stay right here. Talking boulders and flying creatures, I am not moving," Threngrin said as he stomped his foot on the ground.

"Fine, it shouldn't take too long for whatever creature that is out there to reappear and eat you for dinner. So you just stay right here."

Threngrin looked up toward the mountain and then behind him—not much of a choice. "Fine, fine, wait for me."

Sirra and Threngrin slowly worked their way up the mountain slope. Sirra rested her hand on top of a boulder. "That hurts." Sirra jumped, almost falling back down the mountain. She stood there looking around her but saw nothing. She continued on her way. "Do you mind?" Sirra froze in her tacks.

Threngrin put his hand on her shoulder gently. "See, I told you, boulders talk."

Sirra gave Threngrin a quick look. "Boulders don't talk," she snapped back. She placed her foot on another boulder.

"My head." She quickly moved to her right.

"Ouch." She then moved to her left.

"Ouch." She looked around but didn't see anything. Then the ground right under their feet started moving, and one by one the boulders around them started to come to life. They had appendages that acted like hands and feet. Sirra slowly moved backward.

"Hey, what's this," and it raised itself up, knocking Sirra and Threngrin down the mountain again.

"See, I told you that the boulders talk, but no, you never listen to me," Threngrin said with his arms crossed.

Sirra turned toward him. "Fine, we will just have to find another way up the mountain and be careful not to step on any boulders."

"And how do we do that? There are boulders everywhere."

They started walking along the mountainside, when Sirra noticed a small path leading up the mountain slope. They were halfway up, trying not to step on any boulders. Threngrin then spotted something red. It was glowing. He slowly made his way around the boulders, and just as he was close enough, he reached down to pick it up. Then the boulder right next to him moved straight up, knocking him back down the mountain.

Sirra walked down the mountain and looked down at Threngrin, shaking her head. "Did you get it?"

"No," he said as he got up to his feet.

"Good, now let's go." And she turned away and headed back toward the path.

About a quarter of the way up the mountain, their entire surroundings of boulders started to rise up, and this flying dragon came out of nowhere and started circling right above them. The dragon soared toward them, and in that moment, Threngrin knew they were going to die. They hit the ground, lying facedown, as the creature flew right past them, landing only a few feet away.

Threngrin tugged at Sirra's shirt. "We are surrounded by talking boulders and a huge flying creature. We are going to die again."

Sirra pushed his hand away. "Would you stop it! And no, we are not going to die."

"Sure we are. Take a look around us! We are surrounded."

Sirra got up to her feet and brushed herself off. "Let's go."

They only went a few more feet, and the dragon jumped up into the air and flew right over them. They could feel the breeze from the dragon's wings as it passed by them.

"Sirra!" Threngrin cried out. He felt the ground underneath his feet begin to move, feeling like it was gong to open up to swallow him whole. The ground became mushy and soft, and before Threngrin knew it, he was standing in mud.

"Nice, nice, now I am stuck in mud. Sirra, get me out of here!" he yelled.

Sirra turned around quickly, and she couldn't believe what she was seeing. She grinned from ear to ear, trying not to laugh. "You're stuck in mud."

"Not funny. Get me out of here!" Threngrin shouted as he tried wiggling his way out.

Sirra reached down and grabbed his hand. She pulled with all her strength, but he wasn't moving. It was like something had a hold of his feet, keeping him there.

"You're really stuck in the mud," she said with a sight giggle. "Get it? Stuck in the mud."

"Ya, I got it, funny, and it also feels like I am sinking. Get me out of here."

"I am trying." Sirra grabbed his hand again and pulled and pulled. The dragon flew down toward them, getting just close enough that they could feel the wind from its wings, and with one last pull, they both went flying, Sirra landing on one of the boulders.

"Ouch, that hurt."

"Sorry," Sirra said as she moved away.

Sirra looked at Threngrin and smiled. "Looks like you had a mud bath."

"Funny. Can we get out of here now?"

They continued on, but a moment later, the dragon swept down again, with its wings spread out, getting so close to them, and again they hit the ground, covering their heads.

"What is it with this creature?" Threngrin said, looking up at the dragon.

"It's waiting for the right time to eat us." Sirra shrugged her shoulders.

They continued on again, but to their surprise, there was a stone wall right in the path, blocking them from getting to the other side. Sirra shook her head. She tried climbing the wall, but there was nothing for her to grip, and her feet kept on sliding. Threngrin found a small boulder up against the wall. He patted it, making sure it wasn't one of those live boulders. Threngrin got a good grip on the wall, and he was barely halfway up when the dragon flew right past, knocking him off the stone wall and back on the ground. Threngrin lay there looking up at the sky, watching the dragon circling above them. Threngrin finally made his way to the top of the wall. He lay across the wall, trying to catch his breath, and in the blink of an eye, the wall disappeared. He found himself once again facedown on the ground.

"Ouch, that hurt! What happened?"

"The wall disappeared. We have to go."

"The wall disappeared? Where did it go?" Threngrin said as he looked around.

"I don't know. Now get up." Sirra reached down and grabbed Threngrin's hand. "Now!" she yelled.

The dragon was circling above their heads, but this time there was something different about it. The dragon never came back down. It made Sirra nervous, wondering what the dragon was up to. With the terrible fear that she had, Sirra pulled Threngrin up off the ground, and they climbed, shaken and exhausted, to the top of the mountain.

Looking down the mountain across the land, it was once again forest. Sirra looked back behind her and noticed that the dragon had disappeared, but the boulders still remained there, and they were all standing, watching them. It was much easier going down the mountain than it was going up. They quickly made their way down, hoping that the dragon wasn't following them, and within minutes, they were lost once again in the forest.

They slowed their pace once they entered the dark forest. Threngrin felt so lost and had no idea where they were going or where they were. He stopped in his tracks and called out to Sirra.

"Why don't we go that way?" He pointed. "Why are we going this way?" he demanded.

"We are going this way because I say so."

"Because you say so," Threngrin snarled. "Because you say so."

"Certainly," she answered with a grin on her face.

"What if I want to go this way?" He pointed to the left.

"You go that way. I will go this way," she said with a grin on her face.

"You are so bossy." He threw his arms up in the air and decided to follow her. "Bossy, I tell you, just plain bossy."

There was a moment of silence as they continued on what appeared to be a trail. The warmth of the sun sent a damp, cold air through the thick forest. They moved quickly, their fingers almost numb from the cold. The forest was well sheltered, and you could barely see the sunlight shining through. Threngrin could see in the distance that the weather conditions were changing. A heavy storm was heading their way. It was bitter cold, yet there's warmth from the sun—this was not a good thing.

After walking for what seemed like hours, Threngrin found a good place for them to camp, to rest, in hopes that the storm would pass by quickly. The fire crackled and snapped as Threngrin threw wood to the fire. Sirra leaned back against a tree and folded her arms for warmth. Several hours passed by, and the sun went behind the clouds. The wind blowing was chilly, coming from the west, and they sat close to each other, watching, waiting. They couldn't say what they were waiting for or why, only that they felt a sense of threat, a sense of eyes watching and ears listening. Who or what could be out there? What was waiting for them?

Sore and tired, they curled up by the campfire. They could not move anymore. Threngrin's muscles in his legs and arms were on fire. His body had cuts and bruises. He just wanted to sleep for the next few days. Sirra's body felt like she had been through a wringer. She could barely feel her fingers, and every muscle in her body felt like it was on fire. Threngrin threw another log to the fire, and they both lay on the ground as close to the fire as they could. Sleep was what they needed, wanted, but they were too afraid to do so.

Sirra turned to Threngrin, and she placed her hand on his shoulder. "You sleep first, and in a few hours, I will wake you. Then I will sleep."

"You think I can sleep? Disappearing dog and talking boulders and flying creature. I can't sleep."

"I bet you can if you just close your eyes. Give it a try," she stated as she rubbed his head.

Threngrin didn't put up much of a fight. He curled up in a ball and closed his eyes, and within seconds, he was sound asleep. Sirra sat up against a tree, on the lookout for whatever might be out there, but she just couldn't keep her eyes open any longer. She figured on closing her eyes for only a minute, but before long she was sound asleep.

Chapter Eleven

Off in the distance, there was a growling, hissing sound that echoed throughout the valley. It was so loud and creepy, it made the hair on Threngrin's back stand straight up.

A clatter of falling rocks coming from behind them made Sirra jump to her feet. Sirra looked around and saw nothing there. Nothing was around them that they could see, but something was coming toward them. Another clatter of falling rocks sounded like it was getting closer and closer. Sirra watched as something from the distance started to grow. It was standing there on the edge of the mountain.

"What is that?" Threngrin asked as he ran behind a tree.

"I can't tell. It's too far away."

The creature stood there, staring down at Sirra. She could barely make out what it was until it finally took one more leap toward her. She noticed it was the creature they encountered earlier, the one that disappeared. The creature was gradually making its way down the mountain toward her. The creature took another huge leap and was now face-to-face with Sirra. She slowly drew her sword and swung it up in the air, ready to attack. The creature moved quickly and knocked her to the ground before she could even get a hit in. Threngrin ran up toward the mountain to get behind the creature, and he picked up a rock and pitched it at the creature, hitting it straight in the back of its head.

"Threngrin, watch out!" Sirra yelled out, as she was scrambling to get back to her feet.

The creature moaned, and rubbing the back of its head, it slowly turned toward Threngrin. Its mouth was wide open, looking at his next meal, and Threngrin could see its long pointed teeth.

"Don't worry, it will disappear soon just like it did before and everything else that we have encountered!" he shouted.

"No, it's not!"

"Sure it will. Just watch." Threngrin picked up some more rocks just in case the creature didn't disappear.

The creature leaped toward Threngrin, and as the creature was getting closer and closer to him, he realized that it wasn't going to disappear. He picked a huge boulder and threw it at the creature, but the boulder went right past the creature's head, missing Sirra only by an inch, as she was working her way toward Threngrin.

Threngrin picked up another rock and held it over his head, waiting for the creature to get close enough to him. The creature's eyes stared at him. It was so terrifying that Threngrin started to tremble. Carefully he waited till the creature was close enough, and timing it just right, he pitched the rock at the creature. With all the strength and muscles he had, he struck the creature, crushing its leg.

"I got it." He jumped up and down with joy as he heard the creature's leg snap. The creature stumbled backward as it let out a low groan of pain.

Threngrin picked up another boulder, held it up over his head, and was ready to pitch it at the creature. "Don't throw me." The voice came from above him.

Threngrin jumped. He looked at the boulder and quickly put it down in its place, and carefully he grabbed another one. He lifted the boulder up, and he pitched it as hard as he could, hitting the creature in the shoulder. Sirra ran up to the creature and took out her sword. She held her sword up above her, and just as she got close enough to it, the creature fell to the ground, lodging itself between two rocks.

Sirra stood over the creature, watching its leg twitch back and forth. Sirra and Threngrin both jumped when they heard a strange sound. It was like someone was rubbing two rocks together. The creature took his leg into his warty hands and arranged it where it belonged. Sirra slowly moved in to get a better look, Threngrin squinted and covered his eyes with his hands and turned his head slightly. The creature stared at Sirra and groaned at her, reaching out toward her with his claw. She jumped back quickly. But the creature turned back toward his leg.

Along with the rubbing sound of two rocks, bubbles were forming under the creature's skin, and it suddenly eased with the groaning sound. Sirra didn't realize right away what was going on, and the creature turned his eyes back on her, focusing its attention on her. Before she knew it, the creature was standing on its two feet. The creature positioned itself ready to fight. It slowly moved toward her. The leg limb was healed, the creature was standing on two good legs, and it was once again supporting its own weight.

"Oh no, it can regenerate!" Sirra yelled.

"Why isn't this thing disappearing?" Threngrin said with a puzzled look on his face.

"Did you hear me? I don't care that it's not disappearing. I care that it's regenerating."

"What do you want me to do?"

"Don't just stand there! Help me kill it." Sirra caught the creature by the corner of her eye as it slashed out with its claw again. Sirra quickly turned, hitting the creature with her sword. Striking it quickly, she sliced the creature's hand clear off, landing on the ground in front of her. It made a strange sound, and green blood squirted all over the ground. Sirra cast a quick look over at Threngrin. He was still standing there with his hands over his eyes.

The creature was stunned, he had lost one of his hands, and Sirra took her sword and swung it back and forth, pushing the creature backward. Although the creature was taller than Sirra, she continued on striking, dodging, and striking at it. The creature dodged every swung as it held its oozing arm up in the air. Then Sirra saw the most sickening thing. She saw three small claws forming from its arm where she sliced its hand off. She heard popping sounds and saw its skin being stretched out. She couldn't believe just how fast it was growing another claw. Within minutes, its hand was complete, and the creature had a new disgusting hand. Then there was another strange sound that came from the creature's mouth, it was a popping sound, and then white and yellowish foam came oozing out of it. Sirra thought the creature was going to collapse on the ground, but instead the creature slowly crept its way toward her.

Sirra backed up as the creature moved closer and closer to her. She struggled to keep her balance, while loose rocks around her were sliding from underneath her feet with every step she made. The creature got close enough to her, and it swung its clawed hand at her. She dodged quickly but lost her balance and fell on a large boulder. The creature held up its claw as he took another step forward to take in its final strike. Threngrin peeked his head around the tree and saw Sirra was lying on a boulder and the creature was moving in for its final kill. Threngrin picked up a heavy rock and pitched it at the creature, hitting it in the back of the head. The creature jerked its head up and turned around quickly toward Threngrin.

"Threngrin!" Sirra cried out.

Sirra didn't even notice where Threngrin was. All she knew was that the creature was now going after him. "This is not like before! Run, you numskull!"

"I can kill it!" Threngrin shouted.

"With what? Your finger? Or are you planning on stoning it to death?"

Threngrin didn't really know how he was going to kill it. All he knew was that he had to do something. The loose rocks made it hard for him to keep his balance, but he kept on throwing the rocks at the creature, pushing it back for only a second until the creature regained its footing and continued its way toward Threngrin.

Sirra, filled with fear, scrambled to get to her feet and ran after Threngrin. She crept up close enough to the creature, took out her sword, and stabbed it in its back. Green blood gushed out, spraying on Sirra. The creature stood there, groaning, stumbling to keep its balance, and Sirra slowly made her way around the creature toward Threngrin.

"Don't you move! Stay right there!" Sirra shouted, waiting for the creature to move a little closer, and then she took another swing at it.

The creature slowly moved forward, and with all her strength, she stabbed the creature in the belly. Sirra noticed the creature was starting to regenerate again, but with the blow to its stomach, the creature fell to the ground, rolling down the mountain. Threngrin turned to head down the mountain toward the creature.

"No!" Sirra grabbed Threngrin's arm. "We have to go now!"

"We can kill it! It's down, hurt," Threngrin stated as he pointed down the mountain.

"It's regenerating, growing back, and healing itself. We can't kill it."

"We can cut off its head." Threngrin chuckled.

Sirra grabbed Threngrin by his shirt and pulled him toward her. "It will grow another head or maybe two. The only way I know that might work was to kill it by fire. Do you have fire in your pocket?" Threngrin shook his head. "Then we must go now before the creature completely heals itself."

Sirra led the way, and they raced into the forest as fast as they could. The creature was no longer in sight. Sirra ran back over the plans they had formed. If the creature discovered where they were, it might warn others, and then all the possible trails would be watched. Sirra had to assume that there were more than one of those creatures, and they were probably watching the valley. They would have to continue on, forcing themselves, which meant very few hours of sleep or rest. This would be tough enough, but the real problem was where to go from there. They were very low on supplies and not sure where the next town or village was. It could take them days or weeks before they would reach one. Given their situation, it would be impossible to do much more than choose a direction. But which way should they go? Which direction would the creatures least expect them to go?

Sirra considered all angles carefully, though she had already made up her mind. West was all open land as far as she could tell, so going south would be a better choice, since they had a better chance of running into a village or a town than going west. But this was the logical route for them to take, so the creatures would be watching the trails and waiting. The open country offered them little cover, and it made it easier for them to get caught and killed.

They headed southeast, through miles and miles of rough ground. This direction was a dangerous one, but the creatures wouldn't expect to be out this far, they hoped. They went through a murky forest, treacherous lowlands, hidden swamps, and many dangerous creatures that killed travelers, but for them, this was still the best choice to take.

They reached a very small opening of land and halted, breathless, beside a huge oak tree. She looked cautiously around them. Sirra had no idea where the creatures might be by this time. They heard several dogs barking furiously in the distance, so something must be close. Dawn was only a little over an hour away, and Sirra knew they couldn't stay here. If they were to stay in the open when it became light, the creatures following them would see them in the open, and they could be caught.

Sirra slapped Threngrin on the back and nodded, breaking into a jog as they moved away from the open field and went into the heavy clumps of trees and bushes. The night became silent again, except for the sound of their feet padding on the wet ground. Leaf branches whipped at them as they ran past, slapping their hands and their faces. They ran quickly, dodging in and out of the heavy oak and pine trees, bounding over loose gravel and fallen twigs that were scattered around them. They spotted a hill up ahead, or it could be a slope. They scampered up the open grassland as fast as their little legs would carry them, not pausing to look back, but only looking ahead to the ground that rushed by them. Slipping on the damp grass, they reached the top of the hill, where their eyes were greeted with a great view of the valley below them.

Sirra had no trouble running across the uneven ground, moving around the bushes and boulders that blocked their path, but Threngrin followed doggedly. The muscles in his legs were working hard trying to keep up with her. He watched Sirra run ahead of him, bounding over scattered gravel, intent on reaching the other side of the valley about two miles ahead. Threngrin's legs were beginning to hurt, but his fear of the creatures somewhere behind them kept him from falling behind.

Hours passed quickly, and the woods ahead grew closer as they ran wearily, silently, through the chill night. There wasn't a sound, and nothing moved around them. It was as if they were the only ones around. Did the creatures give up? The sky was growing lighter as the night began to fade, slowly disappearing into the morning light. They ran on. They needed to run faster. Being caught was not a good thing.

They finally reached a wooded area, and they collapsed on the twigs that were covering the ground beneath a tall oak tree, their ears hearing nothing but their hearts pounding loudly from the strain of running. They lay motionless for several minutes, trying to catch their breaths. Then Sirra dragged herself to get to her feet and looked back and saw nothing but open land. Nothing was moving either on the ground or in the air, and it appeared they had gotten this far not seeing a single creature. But they were still in a dangerous place. Sirra reached over and dragged Threngrin to get on his feet, pulling him along as she moved through the trees. Threngrin followed, no longer thinking, but concentrating on putting one foot in front of the other.

They soon came to another slope, but this one was more rugged, and its surface was of boulders, fallen trees, prickly bushes—a very uneven ground that made the climb difficult. Sirra set a pace, moving over large boulders as fast as she could, while Threngrin followed her footsteps. The two scrambled their way up the slope. The sky began to grow lighter, and the stars began to disappear. Ahead of them, they could see the sun was beginning to grow with orange and yellow, reflecting the outline of the horizon. Sirra was beginning to get tired. Her breath was getting slower and slower, becoming more difficult as she stumbled on. Threngrin forced himself to crawl, dragging his body after Sirra. His hands and forearms were scratched and cut by the sharp rocks and prickly bushes. The climb seemed endless. Their move became slower and slower, over the rugged ground, but their fear of the creatures alone forced their sore legs to continue moving. If they get caught now after all their effort . . .

Then finally as they reached the halfway mark, Threngrin cried out in warning and fell against a large boulder. Sirra whirled around fearfully. Her eyes caught a huge black object that rose slowly from the distance, climbing like a great bird. Sirra dropped behind a huge boulder. She slowly peeked out and waved at Threngrin to crawl quickly over to her in hopes the creature had not seen them. It circled around them, and then a sudden cry busted from the creature. Their terror grew as the creature moved directly toward them, Threngrin knew this was it, they were caught, and they were going to die again. But instead the creature turned north and headed toward the horizon until it was lost from their sight.

They lay there on the loose rocks for a few minutes, afraid the creature would come back the minute they tried to move. But when their fear faded away, they slowly got to their feet and resumed to climb to the top of the slope. It was a short distance to the top, and they hurried down to the open field and toward the concealment of the forest. Within minutes, they were lost in the forest once again.

They had lost a lot of time, and they had to make it up fast. Night was closing in on them, and still they kept a steady pace, getting as far as they could from the creature.

Threngrin was getting so weak, he no longer cared where they were going. He even lost track of how long they had been running. All he knew was that he could no longer go on without rest. Threngrin found a good hiding spot. He pushed his way through bushes to an oak tree and collapsed to the ground. His legs and feet were on fire. Sirra noticed that Threngrin was no longer behind her. "Threngrin!" she called out.

"Over here," he said in a very weak voice.

Sirra made her way to him, and she saw him lying there lifeless. "We have to continue on. Get up," she stated as she tried to get him on his feet.

"I can't. I am done. I can't move!" he cried out.

"You got to. Now get up and let's go." She tugged at him again.

"My feet, my legs, they feel broken." He let out a slight groan.

"Okay, here, I have found something for you."

Threngrin gave her a puzzled look. "What am I supposed to do with that?" He chuckled.

"It's a stick. Use it to help you walk. Now get up. We will stop at dark to rest for the night."

Still giving her a puzzled look, Threngrin took the stick and slowly rose to his feet. They headed out once again. Threngrin tried to use the stick, but it was no help. He soon gave up and started to use the stick to hit pebbles that was on the ground, as well as bushes, even hitting trees that they ran past.

Sirra stopped quickly and turned toward Threngrin. "Are you trying to get us caught? Stop that!" she snapped at him.

Threngrin paid no mind to what she said, and he continued on hitting everything they ran past. But his luck soon ran out. He came up to a big oak tree and hit it as they were passing. "Ouch!" it cried out.

Threngrin froze. He stopped dead in his tracks. He looked around but saw nothing. He shrugged his shoulder and continued on. He continued hitting everything he passed. Again he soon came up to another big oak tree. "Ouch!" it cried out.

Threngrin stopped again but saw nothing. He was beginning to think he was losing his mind. Sirra turned and saw Threngrin standing there, and she slowly walked up to him. "I thought I heard something," he said, looking around.

"Sure you did. We have to keep moving."

"You didn't hear anything?" he stated.

"No! Was I supposed to? Let's go." She reached and grabbed his hand.

Threngrin shook his head and continued on. Once again he went back hitting everything he passed. He again came up to a big oak tree, and he hit it as he passed, but this time the outcome was different. A tree branch reached down and swiftly grabbed Threngrin by his ankle. "Hey! What is—?" That was all Threngrin got to say. He found himself hanging upside down by his ankle from a tree. Sirra heard Threngrin cry, and she stopped and turned around. She couldn't help but giggle as she saw Threngrin swinging from a tree by his ankle.

"Ouch, you little person, why are you hitting me? That hurt! You hurt me."

Threngrin didn't really know how to react to a talking tree. He was stunned and surprised to find himself hanging from a talking tree. All he could think of was to say, "I am sorry."

Sirra tried not to giggle but found it really hard, and her little giggles became a laugh. She started to laugh so hard, she fell on the ground rolling. "Stop laughing! Help me down!" Threngrin yelled out.

But every time she looked at him, she started to laugh again. "I am sorry, glad you find this funny, go ahead laugh, and get me down!" he demanded.

"Little person, why did you hit me?" the tree asked again.

"I said I am sorry," Threngrin begged.

The tree kept on swinging Threngrin left and right, and Sirra couldn't herself. She laughed so hard just watching him swinging from his ankle. "Sorry! Sorry! Stop!" Threngrin cried out.

"Little person, you hurt me!" the tree said again in a low voice. "Ouch!"

The tree continued swinging Threngrin in midair for what seemed like hours. Threngrin kept repeating himself. "Sorry!" Soon words stopped being exchanged, and the tree quickly stopped moving. The tree slowly lowered Threngrin back to the ground, and it formed itself once again into a tree. Threngrin quickly got to his feet and backed away from the tree. Threngrin raced over to Sirra, who was still rolling on the ground laughing. He placed his hand on her shoulder. "If you can stop laughing, we must go," Threngrin whispered to her.

Sirra slowly got to her feet, giggling a little, and she glanced at him. "Are you done hanging around?" And she started laughing again.

"Ha-ha!" And Threngrin headed back toward the path they were on. Sirra quickly caught up to him.

After hours of running, they finally collapsed, exhausted and tired, their legs hurting, in a small clearing of the forest among the oak trees. Even as dark as it was, Sirra was afraid to start a fire, afraid that something out there would find them. They sat down on the cold ground and leaned up against the oak tree, although Threngrin had to poke the tree first, making sure it was a tree. They sat close to each other, trying to keep warm. Sirra knew that soon it was going to be colder as night continued and they would not be safe here. They had to find a safe place to camp for the night.

After resting for a moment, Sirra helped Threngrin get on his feet. They continued on until they finally found an isolated area among a bunch of trees, with a huge boulder they could hide behind. Sirra decided it would be safe here to start a fire and set up camp for the night.

By late afternoon the next day, Sirra and Threngrin had reached a road that curved into a narrow valley and began climbing steeply. The road they were following showed heavy wagons going up and down, clearly a steady flow of traffic.

As they continued on, they were getting closer to the mountains, and the hills surrounding them had gained sharp definition, hills as high as thousands of feet in the air, with jagged, bare rocks sharp enough to cut you.

Threngrin groaned and struggled up the mountain, and he cursed under his breath with every step he made. They had been walking all day, and his legs began to burn. Every muscle in his body started to ache, and on top of that, they had no idea where they were going. The view of the jagged mountain stretched for miles, and from a distance, Threngrin could hear the crushing sound of a mountain river.

The sun was beginning to drop behind them when the road they were on ended, and they came to what appeared to be a shallow stream. It appeared so quickly as if something had swept the rutted trail away. The bank on the opposite side had risen steadily, and there wasn't a single hoofprint or rut near the bank. The three-foot river was so clear, Threngrin and Sirra could see the gravel at the bottom. Big snowflakes began to drop into the river and melted as soon as they hit the water. "When did it start to snow in midsummer, especially in a forest? It is strange enough that a river appeared in the middle of a forest, but snow?" Sirra said, trying to catch the snowflakes in her hand. Threngrin turned toward Sirra with a slight grin on his face and started laughing.

"Someone is playing the oldest trick on us, hiding the trail. Whoever it is doesn't want us to follow the trail."

"What, you think someone is doing this? I guess that person snaps its fingers." She chuckled.

"Sure! Anything is possible," he said with a grim.

Threngrin stood as close as he could to the edge of the river without falling in. He looked upward and downward. Then out of the corner of his eye, he spotted something shining or something glowing. He slowly walked over and kneeled down next to the water to get a better look at it. It appeared to be a green gem that someone had dropped along the way. "Sirra, come quickly," he said, pointing at the gem. "I think the trail leads across this way."

Sirra moved in closer to get a better look. "I believe you are right, but where did the trail go, and why would someone hide it?"

Threngrin turned toward her with a puzzled look on his face. "Don't know, but we are going to cross here." They both took a step slowly toward the river. Threngrin suddenly, without any hesitation, grabbed Sirra's arm to stop her. A river. A river that strangely appeared out in the middle of nowhere had to be someone's doing. A river that was really wide, they could barely see the other side. Threngrin began to shiver, and a cold chill went right through him. Something wasn't right. The river had no bank. It appeared out of nowhere, and it was at least twenty feet wide.

"What's the matter with you?" Sirra asked, jerking her arm back. "Are we going to cross the river?"

Threngrin struggled to keep her from seeing the fear in his eyes. He couldn't let her see that deep down inside, he was afraid—something didn't feel right. He himself was having a hard time admitting that he was afraid.

"Threngrin?"

"What, can't you see I am thinking? Give me a minute," he snapped. He knew there was no choice, no other way. They had to cross the river. "Fine, let's move!" He pulled up his pants, and with his left foot, he slowly took a step into the water, but only to find he could not move.

"Don't tell me you are afraid to get a little wet? It's only water. It's not going to hurt you." Sirra giggled.

Threngrin gave her a quick glance, taking a deep breath, and he slowly took two steps into the water. Nothing happened. Maybe it's nothing. Slowly he put one foot in front of the other. He could feel the cold water rushing over the top of his boots. As he placed his foot down, something strong grabbed his right leg, sending him sliding off the uneven rocks that lay underneath him.

Sirra reached her hand out. She caught him by his arm and held him tight before he fell face-first into the water.

"There is something in the water," he said, trying to struggle free from Sirra's grip. "Let me go. I am telling you, something is in here," he said as he regained his footing. Threngrin knew something was in the water, and it grabbed his leg.

"There is nothing in the water. A rock or twig is more likely what hit you." Sirra chuckled.

Threngrin glanced at her quickly, his eyebrows turned down. *I know it was not a twig. It was something, even if she doesn't believe me,* he commented to himself. Threngrin had one thing on his mind now, and that was getting across the river as fast as he could.

Threngrin started off slowly again, watching every step he took, watching for whatever it was to come back. His toes were cold and numb, and he could barely feel his legs. Sharp rocks jabbed at the bottom of his feet through his boots, with every step he took, but he wasn't going to stop.

They had gone maybe ten feet when Threngrin heard something, though at first he thought it was Sirra splashing water with her hands. No, it's more the sound of wings, something trying to fly. No, it sounded like a wagon, but really, a wagon coming through there? Threngrin held up his hand to stop Sirra, and he listened closely for the approaching noise. It was coming from behind them, and it was coming from underneath, and the water began to swirl slowly at first, then faster and faster. They had to get out of the water fast, but they couldn't backtrack. There wasn't enough time. Threngrin spotted some branches hanging over the river. Maybe if they ducked low enough and if the branches covered them, whatever it was wouldn't see them.

Quickly Threngrin moved the branches, waving for Sirra to follow. Threngrin held his breath and dropped to his knees, letting the cold water rush over his shoulders. He felt every nerve inside him tingling as the coldness of the water set in. He felt Sirra shaking at his side.

"Hurry, get down here," he said softly. "Get down here before it sees you, whatever it is."

"Threngrin," she whispered under her breath, "wait here. I have an idea."

Threngrin grabbed her arm. "What? No, stay here where it is safe, or I am going with you," he demanded, and then he saw the look on her face. "You need—" He paused for only a second and released her arm. "Look, Sirra, we are not sure what is out there. You can't fight what you can't see, and you can't leave me here alone."

"I am not leaving you, and I will be fine. I'll be okay!"

Something was steadily appearing up the river through the knee-high water. Sirra closely measured her distance and timed herself to see what it was.

Threngrin broke her concentration by grabbing her hand once again. "Get back here!"

The water continued to swirl in circles. Sirra watched as the water parted, creating this big hole. With Threngrin still holding Sirra's hand really tight, they stood quietly as they watched the ground opening up and this creature rising from the water.

A dragon. A huge dragon flexed his wings and lifted his huge body from the waters. He braced himself in midair, he took a deep breath in, and the cool air stung his nostrils and his throat. The dragon slowly made his way to the ground. The ground cracked and broke beneath him. He spread his wings, and the sun lit his gold scales. The dragon shivered again, stomping his feet upon the ground, and he felt free. The dragon turned his head slightly, looking down the river. He smelled something lingering in the air, a smell he knew too well.

The dragon was completely in front of them now. The two-legged dragon was staring right into Sirra's eyes. Without hesitation, the dragon quickly swung himself around and grabbed her with his claws. Sirra managed to wrap her arms and legs around the dragon, and she held on for dear life, dangling beneath the dragon just above the waters, waiting for some large claw to impale her.

The dragon bounced slightly as its left claw sprang to the ground and hit the water with a splash. Sirra hugged the dragon so tight, trying to make herself as small as possible. It was like the dragon had never flown before and it was its first time. Threngrin stood there as he heard Sirra yelling for help in the distance.

Threngrin lowered his head just slightly to the right, looking under the brush, but the thick bush blocked his view. He could only see branches and water. The sound of the dragon's huge wings rolled a short distance, and then the only sound left was the sound of the river in front of him.

The sun was starting to go down, soon it would be dark, and Threngrin knew he had to do something. The only thing he knew was that the dragon was heading off to his right. Where it was heading, he had no idea. His arms began to ache. He was gripping the branches so tightly, his fingers went numb, and he could no longer hold on to them. He unclenched his hands and legs and made his way to the sandy ground, being careful to avoid anyone or anything seeing him. He crouched down in the darkness next to a big oak tree, waiting to make sure it was safe enough for him to move.

Threngrin took two steps, his boots crunching softly on the ground. He was trying not to make a sound although they were filled with water. Then he froze. A clicking sound came from his left. Then another and another. It was too dark for him to see anything. When he heard something snap directly beside him, he quickly turned desperately and threw himself to the left, behind a tree, but it was too late. A small cage with bars slammed down around him, and he crashed into it. Threngrin grabbed the bars with both hands as he tried to push and pull, even tried lifting it, but the cage was too heavy for him to handle. He dropped to his knees and started digging at the ground, but the ground was too solid. There was no way of digging himself out.

"Damn," Threngrin said as he leaned back against the bars. "Now what?"

Chapter Twelve

They took all of Threngrin's belongings and his weapon away from him, and he had no way to protect or even defend himself. He didn't like the feeling of that. Still feeling angry with himself, he couldn't believe he had been captured by some unknown being. Of course he had other thoughts on his mind. Like where would his sword end up? That was his favorite sword. Not to say all the belongings that he had. He had found some really neat things. But the worst part was what they were going to do with him. *If Sirra were here, she would know what to do*, he said to himself. Threngrin was under the watchful eyes of what appeared to be some kind of guards, ten of them. Their skin was black and pale-looking, and they were wide- eyed. They wore what looked like black and blue plated armors.

Although Threngrin was no longer being held in a cage, the guards made him sit in a corner. The guards stood in a circle, whispering something among each other. The tall guard stepped out of the circle, and another followed. They halted against a large boulder and continued their conversation as they kept their eye on Threngrin. He knew what they were thinking, even thought he couldn't make out what they were saying. His life to him was precious and so was his pride for Sirra. He had to find a way out before it was too late. Escaping was clearly out of the question, and he had no weapon to fight his way out, so all he could do was wait for the right time if all was possible.

The tall guard shook with a jerk of his head, and they walked back into the circle. He was so curious of what they talked about. In the meantime, he sat in silence.

After what seemed like hours went by, Threngrin finally stood up on his feet. "Where am I? Who are you, and what do you want?" he said, trying to remain calm.

One of the guards looked toward him with a cold gaze. His pale eyes were so cold, it was like looking at a dead fish lying on the ground. "Shuddup!" he shouted. Threngrin slowly sat back down on the ground.

Minutes later, Threngrin heard footsteps coming toward the doorway. The guards quickly lined themselves into a single file against the cold stone wall. The footsteps came closer, but Threngrin couldn't see who it was through the narrow opening of the doorway.

"What do we have?" he spoke in a deep, harsh voice.

The two guards grabbed Threngrin roughly to get him on his feet. He found himself facing some kind of mountain being. He blinked rapidly to keep focus on the axe in the being's hand. He was carrying a small axe, unlike any battle-axe Threngrin had ever come across. He wore some kind of yellowish brooches inscribed with some symbol of the merchant. Threngrin couldn't make out what the symbol was.

His rough face and hazel eyes set him immediately apart from the others. His long wild white hair flowed across his shoulders every time he moved his head from side to side. His chain mail sleeves revealed his arms of muscle, but the steel breastplate he wore suggested the fullness of his shape.

"Why am I here?" Threngrin blurted. "I demand to—" He was suddenly cut off by the slap of a guard's hand across his face, knocking him to the ground.

"You have no right to speak," the guard's voice was deep, harsh, and he was taller than the others. "Keep your tongue still. Come." The guards dragged Threngrin to get him on his feet.

The guards surrounded Threngrin, and in silence they made their way deeper into the tunnels. Threngrin had noticed the passageway had recently been widened. There were jagged rocks on the wall, and the floor showed fresh chisel marks. This was all too new.

The tunnel swung to the right, into a huge open cave. Huge heavy iron tools hung around him, clashing into one another, echoing around the cave.

"Making tools, I see," Threngrin suggested.

The little being seemed not to hear him, and then he stopped, turned, and looked at him straight in his eyes. "I would advise you to curb the curious nature that lies within you and watch your clever tongue, if you want to keep them both."

Threngrin studied the little being curiously. What manner of person was this little being? He did not fit into any mental picture of creatures he had seen before, and his eyes and hair did not seem to match those of any little being that he had seen in the past. He had no recollection of ever hearing about any stories that mentioned creatures like this, and he had heard all kinds of stories. Yet he seemed to be one of the guard leaders.

They left the huge cave and entered another maze of tunnels. Uncountable tunnels led in all different directions. Some looked old, and some looked new. Some of the tunnels appeared to lead toward small rooms. They appeared to be built from stone and bricks, while others seemed to be carved from the mountain. As they wound along a row of stones that was being piled, Threngrin began to feel like this was some kind of underground city. Just how many of these little being were there, and where did they come from. He had seen a lot and had been to a lot of places, but this place was all too new to him.

They continued down the wide tunnel in almost total darkness. The only lights they had were the small torches hanging on the walls. Threngrin had no trouble seeing, but to his surprise, neither did they. This place was huge. He had never seen or been in any place like this. For the first time, Threngrin began to grasp that he had no idea where he was.

Finally they turned and entered a very old, run-down cave. The sound of metal clanking together drew Threngrin's eyes up above him. It looked like the same cage he was in before, but this one was just a little bit different. It was suspended in midair just above him. The cage was lowered, and it settled on the ground right in front of him. The guard stepped forward and opened the cage.

"What is going on?" Threngrin asked.

"Get in, you," he said with a sharp tone in his voice.

"Then what?" Threngrin was trying really hard to cover his nervousness as the cage door closed.

"You will see," he said, staring deep into Threngrin's eyes. Then he turned and walked away, and all Threngrin could do was watch as he disappeared from his sight.

....

The guard made his way down the narrowest tunnel there was until he reached the doorway leading into a huge chamber. He slowly stepped through the doorway, and quickly there were two guards that appeared behind him.

"What news do you bring me?" the voice spoke very calmly.

The guard took two steps forward. She was sitting in a very hard chair made out of stone, wearing a yellowish robe, looking at the guard with great interest. "We've found a dwarf just outside the tunnel. We have him captured," the guard said nervously.

The young female sprang quickly to get to her feet. "Really!" she stated, rubbing her hands with great delightfulness.

"To me the dwarf seems to be harmless. I believe he was lost," the guard added.

"I don't want your opinion," she snapped. "His fate I will decide." With such gleam in her eyes and excitement in her voice, she moved closer to the guard. "Now take him to the dungeon."

The guard glanced over and looked up at her, her face pressed tightly against his. She showed cruelty and excitement in her eyes. "I have great control over all the tunnels around here, and that goes even for you. Have you forgotten about my little pet, or do I need to remind you?"

The guard shook his head, and she slowly turned away from him. "Now, take the dwarf to the tunnel just beyond the south tunnel. You know the place." The guard knew the place all too well.

"Oh," she added as she quickly turned the guard around to face her again. "Bring along one of those so-called gully that lingers around here," she said with a thin sly smile. "Have them there in two hours."

"A gully? Why?" The gullies were known to be pests. They were dirty, smelly, and stupid. Many of them around here just went through garbage, they did a little work, but they mostly kept to themselves. Overall they were harmless. The guard noticed the look on her face, and he responded very quickly, "Never mind."

"You will do what I say! Or"—her voice dropped quickly—"or you will pay the price for disobeying an order." There was no doubt in the guard's mind as to what the price would be.

....

Threngrin was startled by the guard's facial expression as he entered the room. He wouldn't look at Threngrin or answer any of his questions. The guard motioned Threngrin to follow, and again they walked down these narrow tunnels. Threngrin noticed everywhere there were these little beings. Some looked to be workers. The others were all busy, moving around so quickly. Again Threngrin was more amazed about a place like this. He never knew such little beings even existed.

They soon came to another empty cave, where several guards stood along the cold stone wall next to the doorway. Threngrin again was shoved into the cave, where he waited so patiently. This was becoming so ridiculous to him, going from one cave to another. It was like they were purposely trying to get him confused so he couldn't remember all the tunnels they went through. There was no way for him to escape. Remembering what tunnels or caves he had been in was impossible. There was no way for him to escape to save Sirra. More or less he couldn't even save himself, and he believed that's what they were expecting, to get him lost.

Several minutes later, two guards pulled Threngrin out into a narrow tunnel, where he was greeted with two more guards. One of the guards was holding a miserable-looking gully. The gully's nose was running, and his eyes were red. He looked fearful.

Threngrin was really surprised to see a gully around here. The guard pushed the gully next to Threngrin. The other guard that stood in front of them did so firmly, and his eyes stared at the gully very closely. "Follow me."

The only sound Threngrin could hear other than footsteps stomping on the ground was the sniffling of the gully. One of the guards had ordered the gully to stop, but the gully persisted, and the guard walking next to him slapped him across the face for disobeying on order. They continued walking through tunnels, entering one after another. At one time Threngrin thought they were back to the beginning, where they were once before. The thought then crossed his mind that they had no intention of releasing him.

He was right, and they soon turned down a really, really narrow tunnel. It looked to be a forbidden area that branched off the main tunnel. There were more guards around than he had seen before. *You've been in worse situations than this*, Threngrin told himself, although he couldn't remember one.

They stopped at the edge of what appeared to be a dark, empty dungeon. The edge of the dungeon was stony and dropped away suddenly. Threngrin noticed the scratches around the edge. What kind of creature could make those scratches? He studied the scratches closely, and as fast as the thought entered his mind, he quickly dropped the subject.

The opening of the dungeon was quite large. Threngrin took a glance down inside the dungeon, and there was a distinguished darkness. He couldn't see what was down there. The sides looked crumbly, impossible for anyone or anything to climb out of. The sides were angled slightly, forming a rough edge.

The guards were standing in a semicircle around the gully and Threngrin. Threngrin got the distinct feeling in the pit of his stomach that they all were waiting for something and it wasn't good.

Before long, they heard the sound of footsteps approaching them. The footsteps were followed by a scraping sound. The sound was being repeated over and over. Threngrin saw why.

A female entered the room, and she was the most repulsive thing that Threngrin had ever seen. She had a distorted posture, thin lips, and very little hair. She had many scars all over her face, like she had been to many wars.

It was those eyes, when she looked at you. Then those eyes locked on to Threngrin's, opening wide, and it was the stare of death. "So this is the dwarf." The female made it sound like a curse. "The one that is snooping around?"

Threngrin tried to maintain his cool. "I was not snooping, and you are?"

The guards stepped back, making a path for the female to Threngrin.

"I am called Lolth. I hold a very high place in this society. I run and control everyone here and the tunnels going in and out." The female stared at Threngrin for a moment before speaking again. "I am going to ask you two questions. You must answer them correctly. But first, I have arranged a little show for you, if you should fail me, to ensure that I have your full attention." The female looked over to the guard and nodded. Threngrin got this sick feeling deep inside. He knew what was coming.

The guard pitched the gully off the edge of the dungeon. Threngrin heard the gully scream and cry. He saw him desperately scraping at the sides as he slid down. Rocks slipped down with him, falling all around him.

Suddenly to Threngrin's surprise, the gully managed to break his fall. Threngrin saw the gully's little fingers grasp the edge of a rock. Slowly the terrified gully managed to pull himself up to the next rock. Adjusting his grip, he braced one foot on a rock and slowly began to lift himself up higher. The gully's struggle seemed to amuse the female. She showed great pleasure in watching him.

Something then moved from below, and it shifted Threngrin's attention back to the dungeon. A huge indefinable creature moved beneath the gully. It quickly moved upward, striking the gully in the back, and leashed around the gully's waist.

The gully froze for only a second. Threngrin saw the fear in the gully's eyes as the thing pulled him back down into the dungeon. "No!" the gully cried out, scratching and grabbing at the rocks. Threngrin saw the frantic gully and the pain on its face. It only lasted for a moment, and then he disappeared into the dungeon.

The scream that rose from the dungeon was a sound of terror. It echoed throughout the room. Threngrin closed his eyes, but to his horror, what happened next was even worse. A snapping, crushing sound that rose from the dungeon made Threngrin quiver. Then it was quiet, and the sound died away.

When Threngrin opened his eyes, the female was standing right in front of him. "Now, do I have your attention? I will ask you two questions, maybe three." She laughed. "If you fail . . . I'm sure you don't need me to explain what will happen."

Threngrin saw his chance to make his move. If Sirra were here, she wouldn't stand for this. Threngrin busted between the two guards that were standing next to him. He clamped his hands around the female's throat, and both of them tumbled to the ground, rolling to the edge of the dungeon.

Threngrin was surprised by the strength the female had in her arms. They wrestled from side to side, and Threngrin's grip tightened as the female's nails dug in to pry his arms loose. The female's nails dug into Threngrin's arm until blood flowed down her arm and spread across the floor. Threngrin twisted and rolled across the ground, trying to avoid the guards in their attempt to break them up. Yet every time he tried to get her over the edge of the dungeon, she managed to twist away.

Many of the guards pulled at Threngrin's arms and legs, trying to get him away from the female, and then something hard cracked Threngrin in the back of his head, nearly knocking him out. Something then hit him in his knees. He lay flat, stretched out, belly down and pinned. His face grounded into the dirt, into the cold, clammy dirt that invaded his eyes and nose and mouth. Threngrin tried to cry out, but all he did was get a mouthful of dirt. Threngrin tried to get free from the grip that held him with unrelenting strength. Faintly Threngrin heard the female shouting and talking, but her words made no sense to him. He was then dragged off the female's body and flung against the cold stone wall, where one of the guards stood over him with his sword, ready to attack if he so much moved a muscle. Threngrin hacked and coughed, trying to breathe, trying to spit out the dirt that was in his mouth.

The female stumbled around the ground, trying to get up on her knees. Two of the guards bent down to help her up, but she drove them away with a snarl. She stayed on her knees for only a minute, trying to catch her breath.

The female managed to get to her feet, bracing herself on the wall. She wiped Threngrin's blood from her arm and hobbled her way toward him, who was still standing against the wall.

The young female motioned one of the guards to remove the leather strap from his pants and hand it to her, and she spun around, striking Threngrin across the face. She struck again and again. The female's arm was drawn back for another blow, but she suddenly stopped in midair.

"You are either brave or stupid. I go for stupid," she said as she brought her arms down to her side. "Who are you, and where did you come from?"

Threngrin's eyelids were puffed up, blood running from the cuts on his forehead, cheeks, and lips. Threngrin tried to speak through his swollen lip. "I will tell you nothing."

"You are one stupid dwarf." She laughed.

Gradually his wits were returning, he could barely see from his right eye, but he found he could force his eye to stay open with manageable amount of pain. He wasn't going to show her any sign of weakness. "I will tell you nothing," he repeated.

The female bent down close to Threngrin's ear and whispered, "But you will." She said with a slight grin, "Give me what I want, and I shall be merciful."

"I have seen how merciful you can be," Threngrin lashed out.

The female struck Threngrin across the face again. "Well then."

The mad female grabbed Threngrin by his shirt and dragged him toward the dungeon. Threngrin lunged for the female's throat, but the guards grabbed his arms and brought him to the edge of the dungeon.

"Throw him in!" she yelled.

The guards did not hesitate. The one holding Threngrin gave him a hard shove. Threngrin sailed, headfirst, over the edge. The female's laughter echoed throughout the cave. Every little being in every tunnel heard her.

Chapter Thirteen

Sirra found herself standing upon a pile of rocks at the entrance of a cave. She was gazing with great interest across the plain below her, wondering why she was brought here. The dragon brought her to a place that was dark and cold, a cave that was cut deeply into the mountain and was surrounded by water. She was about fifteen feet up a mountainside inside a cave. Sirra's heart skipped a beat, her body began to shake, and fear set in as she saw its claws dragging on the dirt ground. Her legs felt so rubbery, she could only move a few steps backward before she managed to lose her balance and fell to the ground. Sirra slowly lifted her trembling body up off the cold, damp ground.

"Let me go. Return me to the river," Sirra demanded. "What is this place?" she said, looking at the gold-scaled dragon. But the dragon did not respond. She poked the dragon in its side with the tip of her finger. "Why am I here anyway?" she said as she continued poking the dragon.

The dragon turned to look at her. A long snorting sound escaped him, and he tilted his head from side to side, looking at her as if he was trying to figure her out. Sirra threw her arms up in the air. "Well, what do you want?" The dragon tilted his head from side to side once again, then snorted.

Sirra was startled by the sound of the dragon snorting again. She jumped about two inches in the air. The dragon tilted his head from side to side once again at the sudden move she made. Sirra wasn't sure if the dragon was going to snort again, so she took three steps backward, away from it. The dragon took three steps forward toward her, and she took two steps to her right. The dragon did the same, taking two steps to his left. Sirra let out a little giggle, trying not to laugh, but watching the dragon copying her was too funny. She had never come across a dragon like this. The dragon appeared to be a young one, maybe even a baby. Sirra slowly walked her way up to the dragon, moving her head from side to side. The dragon stared at her for a moment, and then he did the same, moving his head from side to side. As the dragon was too busy moving his head and copying her, she propelled to move forward again, and she stumbled within a couple of feet from it. She forced herself to stand perfectly still in front of the dragon, not to make any sudden movements, and she reached her hand out slowly to touch it. His gold scales felt smooth, soft—too soft. It felt wet, moist, and soft. Most dragons felt rough, ridged, and dry. This one had to be a baby, or a different kind of dragon, different from those she had seen, she commented to herself. Then she remembered stories she heard of species of dragons smaller than other dragons dwelling in high plains, born and bred mostly in mountain regions. These dragons were able to withstand extreme cold.

Because of their smaller size, these dragons were the swiftest flyers of all dragon kind. She heard stories of how people would capture these dragons, train them, and use them for scouting missions. But what happened to this one, and where were the others?

The dragon settled down on the cold, damp ground next to Sirra, feeling the warmth of the sun on his scales. She turned and glanced at the dragon. She held her breath, afraid to move, not knowing what the dragon was capable of. He was powerful. He could rip her apart in seconds. Because she was captured, she wasn't going to participate in anything till she found out why she was here. She managed to crawl up against the wall of the cave, curling herself into a ball. She was cold and tired, and she lay there crying herself to sleep.

Sirra was woken by a startling sound. She knew she wasn't alone the moment the awareness came to her. Who else was in this cave? Her heart began to beat as the air was being forced into her lungs. She felt something next to her, she was on her side, and the instant she felt breath on the back of her neck, she turned. The edge of her hand slammed down on the cold ground. But there was nothing there. Sirra launched her body up off the cold ground, her heart pounding so loudly that it sounded like a beating drum in a confined area. She landed some distance from the dragon, her gaze moving continually, restlessly, in all directions.

The dragon slowly made his way toward Sirra, and before she knew it, the dragon was right in her face, staring deep into her eyes. The dragon was not going to let Sirra out of her sight. The dragon slowly walked behind her, and he bent his head down and nudged her in the butt, pushing her to move forward. The dragon did not realize just how strong he was, and she stumbled forward, taking about three steps. Sirra managed to keep her footing, and the dragon nudged her again, but this time knocking her down on the ground. She slowly scrambled to get to her feet. She threw up her arms into the air. "What? What do you want?" she yelled. Sirra rubbed her pounding head with her fingers. The dragon was trying to communicate with her, and the struggle of understanding it was becoming very painful.

The dragon walked up to her, bent his head down, and nudged her in the belly with his head. She went flying backward, landing on her butt. She started kicking her legs up and down, her arms thrown up in the air, yelling at the top of her lungs, "I don't understand! What it is you want, you stupid creature?"

The dragon slowly nudged her again as if he was telling her to get to her feet. She slowly rose up on her feet, watching the dragon closely. The dragon tilted his head to the right, Sirra stared at the dragon for a few minutes, and then she noticed there was an opening off to her left. *Maybe the dragon was hinting for me to move toward the opening*, she thought to herself.

A rock struck Sirra on the shoulder. She flinched. The stone caused her little pain. The dragon, looking at her pale face and quivering, nudged her to continue moving. More rocks began to fall, but they continued to follow the tunnel that led them deeper into the cave. Sirra tried desperately to continue, but the struggle to push through the falling rocks made it impossible, and one hit her, knocking her off her feet. The dragon bent over, to nudge her again, but Sirra was kicking and flailing about in rage. Sirra was just about on her feet when she was hit on the head with a falling rock, and momentarily she saw stars.

"Hey, dragon, you know what you could do? You could—"

Sirra never got the chance to tell the dragon what he could do, because something huge plucked her up. A hand clapped itself over Sierra's mouth, while two more pairs of hands gripped Sirra's kicking feet. A sack was popped over her head, and all Sirra saw or smelled was burlap as she felt herself being carried away.

Sirra rubbed the top of her head with her right hand. She heard what sounded like booted feet and someone whispering, and then it broke free and ran. When she could finally get to see again, she glanced around quickly. Sirra finally managed to get to her feet, swearing fluently. "What the hell was that?" she roared. "I want—" She stopped and stared, turning this way and that way. "Where the hell am I? So help me—"

The dragon appeared right in front of her, and Sirra then realized that they managed to escape the falling rocks. The dragon was nose to nose with her, glaring into Sirra's eyes.

Sirra choked and fell silent, confused of what just happened. Did the dragon scared off whatever that was? Was he staying close to protect her? Did she now have a friend, although she would never trust the dragon?

The dragon thought for a moment, then shook his head and gave her a nudge to move forward. They entered a small room. It was smelly. As the dragon shoved her forward, Sirra managed to keep her footing. Sirra shook her head dubiously as she entered the room. It took some time for her eyes to adjust to the dimness of the room, which smelled even worse than the rest of the cave.

Her control was crumbling. She could feel it in her bones. She had to find a way to get to Threngrin. She knew Threngrin was alive somewhere, and whether she'd manage to get out of here alive or not, she had to try. Deliberately she bit her bottom lip and concentrated on the pain she self-inflicted, to keep her focus on what lay ahead. Sirra allowed her arms to fall to her side. She was exhausted and scared, and her head hurt horribly. This whole thing was very discomforting, wearing at her defenses down, the voice in her head driving her with its relentless pressure to just give up.

She went reluctantly into the room. She had no choice. She had to survive. Threngrin was her life, she cared for him more than anything, and he was her best friend. If he was gone, she had nothing to live for. At the thought of losing Threngrin, she felt sickened.

There was a bench that was up against the wall and a tall chair that was set in the center of the room. Her eyebrows rose slightly at the sight of the dragon, and it seemed to her that his face softened. Sirra walked forward to the bench, then to the chair. "What is this?" she asked. The dragon just stood there.

Sirra coughed and fell silent, giving the dragon a meaningful, grim look. She shook her head. Her shoulders slumped, and she sighed wearily. She wiped the blood from her cuts with her shaking hand, her features pale with fear. She stood outwardly calm as she looked upon the dragon, wondering what he was up to. The dragon then turned toward Sirra and hesitated. "What are you waiting for?" she yelled.

A shrouded figure appeared in the entryway, then disappeared as quickly. The dragon and Sirra were exchanging glances, and the dragon immediately opened his wings to shelter her, but he never made it in time. Something sharp hit Sirra on the back of her head, knocking her unconscious. The dragon let out a loud screeching sound, he wrapped his wings around her tightly, and they disappeared.

Sirra slowly came to, dazed and confused. She felt the dragon's claws clinging to her body, connecting them in some dark, twisted, ugly way. Her body felt weak, and she felt sluggish hanging in the air. Her heart pounded, and she felt her life being drained as the dragon continued to fly. She felt her eyelids getting heavy. She told herself she had to keep focused, to live, to fight for Threngrin. Sirra began to see yellow dots dancing before her eyes, and she collapsed helplessly in the dragon's claws.

....

Threngrin plunged his way down the steep, rocky dungeon, tumbling head over heels, slamming from side to side. He fought to gain some control over the plummet, but he could barely tell up from down. Jagged edges of the dungeon tore at his flesh and clothing as his hands so desperately tried to grasp at anything. Suddenly his short fingers slapped against something thick and hard and instantly locked his fingers around it. Threngrin growled in pain as his hands slid along the edge of the dungeon walls. Rocks rained down on his head as the weight on his handhold loosened the rocks above him. Tempting to look up, Threngrin saw he had caught something that looked like a tree root. Half of it was sticking out in the wall of the dungeon. He clamped his little fingers around it as tight as he could and clung to the exposed root with all his strength and desperation.

His feet came to rest on a rock that was sticking out of the wall. Expecting the rock beneath him to come loose under the impact of him stopping so suddenly, Threngrin tightened his grip on the root as he tested the rock with his toes. He was surprised to find that the width of the rock was seven inches wide, twice the width of his feet. He managed slowly and carefully as he pressed his back against the wall and tried to think as he caught his breath.

Threngrin barely had time to think when something heavy crashed down around him.

"Help!"

Stunned and almost knocked off the edge by the weight, Threngrin nearly lost his grip, but he quickly managed to lock his fingers around the root. Threngrin heard the terror in the voice, and he recognized the person, but he didn't dare to move an inch to look up.

"I can't hold on!" he squealed.

"Get your feet onto the edge that is below you!" Threngrin yelled. "And stay close to the wall."

Threngrin tried to hold on as tight as he could, and he grabbed the young man's arm in one hand and held on to him tightly while he scrambled for footing. Threngrin guided him close to him, and together they clung on to the root, panting from exertion.

After a moment's rest, Threngrin peered at the young man. "What are you doing here?" he asked bluntly as he rubbed his cheek to his shoulder. "Trip?" He coughed, clearing his throat.

The young man opened his mouth, shut it, considered the comment Threngrin made, and then opened his mouth again. "Hardly!" the young man shot back, afraid to move. "I was pushed in behind you by that evil swine. She'll roast on a slow spit over an open fire for this."

"That's if we get out of here ourselves." Threngrin laughed. "Do you know how far down the bottom is, or how to get out of here, or what exactly is at the bottom?"

"Of course not!" he snapped. "This is a dungeon. We just don't go exploring around here for the fun of it. No one comes down here with any hopes of getting out alive. No one has ever survived."

"Of course, what was I thinking?" Threngrin grinned. Threngrin studied the walls of the dungeon to find a place where they could climb up, but there was no safe place they could climb. The stones were either too small or too slippery.

A noise from below froze the young man in his place. His eyes turned toward Threngrin with fear.

"Don't worry, I heard it too." Threngrin moved his position so he could get a better look down into the dungeon. After a few minutes, his eyes focused on what he thought must be a dirty floor about three feet below. Threngrin strained to see if there were any other details that he could see, the sound he heard, a sort of scuffling, he thought, and then he heard it again. And a strange shadow passed below them.

Still looking down, Threngrin asked, "What is that thing?"

"That is what we call a killer," the young man replied. "Otherwise, I don't know, and I don't want to find out. I want my hands to stop shaking and to climb out of here."

"I don't think we will be climbing out of here anytime soon," Threngrin said. "The sides of this dungeon are rough and slippery. Trying to hold on while climbing up will likely send you falling to the bottom. If there was something we could use, maybe we could—"

Threngrin was cut off by the scraping sound from below as if something heavy was being dragged across the rocks. The young man released the root with one hand and grabbed Threngrin by his shoulder. "I can see something moving down there," the young man whispered. "There it is again. Did you see it?"

Threngrin blinked a few times, trying to focus on something at the bottom of the dungeon. He could hear the sound very well. It was dragging something, punctuated with numerous clicks though. Threngrin had some idea what it might be, but he couldn't quite identify it.

The smell finally reached them, the sickening thickness. The smell of rot and waste rose up around them, filling the dungeon. The young man moved back closer to the wall as Threngrin spit, trying to get the taste out of his mouth. "What is that supposed to be?" the young man groaned.

"That is known to be called a crawler," Threngrin answered. "They are the most dangerous creatures around. They will eat anything, but as long as it's dead. And if it's not, they have fun killing it. They also can climb, as you can see. And I expect it is coming for us."

As if on cue, a pink and black flesh-looking thing just went across the bottom of the floor. A few seconds later, a huge brown eye was looking straight at them. The creature's tentacles were glistening, and each one of them was no more than six feet long. Its mouth was filled with hundreds of grinding teeth. Its head was moving back and forth, viewing them closely, and as it made its way closer and closer to them, the smell grew much stronger, and the noise it made got louder.

"Start looking for huge rocks. Maybe we can drive it away by throwing rocks at it," Threngrin frantically said as he released his grip from the root to move across the edge. Within minutes, they had a small pile of rocks next to them. "This will have to do. I hope you feel lucky and have a good throw arm. Go for the eyes. And don't let his tentacles touch you."

"What will happen if they do?" the young man whispered, staring at the creature.

"If they touch you, it will paralyze you, so it can eat you later. Just watch yourself."

Threngrin grabbed a few rocks. Holding them in one hand, he grabbed the young man's hand from the root with his other hand and placed the rocks into it. "When I tell you to throw them, throw as hard as you can. We are going to give it a nice dinner, rocks." Threngrin grinned.

The feel of rocks in the young man's hand gave him something to focus on and hope. Hope to get out of there alive. He rolled them a few times in his palm. A few good shots could knock it back down to the ground, the young man thought. He turned back to the dungeon, he positioned his hand over his head, and he was ready.

The creature burst into view, its tentacles writhing toward them. Threngrin could see parts of its body, twisting along the wall. A pair of thick, short legs, white and slimy, extended with each step it made. Each leg had a pair of suction cups, and they were bigger than Threngrin's head. The smell of rotten flesh from its past meals lingered with the creature, and the smell got worse as it got closer to them. The smell and the taste got into Threngrin's throat, making it difficult to breathe.

This creature was the largest creature of all the crawlers that Threngrin had ever seen. He had never heard of one living long enough to get this big. This one had to be the granddaddy, Threngrin commented quietly to himself. Swallowing hard, Threngrin tightened his grip on the root and threw the rock as hard as he could. With a crack, it bounced off the creature's head and sailed down the dungeon.

Quickly, the young man's arm flung forward, and the rock went straight into the creature's mouth, disappearing quickly. It was really hard to tell if the creature felt any pain, but it moved its head and made a small roar and moved away from the young man. The creature was now at least seven feet below them. Four tentacles lashed out and wrapped around Threngrin's left boot. Within seconds, his leather steamed, and blisters appeared around his ankles. The leather of Threngrin's boot protected him from the real damage. Threngrin cried out in pain, trying to keep his balance, trying to keep from falling down the dungeon. He grabbed another rock and smashed its tentacles. He smashed the first one, then another one, using all his strength. Black stuff stained the edge beneath Threngrin's feet.

The young man threw another rock at the creature, hitting it just at the corner of its eye. The creature swung its head, dragging Threngrin's foot, pulling him right off the edge. Threngrin tried so hard to maintain his grip on the root with his one hand, as well as trying to find something else to grab on to with his other hand. The young man quickly grabbed Threngrin by his shirt collar just as the creature shot up at them, and they both went flying off the edge. "We are going to die! We are going to die!" the young man yelled as he was flying in the air.

The tentacle that was still wrapped around Threngrin's boot tightened, then broke off. Threngrin and the young man skidded down the creature's back and landed on a pile of bones at the bottom of the dungeon.

Threngrin groaned in pain as he scrambled to get to his feet, but his left foot was beginning to get numb. There were still some tentacles from the creature wrapped around him.

Threngrin looked around and noticed that they were now in the heart of the dungeon where the creature lived. He couldn't tell how far the dungeon went, and he didn't want to know, but all he knew was they had to find a way out.

"We need to find a weapon, any kind of weapon!" Threngrin shouted. "Do you have a knife? Any weapons on you?"

"I did, but no more," the young man said in a low voice.

"What do you mean you did?" Threngrin groaned.

"It fell. It fell as we were falling down to our death," he stated as he struggled to get to his feet.

"What?" Threngrin said in disbelief.

"I lost my knife, I was falling to my death, and the knife wasn't on my mind. Considering I was looking at dying," the young man said, shaking his head.

"Maybe we can find it, or maybe a weapon of some kind. We don't have much"—Threngrin looked up where the creature was, but the creature had moved, and he was heading right toward them—"time! Let's move." Threngrin grabbed the young man by his arm and jerked him to move.

There wasn't much light for them to see, so they continued on feeling their way as they went. Threngrin stumbled over something big and hard. Moving closer, he realized it was a corpse, cold and motionless. Fear welled as he touched it to turn it over.

Horror rose when he saw the body was mangled. Its body was ripped open. Threngrin scrambled to get to his feet. There were ragged marks, wounds made by some creature. Determined, they moved forward, looking for a way out.

Searching the floor as they ran, Threngrin's eye caught a piece of metal in a pile of rocks and bones. With a strong kick, he found a rusty but solid blade about nine inches long. Quickly with his free hand, he grabbed it and ran.

"It's gaining on us!" the young man yelled. "How fast can this thing move?"

"It can move faster than us," Threngrin snorted, looking back at the creature. He was scared. The creature was only ten feet behind them and was moving very fast. Despite how big the creature was, it could move, and its legs ripped along the dungeon floor. Then the creature whipped out its tentacles and grabbed the young man around his waist from behind, bringing him to a complete stop.

"No!" Threngrin yelled. "Let him go, you smelly thing!" And with the rusty blade, Threngrin turned around and moved toward the creature. With his one hand, he grabbed the young man's arm, and with the other, he slashed the creature's tentacles.

Thick blood went flying through the air. It took a third slash before the young man was free from the creature. Threngrin flung the young man, paralyzed but conscious, over his shoulders and moved backward, keeping his face toward the creature.

The creature seemed stunned, and it fell to the ground. Threngrin knew it wouldn't stop the creature. It might just slow him down. Threngrin turned and bolted. Frantically he managed to pull himself up on the wall, dragging the young man and his numb foot deeper into the dungeon.

Threngrin thought they could escape, but to his surprise, the dungeon came to a narrow point and a complete stop. Rocks blocked their passage. There was no way through or around it. Threngrin dropped the young man onto the floor, his eyes looked helplessly at Threngrin and were filled with fear.

Threngrin turned quickly at the noise from the creature that was approaching them, and he jerked his arm away from the young man. He stared ahead and took a deep breath, but his only thought was to get to Sirra immediately. Whatever the evil thing was, whatever creature was following them, Sirra was his main concern.

Looking around, Threngrin caught a glimpse of light that was coming from a crack in the wall. With no thought, he lifted the young man's body. He turned and ran, carrying the young man, uncaring of the curious creature. He tripped on rocks that caught the hem of his coat, and he heard it rip, but he continued for the light.

They reached where the light was coming from. It was a small crack. With his hand, he pushed through the crack and found it was a small tunnel. He shoved the young man headfirst. He pushed him as far as he could, but then he got wedged in, and Threngrin couldn't push him anymore. "Forgive me," he muttered as he put his shoulders to his seat and pushed with all his strength. The young man inched forward, and then suddenly something tugged him on the other side. The young man moved forward quickly. Threngrin tried to turn his head to see what was there, but a hand reached out and grabbed him, dragging him through the wall.

"I'll be!" Threngrin said with a grin on his face. "A gully."

"What you doing in there? You lost? You lost something in there? A little being after you?" the gully said with a click of his tongue.

"What do you think?" Threngrin chuckled. "Where are we now?"

The gully held himself up so proudly with a smile on his face. "I think they call this badland." The gully chuckled.

Chapter Fourteen

The gully that rescued them had left, leaving Threngrin and the young man alone in the middle of nowhere. Threngrin had no idea where they were other than some place in badland, and that didn't say much. Threngrin felt the pain in his side from where a rock had scraped him. It made him focus that they had to run. Whatever creature was following them could come though that hole. Sobbing, he flung the young man over his shoulders and followed a winding path into the forest.

Threngrin became aware of the fog coming in, dense, thick. It hung over the trees like a brick wall. He could barely see a foot in front of him. It even felt thick. It was like walking in thick mud. When he tried to breathe in, he found it very difficult. He wanted to scream for Sirra, but for some reason, a feeling he got kept him silent. Determined to find Sirra, he moved forward, keeping his eyes open. The wind rushing through the trees made it hard to hear anything coming. Without hearing, Threngrin moved carefully forward. Every instinct he had needed to be used.

Despite the strong wind and the heavy fog, he found a place where he and the young man, who was still paralyzed, could rest and recover from the horror they encountered. Although the thick fog hid them, Threngrin felt the creature might be able to see them. This was a chance he had to take.

It was late in the afternoon, and Threngrin and the young man continued to lie low, waiting for the right time to move. Although all Threngrin could think about was Sirra and where she could be, this was all he had to do for the last few days. The young man was in no condition to travel. Every once in a while, he would peer his head down what appeared to be a trail. Where it led to was a different story. It was hard for him to tell if it was even a trail, his eyesight was obscured by branches, but as far as he could tell, the trail was about six hundred paces away from him.

Every night Threngrin would hear wagons passing through shortly after sunset, and they'd continue up the trail. Before dawn, another one would pass by.

Threngrin couldn't make out who or what they were, and with the young man still sick, it was safer to stay where they were. Threngrin shivered, his body shaking out of control from the cool breeze. In the sun, the rays were warm, but he was cold to the bone. He just couldn't get warm. Then within a few minutes, he was warm again. Every time the wind blew, the cool breeze sent chills down his spine. The good thing was it didn't last long.

The afternoon turned into another cold evening. Bored as he was, Threngrin dared not leave the young man alone to explore the surrounding area. Nor could he risk starting a fire when night came. The young man was lucky to be alive. Most people who came in contact with a crawler didn't survive, and if they did, they could be sick for days.

Shivering, Threngrin wondered just how long the young man would be paralyzed. Noon came, and still the young man lay there. Then the sky above him was black and starry, and the air was very cold. Threngrin clapped his hands to his arms, trying to keep warm. Mist was falling, and he tried to cover the young man's body with his own to keep him warm. From the distance, he saw a shadow.

Something terrible was about to happen, he could feel it in the air. The wind picked up, and fog started to roll in. He saw movement in the dense fog, and then something screamed. The sound had a very high pitch. Threngrin's heart nearly stopped, he couldn't breathe, and whatever was out there, Threngrin did not want to meet it. Threngrin moved closer to the young man, covering his eyes with his hands.

Threngrin knew they should have left before dark, even two days ago. *If I wait just one more hour*, he kept telling himself, *maybe the young man would move, come out of it.* But Threngrin grew more anxious by the minute. And again he peered out to look down the trail. From it he thought he heard a wagon approaching—it was time for another to scroll by—but the noise grew louder and unfamiliar. Puzzled, Threngrin turned his head to listen closely. It was not the sound of a wagon but more like clomping feet, many feet.

"Hey! Hey, get up!" Threngrin whispered, shaking the young man. "Come out of it now!" Threngrin kept on shaking the young man, harder and harder. "Come on, dude, snap out of it!" But there was no response.

A chill of terror ran up Threngrin's spine as from the distance of the trail marched no more than fifty men. From what he could tell, they all wore breastplates and had sharp axes. They all stopped for only a brief moment, then fanned out in all directions. Threngrin watched as a detachment of ten approached, stomping through the forest right in his direction.

Petrified, Threngrin threw himself on the ground next to the young man and curled himself into a small ball. *What should I do?* he groaned to himself. *Should I run and leave the young man here alone? Should I try dragging him out of here? Are they looking for something? Or someone? Maybe they found out that I escaped and am still alive.* Even in his frantic state, Threngrin knew that was ridiculous. There was no way that evil female would know if he was dead or that they had escaped from the dungeon. But with all these men, they were sure to find them, and then she would know.

Threngrin bit his knuckles, feeling like he was about to jump out of his skin. He couldn't just sit here and wait for them to find him. He turned quickly, grabbed the young man by his arm, and headed deeper into the forest. A few branches crumbled under his feet, and he bit his lip and prayed that they would not be noticed.

"You there! Stop!"

Threngrin heard a frantic voice behind him, but he just threw the young man over his shoulders and drove himself deeper into the forest. Threngrin was a good runner, but carrying the young man, there was a slim chance of outrunning them.

A loud horn blew. "There is an intruder! Stop him!"

Threngrin did not stop to look back. In the darkness, he was concentrating on finding a good place to hide, aware from anything else but his own safety.

He reached a small path in the forest, but instead of following it, he spotted a ledge just ahead of him, and it led into an area where they could be protected by a bunch of boulders. If they could get to those rocks, they might have a chance.

Drawing on strength he did not have, Threngrin flung the young man and himself up onto the ledge. He threw the young man back onto his shoulders and broke into a slight run across the flat limestone. Legs pumping wildly, he closed with a huge boulder and tossed the young man behind one to catch his breath for just a moment. He peered back behind him and saw no signs of the men. Hope filled his heart, but he could not stop just yet.

He threw the young man back onto his shoulders, keeping low. He made his way through rocks and the boulders. The rocks gave way to a thick grove of pine trees, and he pushed his way through them, uncaring of the low stiff branches that slapped him in the face, leaving scratches on his cheeks. He could hear nothing but his own footsteps crunching on the dried-up needles and his heart pounding in his ear. The stand of trees ended, and Threngrin ran into a clearing of land. He skidded to a complete stop and looked around, and then all hope was gone.

He had burst into a gathering of men from all directions.

The men were equally surprised to see Threngrin in their midst, but they recovered quickly and surrounded him. Threngrin counted twenty of them. Weaponless as he was, he knew he could not overpower them. He laid the young man on the ground next to him.

"What do we have here?" one of the men spoke out, stepping toward Threngrin. The old man's yellow hair stuck out, and his large eyes reminded Threngrin of eyes he had seen once before.

"Well, answer me!" he said as he poked Threngrin in the chest with the point of his spear. "You're obviously not from around here," he said, taking in

Threngrin's tanned face, his thin leather jacket, and his muddy boots. "What are you doing out here?"

Threngrin tried to keep his knees from shaking as he ransacked his mind for a quick response. "I-I was hunting!" he finished quickly. "I was only hunting, nothing else," he said with an innocent look on his face. "I guess I didn't pay any attention on where I have wandered off to."

"What, hunting at night? What could you be possibly hunting at night?" The old man said, eyeing Threngrin skeptically. "And no weapons?"

"Squirrel," Threngrin supplied hastily. "You can trap a squirrel at night. You don't need a weapon."

The old man appeared to be considering Threngrin's answer, rocking back on his heels and searching Threngrin's face for deception. All he detected was fear. "And what is wrong with him?" the old man said, pointing to the ground.

"He fell while we were chasing a squirrel," Threngrin said with fear in his voice.

The old man's eyes got real narrow. "I saw you when you came through those trees. It appears to me that something was chasing you."

Threngrin nodded. "I was tracking a squirrel when I saw . . ." He thought about making up another lie about seeing a wolf but decided to stay close to the truth so he wouldn't slip up. "I saw something huge coming our way, and we panicked and ran. That's when he fell."

"He's lying," said a deep voice from behind Threngrin.

"Who really cares? Let's just kill them both and move on!" yelled another.

"Yeah. We have a lot of ground to cover tonight. Let's get a move on."

Threngrin could feel the circle around him drawing tighter and tighter. Suddenly someone pushed him from behind. Threngrin stumbled forward, only to have someone's spear jammed into the pit of his stomach. He doubled over, unable to breathe, and another spear struck him across the back of his neck. Gasping, he fell to the ground.

The ring of men erupted in laugher and taunts. "Look out!" one man yelled.

"The squirrels are going get you!" shouted another.

"Oh, look, here comes one now! Better watch it!" Threngrin saw one man stepping forward, and then felt his rib cage crack as the old man's boot crashed into him. The force of the blow rolled him over onto his stomach.

"Get him up on his feet," one of them growled. "I want my turn to knock him down." Then Threngrin felt a pair of hands lifting him to get him on his feet. Someone slapped his face. He looked up just in time to see someone's fist smash into his nose. Excruciating pain exploded in his skull as he stumbled backward, landing on his right shoulder.

Threngrin drew his knees in an effort to stand, when something forced him back down to the ground. A muddy boot pressed down on the back of his neck, grinding his face into the ground. The night sky was filled with colors before Threngrin's eyes as the men pelted him with kick after kick and hammered his back and legs with the end of their spears. He bit his lip to keep from screaming, but he could not keep from moving as the blows increased. And then suddenly, they all stopped.

Threngrin felt someone grab him by his arm and jerk him to get him on his feet. He looked up through the blood that was running down his face and saw it was the old man.

"Now that my men had their fun," he said, holding Threngrin's arm, "it is my turn to have some fun."

Threngrin slumped to his left foot, trying to keep his balance. He hoped they would just kill him and get it over with. There was no strength left in him to fight.

The old man forced Threngrin to stand, then smiled. "You'll love the little game I have planned for you. I am going to let you go!" Threngrin lifted his head slightly.

"I see that I have your interest," he began. "I am going to let you go, and we are going to try to catch you again. You will have only a one-minute lead of course."

Threngrin tried to look at the old man with his eyes swollen. "And if you should catch me, then what?" He wheezed. His bruised ribs made it difficult for him to breathe.

The old man shook his head and clucked his tongue. "You really don't want to know what will happen if we should catch you."

Threngrin felt his heart stop. He felt near to fainting from the pain. But he forced himself to stay standing.

"How can I say it?" The old man tapped his chin with the tip of his fingers. "I've got it. You be relieved of the burden of being you!" The men around him hooted with laugher.

"I can't run very fast carrying him. He is injured and can't move," Threngrin said, looking down at the young man lying on the ground.

"Well, then a two-minute lead, no more. Unless you are willing to give up, and we can make your death painful," he warned. The old man shoved him through the circle of men. He fell, struggling to get to his feet, and the men around him started to kick and jeer at him. The old man squeezed Threngrin's left shoulder and pointed him to the clearing just ahead of them.

"Go!" the old man yelled. "We will see you again."

Threngrin tossed the young man over his shoulder, he felt his legs moving, and he found himself half staggering, half running toward the trees.

"Remember, we are right behind you!" the old man yelled, and all the men around broke into laugher.

Threngrin stumbled to the edge of the clearing of the forest, barely avoiding tripping on an overgrown tree stump. He rushed forward down the path and more than once crashed into a few pine trees or lost his feet in a tangle of branches. Desperately he wanted to stop and rest. Carrying the young over his shoulders and running was taking a lot out of him. Or to even stop and listen for sounds of the men. But he knew he could not. If he stopped, he might never move again. He also knew he wouldn't hear anything over the sound of his own heavy breathing or the blood rushing through his head, pounding so loudly. He could hear it echoing in his ear.

He ran blindly and senselessly, not realizing the ground changed from dirt to thick mud. He stepped out into an open area, and an awful smell hit him, a clinging odor that lingered in the air. The spreading of weeds set off an odor, and every time Threngrin breathed in, he could taste it on his tongue. The land had changed, and the scattering of weeds was all he could see in the distance. He could feel the cool air rushing past him, the wind blowing through his hair. Less than seconds later, Threngrin and the young man splashed into an ice-cold stream. He wanted to scream, but his mind kept him in control. His chest felt as if someone had crushed him with stones.

In panic, Threngrin clawed his way and dragged the young man up the muddy bank. There he collapsed on the ground, shivering. All the strength he had was gone. The tiny bit of strength that he still had was keeping Threngrin from weeping. He swore he would not cry, not even if those men found him and chopped him to bits. He heard a soft laugh, a wicked laugh, and the sound of nails scraping on stones. He actually thought he felt fingers along his arms. Threngrin struggled, fought, and kicked in an effort to get free. After struggling and wiggling himself free, he instantly jumped to his feet to find himself fighting with a tree branch. A tree branch was blowing in the wind, and it was rubbing against his arm.

Threngrin took a deep breath to calm him. He tried everything he could to bring himself back to reality. He had no idea where he was or where he was going. Surely it was the howling of the wind, the dark skies, and the cool air that made him think that something was after him. He must hold on to his wits and not allow the still night to fuel his imagination that something was out there.

Threngrin doubted the men would still be looking for them. They gave up a long time ago. He was alone, in complete silence, which was unusually quiet for him. Yet he sensed the unexpected, and it had nothing to do with fear or the discomfort he was feeling. What he felt was more intense. He knew something wasn't right, it had been too quiet for too long, and he relied on his past experiences.

"I know Sirra wouldn't cry," he sputtered through clenched teeth. But he could not stop the tears from flowing—for his fear and desperation and for Sirra.

After a few minutes, Threngrin's breathing became shallow. He could hear the sounds of the forest again. His teeth stopped chattering, and the ringing in his ears stopped. He crawled a few yards away from the stream, dragging the young man behind him, toward the trees. There they lay. Threngrin needed to rest for a while.

Threngrin listened for several minutes but heard nothing, not even birds chirping. "Could they have lost my trail?" Threngrin commented to himself. But he knew that made no sense. They didn't lose trails, and they weren't frightened out of their wits either. They didn't fear easily. He had certainly left a trail that even a child could follow. So where were they?

"They are toying with me or . . . or they didn't follow me, and they wanted me to think they did," Threngrin said, rubbing his chin. The first thought didn't really bother him too much, but the second really pissed him off. The shame was almost more than he could handle.

The young man slowly started to come around. He slowly moved his arms, then his legs. Within seconds, he managed to sit himself up, still a little shaken. He looked around, but nothing was the same to him. Not one thing was familiar to him. "What happened?" the young man said, rubbing his head. "Where are we, and how did we get here?"

Threngrin turned and gave the young man a quick glance. Exhausted beyond endurance, broken in body and spirit, Threngrin lapsed gratefully into unconsciousness.

Chapter Fifteen

The heat had disappeared for the day. The wind coming in from the east cooled the air. Threngrin was still unconscious, and the young man watched the area very closely as he kept up the pace. He could feel his head getting heavy, and his body was getting tired from carrying Threngrin, yet he remained on walking.

The young man carried Threngrin for a distance. He finally found a great spot for them to rest. The young man knew Threngrin took care of him and protected him when he was unable to move, so with great gratitude, he did the same for him.

The young man hoped that the men who were following them really did give up. It had been days with no sign of them. What if they had been following and were waiting for the right place? The thought hindered him. No matter what, the young man felt they would never be safe. The hunters would find them again.

The thought was terrifying. He sat in silence in the dark, with fear in the pit of his stomach. He tried to fight the terror that was rising inside him. As the night got colder, the young man decided to start a small camping fire next to them to keep them warm. He snuggled up against the fire. It took him a very long time to fall asleep.

After hours of being unconscious, Threngrin finally came to from the smell of food cooking over an open fire. The smell of the food cooking woke up his stomach. He was starving. Threngrin slowly sat up, rubbing his head. He was surprised to find that he was alive. He glanced around and saw a nice warm, blazing fire, with what looked like squirrel roasting on a spit, but the young man was nowhere in sight. Threngrin slowly got to his feet and sat down next to the open fire. The heat felt so good. Still in a daze, he had no idea where he was.

"You are finally awake, man," the young man said with a grin. "I was beginning to wonder when you will wake up."

"Where are we, and what happened?" Threngrin said, rubbing his head.

"Well, you collapsed, so I carried you the rest of the way. I think we are safe for now." The young man patted Threngrin on the back. "But where we are, I have no idea yet."

"I need to fine Sirra. It has been days, maybe weeks, since I have last seen her. I must find her." Threngrin tried to get up but lost his balance and almost fell into the fire.

The young man grabbed Threngrin by his arm. "Look, you rest and eat. We will find her, but first you need to gain your strength back." And he handed him a chunk of meat.

"I don't even know your name," Threngrin said, taking the meat from him. Threngrin studied him closely. He noticed he was about three to four feet in height and was lightly built, but despite his size, he was fairly strong. His eyes were blue, his skin was a light tan color, and his hair was white to pale gray, the same as his beard.

"Oh, you can call me Basil," he said as he took a bite out of the meat.

After resting a few hours, Basil and Threngrin packed their things and headed out. The day started out gloomy, and the air felt damp and chilly. Threngrin and Basil found it hard to keep warm and comfortable as they continued on their journey. They could feel the climate changing quickly. There was little talk among them as they followed a narrow path, which went around clumps of dying bushes and fallen trees. Threngrin took the lead. His eyes watched everything that was around them, watching for any obstacle that might lie in their path. Threngrin stopped suddenly as he looked ahead of them. As far as he could see, there was nothing but trees—dead trees, dead bushes. Nothing seemed to be alive. Threngrin felt unsafe. He had no idea what lay ahead of them, but he had to continue on.

The day went by quickly as they continued, and by late afternoon, they finally reached the bank of a river. Threngrin led the way down the riverbank about two miles until they reached a place where the bank cut across to the other side. Here they stopped and looked across more forest beyond them. The sun would be down soon, and Threngrin did not want to be caught. He would feel safer with the water between them and anything that might be following. This time of day, you never know what was lingering around. They both agreed and set out in making a raft. The raft was a small one. It's only to carry their packs and clothing. They would have to swim across the river, dragging the raft behind them. It only took them a short time to complete the raft, strip off their packs and clothes, tie them down to the raft, and slip into the chilling waters. The only problem they had was finding a suitable landing place along the bank for them to climb. The current took them far, almost two miles, when they finally came across an area that they could cross. They scrambled out of the cold water, shivering in the evening air, and after dragging the raft out after them, they quickly dried off and dressed again. The whole venture took them a little over an hour, and the sun was lost from sight beneath the tall trees, leaving only a little red in the sky. Soon it would be complete darkness.

Threngrin was not ready to quit for the day. He wanted to find Sirra as soon as possible, but Basil suggested they sleep for several hours to regain their strength and then resume their journey in the morning.

They found shelter, and the area seemed safe. They found protection beneath an old oak tree and some heavy bushes. The mist in the air soaked their clothing, and the chill left them shivering. Threngrin made numerous attempts to start a campfire to gain some warmth, but the wood was so wet and damp with moisture, making it impossible. Basil wasn't going to give up. He found a pile of dead leaves, and he took some cloths out of his bag. He finally got a small fire going. How long it would last, he had no idea. They took the blanket that Threngrin had wrapped both of them in and settled for what appeared to be a very cold night. They curled up against each other to keep warm as they watched this little fire burn. They shared very little conversation. They were too cold to talk. There was no movement or sound beyond where they were camping. It was the quiet that made Threngrin uncomfortable. It made him focus to listen, in an effort to catch some kind of life. But there was only silence and complete darkness. The only thing that was out there was the cold wind that chilled their faces. Eventually Threngrin and Basil gave up and dropped off.

Basil woke Threngrin with a light shake, and they quickly packed their things and resumed their journey. The day started out very cold. Very little sun was peeking through the trees. Then the rain came in, chilling rain that soaked their clothes completely. Their weary bodies and the discomfort of being wet made their journey very difficult. Everything around them became damp and wet, and the dirt turned to mud, making walking impossible. Nothing moved. They had not seen one animal, and the trail had disappeared. They had no path to follow, and they had no trace of which direction they were going. With the heavy clouds and the falling rain, they had to guess which way to go.

Threngrin began to worry. They had been walking for hours, with no sign of life, and they seemed to be getting deeper into the woods. He began to wonder if they somehow got offtrack and were now lost and had been walking in circles. Threngrin knew with the heavy rain, it would wash out any paths they had made, and with the thought of being lost forever, fear set in. Basil had been following him and relied completely on Threngrin's sense of direction. Threngrin didn't want to worry Basil, so he kept silent.

Hours had passed, and nothing had changed. Threngrin started to feel his confidence slipping away. Threngrin saw a dead tree lying across their path. He came to a halt and sat heavily on the tree.

"I don't know what direction we are heading," Threngrin murmured. "I am not sure, but we might be lost."

Basil dropped his bags on the dead tree, shivering his shoulders. "I don't think we are completely lost."

"You got any idea where we are or what direction we are heading?" Threngrin asked, rubbing his head.

For a moment they looked at each other blankly, and then Basil rose quickly to his feet. "Let's go left."

Left, there was nothing, no path off to the left. Then again there was nothing ahead of them either.

Threngrin picked up his bag, and they headed left. Not a word did they speak as they walked. They looked ahead of them at the unexpected long forest. The chill in the air was finally gone, and the rain had finally stopped. Threngrin no longer felt the despair he was feeling. It seemed like hours went by as they continued ahead, when suddenly they came to a covered green area. With their tired eyes and aching body, feeling so exhausted, they felt joy to see green land once again. Basil thought he heard something prowling behind them and hurriedly warned Threngrin. They listened for a few minutes but could detect nothing moving around them, so they finally concluded that Basil must had been mistaken.

They continued walking, trying to move in the western direction, but it was hard to tell which direction they were really heading to. Branches and rustling leaves masked any view of the moon, and when they finally stopped, they were still not clear of where they were and had no idea how much farther they had to go before reaching any town, if there was even a town. Basil was glad to see the moon rising directly above them, and from what he could tell, they were still heading in what he believed to be the right direction. They put up camp in a clearing area sheltered by big elm trees and thick bushes, tossing down their packs.

Unwilling to start a fire, afraid it might attract attention, they contented themselves with the meat they had left from the previous night and raw vegetables they found along the way, completing the meal with some fruit that Basil found and a little water.

As they were eating, Threngrin had to get something off his chest. "Are you sure there is even any town out here?"

Basil nodded and then shrugged.

"I am sure we are going the right way, and there is a town . . ." He paused for a second. "Somewhere there is a town. This may be a longer way or we could go north, but I am pretty sure this is the right way and it is safer."

"I suppose this is the best way. I just want to find Sirra."

"And we will," Basil reassured him as he rubbed Threngrin's head. "Don't be so gloomy." Basil laughed. "We aren't dead yet."

Threngrin was not convinced by this argument, but he felt that the whole matter was best left alone. He admitted that Basil was right in taking the left, but it was just taking too long for him to find Sirra, and there was no way of knowing if she was alive.

The forest ground was soft and very comfortable compared to what they had been lying on. They lay quietly, gazing at the stars, which they hadn't seen in days.

The green forest insects maintained a sound that was peaceful. A few times they heard small animals rustling through the leaves close by. They were sounds of life, sounds they had missed. The sounds was so refreshing, they both drifted to sleep.

When they woke, the forest was still dark, and the sun had not appeared yet. They quickly packed their things and began their slow, steady pace eastward. A thin mist was still lingering in the air, not like it was before. It was cool, but more of the crisp cool of the early morning. They proceeded through the heavy branches, making walking difficult. Based on the position of the sun, Basil was hoping it would bring them out to a point along the edge of the forest, a little green marsh.

The woods were unusually still, even for an early morning, and they continued walking in uneasy silence through the forest. Threngrin was disturbed by the unnatural silence of the forest. Silence was so strange to this huge forest but uncomfortably familiar to Basil. Occasionally, they would stop, listening to the deep stillness, and then hearing nothing, they would continue walking, hoping to get through the forest by nightfall. Threngrin hated the silence and once began humming softly to himself, but he was quickly stopped by a look from Basil.

They at times would pick up the pace, and at times they had to walk really slow, climbing over dead trees that covered their path. Basil was now in the lead. He was determined to pick the best path to travel. Threngrin followed close behind, hoping Basil's sense of direction wouldn't get them lost. They only made three stops to rest, then quickly resumed their journey.

The day was ending quickly, and soon it would be nightfall. Still there was no break at the end of the forest. All they could see for miles were trees, and what was worse was a heavy mist that was once again covering the area. But this was something new, some kind of new mist. It was very thick, more like smoke, and they could feel it clinging to their bodies, and it had a very unpleasant taste. It felt like hands all over their bodies, weighing them down to the ground.

"We are getting close to the end of the forest. Not much farther!" Basil yelled out.

Threngrin did not like this. He was feeling very uneasy about this whole journey.

The deeper they went, the mist grew heavier, and it made it impossible to see. Basil slowed his pace down. They stayed real close to each other so they wouldn't get separated. The day was almost gone, with the mist and no sun. The forest was in complete darkness. Basil instructed Threngrin to stay close, to hold on to his bag strap. It finally became so difficult to see, they couldn't see an inch in front of them.

The mist was so thick, Basil couldn't see where he was going until it was too late. He had stepped into thick green moss, and he was already up to his knees. He pushed Threngrin back, preventing him from joining. The chill, cool moss clung to Basil's body, causing him to slip deeper and deeper into the hole. Responding to Basil's cry, Threngrin ripped the straps from their bags, making a rope. Threngrin had to do something quickly. Basil was in something like a quicksand. Soon he would be covered to his head and would suffocate. He threw the strap to Basil, and slowly, as hard as he could, he pulled Basil out. The two stared at each other. Their fate came so close to an end.

"What was that?" Threngrin suddenly spoke, breaking the silence. "We should have gone the other way."

Basil jumped to his feet and shook his head. "We've made it this far. We just have to follow this path until we get through this area. We will soon break through to the other side."

Threngrin rubbed his head, looking up at the sky. He noticed where the sun was. He turned to look at Basil with a concerned look on his face.

"I'm not spending the night in this awful place. We will continue on through the night. All day tomorrow. No stopping for anything! No food, no sleep, nothing. I want out of this place!" Threngrin said in a shaking tone of voice.

Basil nodded his head in agreement, and they continued on until they reached the end of the forest. Or until they reached an open land. Then they would rest. This place brought great fear to Threngrin. He had concerns if they were even going to make it out alive. They slowly moved along the uneven ground, and Threngrin kept his eyes on the path ahead of them. At times they came across roots from trees and fallen branches, even huge trees that blocked the path, which took them off the path. Threngrin quickly got a sense that something wasn't right. The feeling gradually overcame him. Not saying a word, he continued walking in silence. He listened for any sudden movement. Something then touched him on the leg. Threngrin jumped but saw nothing. Something touched him on the arm, and he jerked back but saw nothing there. He heard a faint sound coming from something standing next to him, but when he turned his head, nothing was there. Then off to the right, he saw something running. A chilly feeling went through him. They were no longer alone, and there was something out there. He just couldn't see it. Threngrin was so terrified, he was unable to speak out. He walked very close behind Basil, waiting for something to happen. It took all his effort to remain calm.

Basil stopped in his tracks. He saw Threngrin jumping around, moving from side to side. Threngrin spotted Basil standing there, looking at him like he just flipped out.

"I saw something. I know I heard something," he said, being so hysterical. They stood there motionless. Nothing happened.

"Maybe you are seeing things. No sleep or rest, it is so easy to start imagining things," Basil commented as he was walking in circles, looking around but seeing nothing.

"I don't think so. I really feel something is out there. I felt something touch me. I heard a voice. It is watching us, our every move. I don't like this," Threngrin whispered. "But maybe . . .," Threngrin said, circling around again. "Maybe you are right, it's nothing. Let's keep going. I want out of this place."

They continued on, watching, listening, but after a few minutes, nothing happened, so they dropped their guard. Threngrin's mind turned to Sirra. He was remembering her laugher, her smile, and he could only hope he would see her again.

Basil felt the strap he was holding jerk, and he lost his balance and fell to the ground. The first thing he saw was Threngrin suspended in the air. In minutes he felt a chill as something touched his legs. Basil with a quick reaction took the straps and tied them to a dead tree, hoping it would keep his feet on the ground. Basil could hear Threngrin crying out in the darkness above him. Not sure what they were up against, Basil felt safe staying where he was at. But he knew he couldn't keep Threngrin hanging.

Basil slowly untied himself from the tree and walked his way toward Threngrin. In his right hand, he held a silver dagger as he climbed the tree. Holding on to a tree branch just above his head, he repeatedly cut the thing that was holding Threngrin. Basil yanked really hard, trying to free him, and suddenly the limb that was holding him whipped back into the forest, releasing Threngrin. Then he promptly fell to the ground below.

Basil quickly made his way down the tree. He helped Threngrin to his feet before more of those limbs came out of the dark forest. One of the limbs knocked Threngrin back to the ground, and one grabbed Basil by his arm before he had the chance to dodge it. Basil felt himself being dragged toward the forest. He drew his dagger, trying to cut himself free. Threngrin again got caught in the grip of two limbs. He, too, was being dragged toward the forest. Basil finally broke free by cutting through the limb. Trying to reach Threngrin, he felt another limb grip his leg, knocking him to the ground. Basil struck his head on a boulder, and he lost consciousness.

Threngrin managed to reach for the dagger lying on the ground. With all his effort and strength, he chopped the limb free of his leg. He again made his way to Basil, cutting him free from the limb that was holding him. Seconds later Threngrin found himself chopping and cutting his way to a bush, protecting Basil, who was still unconscious. Soon the limbs disappeared back into the dark forest. Threngrin hesitated at first to pull Basil to any safe area, but before he had the chance to move, limbs again shot out of the dark forest. Threngrin had to think really hard about what they were fighting. If Sirra were there, she would know right away. The only thing that came to his mind was what they called a hangman tree. Threngrin had no idea how to fight it or get away from it. All he knew was they had to get through it.

"Basil!" he yelled. "Wake up, or we are not going to make it."

Threngrin noticed more limbs coming out of the darkness toward them. He started swinging his dagger, cutting and slicing, trying not to get tangled with the limb again.

"Get your butt up!" he pleaded.

Basil struggled as he came to. He got to his knees, but he was knocked back to the ground again. He saw several limbs waving in front of him. He turned his head slightly to the left and saw Threngrin fighting with limbs that were attacking him. Basil leaped to his feet and launched toward Threngrin. He slipped between flying limbs and grabbed Threngrin by his arm. They took off running, trying to avoid any of the limbs. If they could make it to the edge of the forest, they would be safe. Before they made it to the edge, the limbs were disappearing. The sun was rising, forcing the limbs back, and they were alone once again. Not saying anything, they collapsed silently against a big boulder and took deep breaths. They made it, and they were alive.

They briefly discussed which way to go. The choice wasn't simple. One risk was continuing through the path they were on, becoming lost, and fighting with limbs and strange creatures. Or they could go toward the mountains, which were not easy to climb. No one had ever made it through the mountains. The legend had it that no person had ever made it to the top. They had either disappeared or been found dead. The choice was not easy, and they decided to head toward the mountains. There was some woodland to go through, but it was a little safer.

They were tired and frightened. The journey was into a world of the unknown. Which in a way was more than Threngrin had expected. They struggled and pushed themselves to get through the pain and aches in hopes of getting close enough to the mountain. There they might to able to get a few hours of sleep.

The journey continued for hours, and they found it very hard to stay focused, their eyes straining to keep open. It seemed like minutes had went by, and they started to walk really slowly. Their eyesight began to blur, they needed sleep, but they continued to walk slowly. They were determined to maintain their course on the path. They had no idea how long they had been traveling or how far they had walked. To them it no longer seemed important. They were now sleepwalking, their minds struggling to keep going. To Basil, passing trees became buildings, and he started counting trees as if they were buildings in a town and they were walking down a street. He heard a voice, a faint cry in the wind. With every step, he fought to keep going, and he concentrated with all the strength he had to put one foot in front of the other to move forward.

Basil tried to stay focused. He was following Threngrin. Basil saw Threngrin walking ahead, and he turned his head, looking back at the trees, counting. He looked ahead again, but this time Threngrin was gone.

At first he thought his sleepy mind was playing tricks, and he continued to walk, looking for Threngrin up ahead. Then he stopped, and fear overcame him. Somehow Threngrin was nowhere around. The wind began to howl, and he called out for Threngrin, and he heard only his voice echoing. He continued to call out, with desperation and fear. The only sound he heard was his voice, muffled by the wind and silenced by the rustling leaves.

Basil heard his name faintly being called, and he ran through the trees toward the cry. But there was nothing. Basil fell to the round, and he kept on calling. He then realized Threngrin was gone and he was left alone.

Chapter Sixteen

Sirra felt sick, dizzy, and she was finding it hard to breathe with the wind blowing in her face. She finally got to see the treetops as the sun began to rise.

After flying for what seemed like hours, the dragon made a motion with its head, slowly circling around, and finally landed on a forested mountain. The dragon landed in a small area barely between two trees.

Sirra glanced around the surrounding area, fear growing, still not knowing what the dragon wanted. The dragon slowly released Sirra from its grip. There was no sign of any animals. No sign of any life. It was like everything had died off or disappeared. They were surrounded by tall trees and limbs so thick and tangled, it shut out most of the sunlight. The forest was dark and felt empty. At the end of the forest, Sirra saw a small cave. It was smaller than the one she was in before.

"Where are we?" Sirra asked, staring at the dragon. "Why are we here?"

Moving closer to Sirra, the dragon gave her a little nudge on her back, and she stumbled and fell to the ground. For a moment she stared at the dragon, and then she slowly got up to her feet. The dragon took its head and pushed her toward the forest. She studied it. She couldn't understand why the forest. They had been staying in caves.

The dragon nudged her again to move forward. Sirra placed her hands on her hip. "I am not moving," she demanded as she stomped her foot on the ground.

The dragon tilted its head to the side. Sirra saw the dragon's glowing eyes swing toward her. Suddenly she felt this frightening tingle inside her, fear that the dragon would hurt her or, even worse, step on her like a mushroom.

The dragon circled around her a few times, like it was studying her, trying to figure her out. The look on the dragon's face was so frightening, Sirra felt butterflies flying in her stomach. But she could not show any fear, and she tried to remain calm. With a slight growl, she leaped in front of the dragon. The dragon reacted quickly, and it brought its face right into her face, and they connected, knocking her to the ground.

With frustration, Sirra jumped to her feet and charged at the dragon again. She lowered her head and drove it into the dragon's gut. The dragon moved slightly, surprised by her little blow. The dragon let out a little puff as it watched Sirra bounce off and land on the ground again.

The dragon moved toward her, looking down at her, and it shook its head from side to side. Sirra, feeling the blow to her head, realized that wasn't a good idea. She watched in a daze as the dragon swung from side to side. It was almost like the dragon was laughing at her.

Sirra got up to her feet, and she brushed off the dirt on her. Confused and not understanding what the dragon wanted from her, she headed toward the forest. The dragon followed her close behind, so close she could feel its breath on the back of her neck.

They walked for hours, and Sirra was getting hungry. She needed food and rest. She started looking for any berries along the path. It wasn't much, but it was better than nothing.

It didn't take long for her to come across a berry bush. It was full of blueberries. Sirra walked up to the bush and started picking. The dragon came up behind her. The dragon took its paw and pushed her away. Her first thought was the dragon wasn't going to let her eat. Instead the dragon took a deep breath and blew at the bush, and all the berries fell to the ground. The dragon took its paw and nudged Sirra to the bush, as if it was saying, "Go ahead and eat."

The dragon lay down on the ground next to Sirra as it watched her eat. Sirra had no idea what to think about this dragon, but it wasn't going to leave her side. Sirra ate her portion. Although it wasn't much, it was enough to fill her up. Sirra headed back on the trail they were following, and the dragon got up and was right behind her again.

Sirra couldn't understand why they were walking and not flying. To her this was one strange dragon. The forest was dense with overgrown tree limbs, making it difficult to stay on the path. At times the land sloped upward and then downward. Once in a while they would get a glimpse of the sunlight peaking through the trees. Slowly they made their way through the forest. The forest soon became too thick for Sirra to walk through, and the dragon pushed her out of the way to take the lead. With the swing of its paw, it hacked away, clearing a path.

Soon they came to a gravel path that led to the east and led off into two other paths. One of course led to the mountains, and the other led west. Sirra had no idea where the dragon was leading her to, and many times she thought of just running, but with the fear of what the dragon might do, she decided it wasn't a good idea. The dragon took the path heading south. The path was dirt and mud, a path that didn't seem to go anywhere. They stayed on this path for what seemed like hours, and then they reached a dead end. Dead trees had fallen, and plants, grass, and moss had covered and taken over the path.

The dragon pushed the dead trees out of the way, clearing the path for Sirra. Sirra couldn't help but wonder why the dragon chose her. After walking for miles, they finally reached a small grassy area. Sirra saw a nice oak tree that had fallen next to some huge rocks. It was the perfect spot to rest. Sirra knew it was going to be dark soon, and she just hoped the dragon would let her camp instead of walking through the woods in the dark. The dragon made circles around Sirra as she sat there to rest. The dragon turned quickly to its left. It heard a sound coming from the forest. Sirra quickly jumped to her feet as she watched the dragon staring off into the forest. As Sirra was about to speak, something cold and strange-looking curled around her leg and worked its way up her body, at first not touching her. Then just as Sirra saw it, it was too late. It squeezed her really tight and snatched her up.

The dragon let out a high-pitched screeching sound as it watched Sirra being dragged off. Without any hesitation, the dragon flew up in the air, trying to spot Sirra moving below. The trees below were so thick, it made it really difficult to see anything, but the dragon was determined to keep her in its sight.

At times the dragon would lose her, then spot her, then lose her again. The dragon followed her for miles, and then it spotted an open area, where it got a good look at Sirra. The dragon flew down and stood right in the path of the creature and Sirra. The creature came to a complete stop. The creature holding on to Sirra as tight as it could was now face-to-face with the dragon.

The dragon stood in front of the creature and swung back and forth, trying to challenge the creature to a fight. Sirra, trying to kick and wiggle herself free, was not getting anywhere. The more she wiggled, the tighter the creature's hold got. The dragon studied the creature carefully for several minutes, noticing it had four legs, one of them attached to something in the ground, holding it in its place. The dragon took in a deep breath and blew out as hard as it could in hopes it would release Sirra, but it didn't. It just knocked the creature back a few steps.

The dragon then leaped forward, grabbed Sirra with its claws, and flew up in the air, not realizing that the higher it went, the tighter the legs around Sirra got. Sirra tried to cry out, but the air was getting crushed out of her. When the legs refused to give up, the dragon did one last attempt. It flew down just above the tree line where the creature was standing, and with all its strength, it took the leg of the creature in its mouth and bit down as hard as it could until the leg snapped in half.

The dragon flew only a short distance and landed where it was clear, with only a few trees. It gently placed Sirra on the ground. Sirra, struggling to breathe, managed to get untangled and out of the legs that were still wrapped around her. Sirra stood there staring at the dragon. It just saved her life.

The dragon knocked down some tree branches, and Sirra took the hint that they were going to camp there for the night. She collected the branches and a few twigs for the fire and gathered some berries to eat.

After she finished eating, she lay down on the ground next to the fire to keep warm, and the dragon lay next to her. The night was filled with stars that lit up the sky. The moon was so bright, it lit up the treetops, and she could see the cool mist in the air.

The night echoed with the sound of little creatures, and the wind blew through the trees. Sirra took a deep breath of the cool, crisp air. Sirra curled herself into a ball, so lost and worried she was never going to see Threngrin again. She would be lost out here forever. She quickly sat up as she saw the dragon rise and begin circling around her. Something got its attention. Although she didn't hear anything, the dragon did. At that moment, Sirra looked up at the dragon, and she could tell something was bothering it. The dragon circled around a few more times but saw nothing.

The dragon gave a low puff and lay back on the ground next to Sirra. She could see how uptight the dragon was. It was having a hard time relaxing.

The dragon had spent most of the day learning from Sirra even though communication had not been established. It had picked up other things from her. Sirra was still getting used to the idea of having the dragon with her. She didn't understand what was really going on, but she decided to stay with the dragon. She was grateful the dragon saved her life, but she needed to find Threngrin.

She stared up at the sky, and her thought for a moment turned to Threngrin. She was so confused, and emotions swept over her. The thought of never seeing him again brought tears to her eyes.

She could feel the air getting colder, and she moved herself closer to the fire. The dragon saw Sirra shivering. It curled itself around her to keep her warm. She took a deep breath in and closed her eyes. She figured it would be best to get some sleep.

Daylight was finally breaking through the trees. Sirra could feel little of the sunrays on her. She slowly got to her feet, rubbing her eyes. She noticed the dragon was already awake and pacing, watching her.

They started the day as they had before. Sirra would lead until the path was no longer a path, and then the dragon would take the lead to clear it. They would travel for hours before taking a rest. The sky was gray, with a little haze from the morning dew. They couldn't see much. The forest was still dark, with little sunlight coming through.

The haze grew thicker as they got deeper into the forest, and Sirra could barely see two feet in front of her. This had to be the chance she could take to break free. She was grateful the dragon saved her, she at first was going to stay, but she had to find Threngrin. If she broke free now, the dragon wouldn't be able to see her. But she had to time it just right. She walked a little bit faster, putting some distance between her and the dragon. Then she saw the perfect opportunity. She dodged between two trees and took off running. The dragon was quick, and it swung its tail in front of her, causing her to trip. Sirra quickly got to her feet and saw the dragon was standing right in front of her.

"Don't. Don't do that," the dragon finally spoke.

Sirra was stunned that the dragon could speak, and she took two steps backward. "You. You could speak? This whole time you could speak?" Sirra shouted. The dragon tilted its head off to the side, just staring at her. "Don't look at me. Say something." Sirra stomped her foot on the ground. The dragon quickly brought its head down to her and nudged her to move forward.   "I am not moving until you tell me where we are going. What I am doing here?" Sirra demanded. "Or I just might try to run away again."

"Don't. Don't do that," the dragon repeated again.

Sirra folded her arms and started pacing back and forth. The dragon watched her, following her every move with its head, and then the dragon started doing the same thing she was doing.

"Fine! Fine! Do you have a name?" Sirra asked. The dragon tilted its head to the other side. "What is your name?" Sirra asked again, taking a step closer to the dragon.

"What is your name?" the dragon repeated.

"My name is Sirra," she answered.

"My name is Sirra," again the dragon repeated.

"No, my name is Sirra," she stated, shaking her head.

"No, my name is Sirra," the dragon commented as it shook its head.

Sirra threw her arms up in the air and stomped her foot on the ground. "No! My name is Sirra. What is your name?" she said, poking the dragon in the chest.

The dragon stared at her for a moment. Then it stomped its foot on the ground and nudged her with its head, knocking her to the ground. "No, my name is Sirra. What is your name?" the dragon said.

Sirra sat there on the ground, staring up at the dragon. She had no idea that the dragon was a baby dragon and it had been learning from her. Learning her language, her walks. To her this was just a stupid dragon.

The dragon nudged Sirra to get up and start moving. She slowly got to her feet, and she turned toward it. "So I guess you're not going to tell me where we are going?"

The dragon shook its head back and forth, nudging her again.

"I see you are not speaking. Fine, let's go." Sirra drew in a deep breath and started walking toward the path.

Sirra's mind started to wonder about the dragon. Where did it come from? What message was it trying to tell her? Does it know where Threngrin was? Then she thought about Threngrin. Where was he at? Was he still alive? Was he safe? And then back to the dragon. Trying to figure out the dragon was more of a mystery to her.

Sirra was too focused on the dragon that she didn't even notice the creature that was following her. Just as Sirra turned the bend, she noticed a sweet but bitter smell. Soon the dragon caught the smell and pulled Sirra back toward it.

Sirra could feel her body begin to shake, and she felt her legs weakening, her heart racing. She saw in front of her, about five feet away, a huge creature. From what she could tell, it looked like a lizard. Its fur appeared to be dirty brown, maybe golden. It had horns coming from the top of its head. Sirra saw it had six toes with claws that were about seven inches long on both feet. The creature had its mouth opened, and Sirra could see its teeth, and every time the creature breathed out, the smell alone could kill anything.

The dragon stood next to Sirra, its head low to the ground. It was locked on to the creature, waiting for the creature to make its move. Sirra stood there watching, then realized she had no weapon to help in the battle.

Sirra slipped farther behind the dragon, her body shaking as the creature moved three steps toward them. Sirra saw its tail twitching, and it appeared to have thorns sticking out of it. Sirra went to move back and stumbled over a stick, landing on the ground. The creature took another two steps forward.

Sirra peeked around the dragon and saw it was just a foot away from her. As the dragon watched, the creature moved from one tree to another.

The dragon pushed Sirra into the bushes that were next to two big boulders. The creature and the dragon were no more than a foot away from each other. Sirra watched as the creature leaped around the dragon, then charged forward with great speed, hitting the dragon so hard in its side with its claw. The dragon quickly fell to the ground.

Sirra watched the dragon lying there, hurt. She wanted to help, but she had nothing she could use as a weapon. The dragon slowly got back to its feet. The creature leaped toward the dragon again, and the dragon quickly moved out of the way, so the creature slammed into a tree.

The dragon flew up into the air, just a few inches above the ground. The creature took a few steps toward the dragon. Just as the creature was ready to leap, the dragon flew down and caught the creature in its mouth. The dragon flew up into the air. Sirra watched as the dragon flew away and was no longer in her sight.

Then Sirra heard a roaring sound coming from the distance. She stood there frozen. She couldn't even breathe. She heard the roar again, and she moved in circles, trying to determine which direction the sound was coming from. There was another roaring sound again. It was more of a squealing sound, and it came from behind her.

Sirra couldn't just sit there. She had to go looking for the dragon. It had to be alive. She had become very close to the dragon. Sirra took off, running down the path as fast as her legs would go. Then she heard the roaring again, and this time it was louder, but it ended quickly. It was coming from in front of her. She froze for a few minutes, then slowly moved forward, not sure what she would see.

She quickly stopped. The dragon and the creature were nowhere to be found. She looked the area over, not sure if the creature was still around. The forest was silent. Sirra couldn't see much in front of her, so she kept herself focused on her surroundings as she moved slowly down the path. Sirra felt something pass by her and quickly dashed for the bushes.

Sirra circled around looking for the dragon and found herself standing about ten feet from the creature. Then she heard from behind her, trees were being pushed aside, and to her surprise, the dragon crashed through them. The dragon latched onto the creature's neck, and they were gone again. But this time, not too far from where she was standing. Sirra heard a thud. Something hard fell to the ground. She took off running and quickly came to a complete stop. The creature and the dragon were lying on the ground, a foot away from each other. They both showed no signs of life.

Sirra dashed quickly toward the dragon and fell to the ground next to its side. Tears began to form, and soon she had lost all control over herself. She could no longer fight back the tears. She laid her head on the dragon as tears ran down her face.

Hours went by, and Sirra finally felt the dragon twitch. The dragon still unconscious, Sirra now knew it was alive. She had to find a way to protect it. She scurried out into the forest. She found tree branches and leaves. She returned to the dragon, and she covered it the best she could to keep it safe till morning.

The sun was dropping quickly, and the air was getting cool. Sirra lay next to the dragon in hopes of staying warm. But the cool wind was blowing, causing her to shake. She needed to start a campfire. Sirra got up, wandering off into the woods to gather some stones, and made a small circle. There she added twigs and braches, and she finally made herself a small fire.

That night, she tossed around, drifting in and out of sleep. She had to make sure the dragon was warm and safe, not to say she was worried about her safety. She curled up against the dragon, feeling the cool air across her face. Once again she tried to drift off to sleep.

Sirra was woken by the sun and the warmth of its light beaming on her face. She turned on her side to check on the dragon, and to her surprise, the dragon was not there. She quickly jumped to her feet and saw the dragon up and moving around. It was moving slowly, still recovering, but she was glad to see it alive.

Sirra looked at the dragon, shaking her head. "I don't know which way to go. Are you well enough to travel? Maybe we should just camp here till you are better," Sirra said as she reached out to touch it "You still look hurt. We—" But before she could finish her sentence, the dragon nudged her to move forward.

"I guess you are good enough to travel. Let's go."

119

The trail they followed led them through a very dense forest of pine, oak, and maple trees. Occasionally the trees were so close to the path, Sirra could feel the bark of the trees brushing against her arm, leaving scratches. After what seemed like hours of walking, they came to a ravine. The ravine was small, and the water was shallow. To her this was the best place to cross over.

The dragon behind her looked around. Then without even a sound, it nudged Sirra, and she fell right into the water. She sat there looking up at the dragon. The dragon took one step into the water, and she took as much of the water she could in her hands and splashed the dragon.

"There, you got me wet. I got you." She laughed.

She slowly got her balance and was on her two feet. Then the dragon took its paw, and as hard as it could, it slapped it down into the water, causing a small wave, which was just enough for Sirra to lose her balance and fall back into the water.

"You know this is unfair. You are bigger than me and stronger." Sirra pulled herself out of the water.

She had to admit the water did feel good.

Once they crossed the ravine, the forest was more sparsely covered with trees, and she could see the open clear skies. She never thought she would see the sky again. She heard birds chirping and even saw a butterfly. The forest seemed peaceful.

Sirra's eyes wandered around the forest, taking in the calm nature and the fresh air, scuffing with her feet the small pebbles that covered the ground. The forest gave her a sense of peace. She looked back behind her, and the dragon was slowly keeping up with her.

The dragon sensed something, and it quickly wrapped its tail around her waist, pulling it back. The path they were on ended quickly. Sirra was a few inches away from a drop-off that was about four hundred feet. Sirra latched onto its tail as the ground was giving way right under her feet.

She stared at the dragon and then back to the edge. "I guess I should have been watching where I was going," Sirra said, backing away. "I think we should find a different way."

They turned back in hopes that there was a path they had missed. Sirra was so in tune with the butterflies and birds, she walked right past the path they should have taken. Seconds after they turned onto the path, Sirra noticed how quickly the weather had changed. The warm air was getting cooler, and the clouds began to cover the sun. Dark clouds started forming, and they were rolling in very fast. Soon after, she felt one drop landing on her head. There was no place to take cover, nor did they have much time. It wasn't long until another drop fell, and seconds later, she was soaked from head to toe. The air became cool, sending chills to her bones. It continued to rain for several hours. They followed the path, which was now covered in mud, until they finally reached its end. She had to make a choice, east or west, and neither looked too promising.

The dragon nudged Sirra to go east. Tired, cold, and soaked, she looked at the dragon, and they continued their journey east. They continued on for another hour, but Sirra was getting so weak and exhausted. She felt like she was about to pass out. She came to a clear area underneath an old oak tree. There were a few dead trees on the ground, where she planned for a campfire. *A campfire*, she thought, *would feel so wonderful right now.* Her body was cold and damp, but everything around her was soaked. Starting a campfire wasn't going to happen, so Sirra sat down on a dead tree, her arms crossed, trying to keep what body heat she had. As Sirra was watching the dragon pacing back and forth, she sneezed. She sneezed so hard, she fell backward, landing on a mud puddle.

"Just great. Not only am I wet, I am now covered in mud," Sirra said, climbing back on the dead tree.

"It will be all right," the dragon spoke.

"Now you speak. Funny," she stated as she reached into her sack and pulled out a rag to wipe the mud off her hands and face.

"It will be all right, you say." And she sneezed again. "I am dying, and you say it will be all right."

The dragon quickly jumped to her side. "Are you?"

She could feel the dragon's breath hitting her in the face. "Well, not really, I just feel like I am." The dragon took its head and nudged her back off the dead tree. She landed again in the mud.

She slowly got up to her feet, standing in the mud, and she looked directly into the dragon's eyes. "This is so not cool."

The rain had finally stopped, and the dragon glanced over toward the path. "Let's go."

Sirra looked at the dragon with a serious look on her face. "Let's go, you say." And she took the rag and blew her nose.

The dragon waited patiently as it watched Sirra gather her bag and climb off the dead tree.

Sirra was lucky she found this bag. It was up against an old pine tree. Of course the dragon was unconscious when she found it. It really didn't have much—a few rags, a spoon, a tin plate, and a hat. She figured it could come in use someday.

Nightfall was upon them. The sun had gone down. Under the bright moon, the road was soon covered with flying insects. The dragon continued to push on. Tired and every muscle in her body aching, she tried to keep up. Sirra got this sense that something wasn't right. A chill went through her body, down her spine. She slowed down but did not stop. Maybe it was something, or maybe it was nothing. She slowly continued.

She heard whispering through the trees, or maybe it was the wind. She started to feel her mind was playing tricks on her. From a distance, she thought she saw red eyes glowing. She rubbed her eyes, it was gone, and nothing was there. Then she heard another faint whisper echoing through the forest. *It's nothing*, she said to herself. She took a deep breath as she tried to calm down, but the feeling she had wouldn't let her.

I am just tired. My mind is playing tricks, she thought. *I am just hearing things*. And she glanced back at the dragon. It was walking very calmly, showing no awareness of threats around. She knew if something was out there, the dragon would be right in front of her. As quickly as she turned back around, the dragon had jumped in front of her. She was so shocked by how fast the dragon was that she straightened herself up, looked around, but saw nothing. Then she saw the dragon clearing an area for them to camp for the night. It was like the dragon could read her mind. She wasn't going to disagree, sleep would be really nice, but deep down inside could she really fall asleep?

She gathered some twigs and a few branches and started a small fire. She lay down next to the fire, trying to warm up, and the dragon slowly lay down next to her. She watched the flames flicker and listened to the sound of the wood crackling as it was burning. She knew she was protected, the dragon would keep her safe, but the feeling she had was very uncomfortable. She slowly closed her eyes, and it wasn't long before she was sound asleep.

Sirra was woken by the warmth of the sun beaming on her face. She rose up slowly, still drowsy, and she saw the dragon was already up and had brought her some berries to eat.

She grabbed a handful of berries and looked up toward the dragon. "Do you ever sleep?"

The dragon shook its head and turned toward the path. Sirra with a handful of berries picked up her bag and followed behind the dragon closely.

The day started off like any other day. The forest was damp from the nightly dew, making the path slippery with mud. Then the dragon turned off the path, and they were walking completely in the forest—no path and no trail. Not saying a word, she followed.

The sun had not heated up the forest yet, and everything was still damp. She could feel the twigs snapping under her feet, and every tree branch was covered with wet leaves and slapped her in the face. Trying to avoid as many wet branches, she ducked under, but somehow the dew from the branches managed to drop and land down her shirt.

Being as difficult as it was, she managed to keep up with the dragon. She was ducking tree branches and avoiding the leaves, and she wasn't paying attention on just how close she was to it. She heard a crackling sound and raised her head up just enough to see, and a small twig came flying and caught her in the stomach, sending her flying backward and landing on the ground, flat on her back.

The dragon quickly turned around when it heard Sirra hit the ground. She was lying on the ground, trying to catch her breath. The dragon looked down at her as she was rolling from side to side, holding her stomach. It took Sirra a few minutes to catch her breath, and she slowly sat up.

"You should really watch what you are doing!" she said, trying to breathe.

"It will be all right," the dragon said, tilting its head to one side.

Sirra shook her head as she got up and brushed off the leaves and dirt off her clothes. She walked up to the dragon and placed her hand on its side. "It will be all right—is that all you can say?"

"Sirra," The dragon spoke softly.

"Oh, now you know my name." She giggled. "I should give you a name," she commented as she picked up her bag off the ground. "I will call you Goldie." She thought for a moment. "Ya, I like it, Goldie. Your name is Goldie."

The dragon jerked its head back. "My name is Goldie."

Sirra giggled a little. "That's right, Goldie."

The dragon glanced at her one more time and started walking forward down the path.

"So, Goldie, are you going to tell me where we are going?" Sirra was hoping for an answer. But the dragon continued on walking. "We are not speaking again, I see."

Sirra kept up the pace, but this time not following behind Goldie too close as she hummed to herself. As they got deeper into the forest, they came across vines that were growing all over the place, making it hard to get through. Vines had taken over fallen trees, and some were covered with moss. There were vines that were so thick, there was no way she was getting through. She tried to keep up with Goldie as it was making a way for them, but it was becoming impossible. She was trying to break and yank vines, but she was having no luck. Goldie would push its way through, but the vines would come right back toward her, blocking her path again. She thought to herself it would be easier to climb over the vines. They were thick and heavy, it would hold her weight just fine.

As she was climbing, she saw a twig sticking up. She yanked on the twig, turning, twisting with all her strength. She yanked so hard, the twig broke off, and she went flying backward, landing on a pile of vines and twigs. She tried to move to get free, but every time she moved, twigs stabbed her in the arms, legs, and back. She was also getting herself tangled up more.

She lay there for a moment, out of breath and angry. "This was a great idea," she said to herself. She finally found a breakthrough in the vines and wiggled herself out. She rolled over onto her back and slowly rose to her feet. The dragon just stood there watching with a puzzled look on its face.

"You were a big help," she stated.

"It will be all right," it said as it turned its head away.

"Sure thing," Sirra said as she was pulling twigs out of her hair.

As they continued on their way, Sirra was still pulling twigs out of her hair. She had so many, it would take her forever to get them all out. Not long after, she heard from a distance running water. They were coming close to a stream.

Sirra carefully followed the dragon along the stream until they came to a spot where they could cross. Trees grew close to the embankment, making it hard to keep her footing, and branches hung very low over the stream. The dragon made it across with no problems, but for Sirra, she had more challenge. She slid just a little down the embankment, she placed one foot on top of a stone, and little water was covering her foot. Slowly she reached out for the other stone, trying to keep her balance. Sirra had a hard time keeping her balance. The cold water covering her feet made her shiver, twigs and small pebbles were hitting her legs, and she was also ducking the low tree branches—all at the same time. She took a deep breath as she reached for the other stone. Then her foot slipped, and she landed in a deep hole. The water was up to her waist, and she could not move. Her foot was caught between a log and a stone. The cold water startled her as she cried out.

The dragon heard her cry out, and it wrapped its tail around her and pulled her close to the embankment. Sirra scrambled to her feet as she reached up to grab a branch. She slowly climbed the embankment. The edge was slippery, and the pebbles were giving away from under her feet. She finally made it to the top, and she collapsed onto the ground. She had cuts and scrapes on her legs and a huge bruise on her arm where a tree branch came across and hit her.

"No more stream!" she demanded as she lay there, trying to catch her breath. Sirra tried to get to her feet, but it was so muddy where she was. She kept slipping, and her feet were going in all directions. She gained her footing, and she stood there, water dripping from her clothes. She was soaked from head to toe. The cool breeze coming from the east brought chills to her body.

"Why! Why! Look at me, I feel like a drowned rat!" she said through her chattering teeth.

The dragon looked at her, turned, and walked away.

The forest was filled with the fresh fragrance of pinesap and maple trees. Still with the taste of water from the stream, she tried to focus more on the sounds coming from around her. It was the sounds of small animals rustling trough leaves, running in and out of bushes. Even though she couldn't stop shaking, with what little sun that was coming through the trees, she was slowly drying off.

She watched the dragon leading the way, again deeper and deeper into the forest, and the path was getting narrow. It was barely wide enough for the dragon to pass. For the first time in a long while, she spotted a squirrel sitting on top of a log, which then quickly ran away. From time to time she would hear the sound of birds chirping, and that brought back memories of her home, which she might never see again, along with Threngrin.

It wasn't long until the sun disappeared, and nightfall was upon them. The forest became dark real quick. Sirra could barely see where she was going. The moon gave very little light through the thick trees. Sirra had to use her hands and feet to guide herself along the path.

Too cold to speak, she continued to follow the dragon close behind, watching its shadow along the trees, made by the moonlight. She really didn't care anymore on where they were going. She was too damn tired and cold to care.

The farther they went, the more difficult it became for them to walk—the trees became closer and closer, and the path became more rugged, making it harder to keep her footing. Tree roots were sticking out of the ground, covering the path, and she tripped over a few. She tried really hard to keep her eyes open and to stay focused, but sleep was what she wanted. Walking with her eyes closed for only a second, she didn't realize what was up ahead of her, and within that second, her feet went right from underneath her. She slid right down into a river.

As she tried to cry out, her mouth was filled with water and dirt. Fear set in as she was being pushed downstream by the current of the water. She tried to keep her head above the water, but the current was so strong, it kept pulling her under. She could feel twigs slamming against her body as she tried to grab something to hang on to. She finally caught a tree branch, but the current was so strong, it snapped in half, sending her farther downstream. She got her head up above water just enough to cry out for help, and she went back under again. Her body flipping and turning, her head slammed into a log, knocking her unconscious. The dragon saw Sirra floating downstream, and it quickly flew up. It tried to grab her with its claws, but it couldn't get close enough because of the trees. It made a dash down the stream, not realizing just how close the tree was to the river. It hit the side of the tree, knocking it into the river. The dragon stood up, shook itself off, and flew back up. It saw Sirra was just inches away from a waterfall. It quickly picked up speed, but it was too late. Sirra went over the edge. It was a three-hundred-foot drop. The dragon nose-dived and instantly snatched Sirra in midair.

The dragon flew around until it found a cave. It slowly flew in and carefully placed her on the ground. She started to gain consciousness. And she flickered her eyes, coughed up some water, and passed out again.

Chapter Seventeen

The following day, Basil was woken up by the bright sunlight shining on his face and the smell of morning dew still lingering in the air. He found himself lying on the ground in really tall grass. He lay there, his memory so vague. He had no recollection of what happened or how he got there. Rubbing his dreary eyes, he sat himself up, and he saw that he was in an open field. Slowly he started to regain some of his memory, of Threngrin disappearing, but he had no recollection of how he got there. Everything to him became blank after Threngrin had disappeared, and he didn't remember leaving the forest. He rubbed his eyes again and sighed for a moment. Although the warmth of the sun felt good, he had to find Threngrin. Basil slowly stood up on his feet. The grass was about as tall as he was. He could barely see over the tall grass. Anything could be out there, and he would never see it. Looking around to determine which way to go, he heard something ruffling in the tall grass about ten feet away from him. He looked closely but couldn't tell what it was. The grass was moving, and that was all he could see. He slowly walked toward the area, taking one step at a time. Just as he was within range, something grabbed his legs, causing him to fall flat on the ground, landing on his face. Before he had the chance to turn over, he felt something heavy on his back. Quickly his hands were tied behind his back, and a brown sack was placed over his head.

"What is this?" Basil shouted as he tried to wiggle himself free. "Let me go now!" he demanded.

Quickly Basil felt the weight being lifted off his back. "Don't move." The voice was low. "If you don't move, I will take the sack off your head."

Slow he took the sack off Basil's head, and Basil quickly turned around. They were surprised, and being two feet apart, Threngrin quickly ran up to Basil.

"You're alive! You're alive!" Threngrin said in a cheerful voice, patting him on the back.

"You're not going to be unless you untie me!" Basil yelled. "Untie me!"

"Oh, yes. Sorry about that. I couldn't see who it was. I didn't know it was you," Threngrin explained. "I thought you were——"

"I know. I know. Now hurry, untie me," Basil said as he tried to wiggle himself free.

"I see we made it out of the forest, but I don't know how," Threngrin stated as he was untying Basil. "I don't remember how."

"Do you remember anything?" Basil said as he reached to grab Threngrin's arm.

"Not much, just that something cold grabbed me. Then it was lights out and waking up here. Why?" Threngrin stated as he jerked his arm away.

"No reason. I can't remember anything either." Basil rose to his feet. "I guess it doesn't matter. At least we are alive."

Threngrin couldn't agree more. They discussed which way to go, considering they really had no idea where they were. They decided to go west, to follow the sun. With any luck, that would take them toward the mountains.

They trampled along the tall grass, heading toward the tree line. Basil hoped they would get close enough to the mountains before nightfall. They had a lot of ground to cover. It was already midday, but they continued on, walking with little conversation. They never brought up the events of yesterday, leaving their feelings unspoken. They came up to a small stream. Threngrin was very thirsty. The water didn't look very clean, but he needed something to drink. He hesitated at first, then bent down, cupped his hand, and gathered up some water. He smelled the water first. It seemed to have a faint smell. He took a small amount to taste it. To his surprise, the water tasted fresh. He quickly gathered as much water as he could, and soon Basil followed. They had been without water for two days.

Basil spotted just on the other side of the river a clearing underneath a maple tree. It was a great spot for a campfire. The sun was going down, and soon it would be too dark to travel. Basil felt it would be safer to camp for the night and travel out early in the morning.

They had no supplies. Everything they had got lost back in the forest. The only thing they had was a pocketknife that was in Basil's pocket. They had no food. Basil came up with an idea, and they would have to go hunting. They walked a little ways into the woodland, not too far from camp, and Basil found some twigs and attempted to make themselves a weapon. Threngrin was not too fond of the idea but went along with it. Basil made a small spear out of wood and gave it to Threngrin. He then instructed Threngrin to climb a tree.

"I am going to gather up some squirrels. Once you see one, throw your spear. Make sure you hit it."

"You want me to do what?" Threngrin asked, shaking his head.

"Throw the spear. Hit the squirrel," Basil said, walking away.

Threngrin shook his head. "This is dumb," he muttered, climbing a tree.

Threngrin sat there in the tree for what seemed like twenty minutes, when he saw Basil running. He positioned himself, and when the squirrel was within his range, he threw the spear. Threngrin threw the spear so hard, he lost his balance and fell out of the tree, landing flat on his back on a pile of twigs

Basil ran up to Threngrin. "You did it!" he said, holding up the squirrel. "We got food," he commented, looking down at Threngrin. "What you doin' down there?"

Threngrin glanced up at Basil, barely able to breathe. "This was not a good idea. I broke a rib or two."

"I don't think so," Basil said, reaching out his hand to help Threngrin. "Come, let's go eat. You will feel better." And Basil started walking back to camp.

Threngrin followed, holding his rib, trying to breathe, but with every breath he took in, it hurt.

They made it back to camp, and Threngrin collapsed on the ground. "I broke my rib. I am going to die thanks to you."

Basil looked at him with a straight face. "You only bruised a rib. You are not going to die from that."

Threngrin still lay on the ground, looking straight up at Basil with his bottom lip sticking out. "I am curious. Have you ever seen someone die from a broken rib?"

Basil giggled. "No!"

"So how would you know if I am dying or not. I can tell you this, I am dying," he said with a slight cough.

Basil tried not to laugh. "I do know this. You will be the first." And he patted Threngrin on the head.

Within minutes, Basil had gutted the squirrel, and he held it up. "I am going to the stream to wash dinner."

"Sure, leave me. You'll see, when you come back, I'll be dead," Threngrin stated, still holding his rib.

Basil walked away, heading toward the stream. It didn't take long for him to clean and wash the squirrel. He headed back to camp and found Threngrin still lying on the ground.

"See, you're still alive." Basil grinned. "But I suppose if you're dying, I get all food," he stated as he started the fire.

Threngrin jumped up. "I'm not dead yet!"

There was a full moon, the sky was full of stars, and it brightened the sky. They ate their meal in silence, listening to the sounds of crickets, watching fireflies around the campfire.

They had a very long tiring day. Threngrin made himself comfortable lying in front of the fire. Basil lay back up against a dead tree. It didn't take long for them to fall asleep.

A disturbing sound from the woods caused both to sit straight up at the same time. They were no longer sleepy. They were wide-eyed, awake now. Basil slowly made his way to Threngrin and sat down next to him. They both grabbed each other's hand and squeezed tightly. They sat there not moving, listening to the stillness of the night, as close as they could be. Minutes went by, and nothing happened. They were still afraid, knowing that something would happen. They just didn't know when.

Then they heard something wading in the water at the river. They looked toward that direction, and they froze as they saw the shadow of a creature that was heading toward them. They froze with terror. They were unable to think and couldn't move, as they watched the creature move closer to them. They had not seen the creature yet. The creature might not have seen them. The creature would know real soon. They had no place to go. Out here they had no place to hide. There was no chance for them to try to escape. Threngrin felt his mouth go dry, and somehow he remembered the scattered planks just around the big oak tree, but he went numb. He sat frozen with Basil, and he knew soon it would be the end.

Strangely nothing happened. Then a few minutes later, Threngrin saw a shadow. It looked like the creature was upon them. A sound coming from deep within the woods caught the creature's attention, and it disappeared. Suddenly they heard the sound again but saw nothing. They stared out into complete darkness, and the creature was gone. But the sound still lingered.

They both remained immobile. They sat real close to each other, not saying a word, listening, but all they could hear were the fireflies around them. A few minutes had passed, and soon they were able to breathe a little easier. They began to relax, enough to release the grip of their hands as they looked at each other.

They still wondered where the creature came from, but more of their curiosity was on where the creature went to.

They dropped their arms to their side, and Threngrin moved over slightly to the right. The night was once again quiet. Still sitting, Threngrin turned around to grab a piece of wood to put on the fire, even though there wasn't much of it. The creature was right there behind him, with its mouth open wide. Threngrin was startled and fell backward. Basil scrambled to get to his feet. Basil stood there frozen as he watched the creature with its mouth open wide face-to-face with Threngrin.

The creature was huge, had brown fur, had four legs, and was about nine feet tall. Basil watched as the creature stood completely on top of Threngrin.

Threngrin lay there with his hands over his face. He could feel the creature's breath hitting his face, and he was too afraid to look at it. He knew his time had come.

Basil took a hard look at the creature, rubbed his eyes, and looked again. "It's a bear!" he yelled.

He turned slowly, trying to remain calm as he looked for a stick, something to chase the bear away, but when he returned, the bear was gone. Threngrin was still lying on the ground with his hands covering his face.

"Where did it go?" Basil asked, walking up to Threngrin.

Threngrin slowly removed his hands, looking around, and quickly jumped to his feet. "I don't know," Threngrin said, shaking. "I-I didn't hear or see it leave."

They carefully looked around, and neither heard nor saw where the bear went. It mysteriously disappeared.

Everything seemed to go back to normal. Still a little restless, Basil threw more wood on the fire and lay down, curled up in a ball. They had several hours before daylight. Threngrin wasn't about to sleep, his heart still pounding and with the fear that the bear was still out there.

Threngrin sat down on the ground, his back up against a dead tree that was lying next to the fire. Even though Basil had no trouble falling asleep, Threngrin couldn't. He was going to stay up and be on the lookout. As he sat there, his eyes fell heavy, and he could no longer keep them open.

"Basil," Threngrin cried out as he rubbed his sleepy eyes.

Basil blinked, struggling to get to his feet. "Hey, we are alive. We made it through the night."

"We need to head out," Threngrin stated.

They headed out, following the same path they were on yesterday. Threngrin had lost any hope of finding Sirra. He started thinking about when they became separated, and panic set in. He was afraid. He feared he would never see her again. He began to think it was pointless to try to find her and that he would never see her again. Feeling exhausted, he pushed through his doubts and continued on. He had to keep some hope they would find each other.

Basil believed this was the right direction to a town. He did make a promise to Threngrin that he knew of a town and he could get them there, but he had not travel the land in many years, so everything had changed. He wasn't about to tell Threngrin that. Basil chose to go west in hopes of cutting down their travel time. They moved rapidly. It was already late in the afternoon, and daylight was disappearing quickly.

It was getting close to dusk when Basil found a trail that seemed to be several years old. He could tell it was a trail because of the ruts that were deep in the ground. Basil hoped this trail would take them near the mountains by nightfall.

They both agreed it was too dark and it would be best to find a spot to camp. Threngrin found some pine trees that were close together, and it would make a great spot for shelter. There was just enough light from the moon for them to see to start a fire. Basil tossed his bag on the ground, and Threngrin started the campfire. They warmed up the leftover squirrel they had from the night before, and they lay down next to the fire after. It didn't take long for them to fall asleep.

They rose the next day feeling well rested. Basil came up with a new idea. They could cut across the woods, come out near the edge of the wood line just a little way off the west, and that should bring them closer to the mountains. Threngrin agreed, so they abandoned the trail they were on and started heading northwest. Basil was hoping they could come across a squirrel or a rabbit— something for their meal.

The smooth path they were traveling changed quickly. It was rough, with small hills that dropped down into steep ravines. This slowed down their traveling. In some places it was really hard for them to see what was ahead of them. At times Basil thought it would be best to go back. It might be because something didn't feel right, or perhaps it was only his imagination. Nevertheless he decided to push through. Soon they would be near the mountains.

Something about this had changed, and it didn't feel right. They were walking, sun shining through the trees, and then in the blink of an eye, it was completely dark. Basil looked around, and he saw nothing really out of the ordinary. The trees just got closer, blocking the sun. Then he got this leery feeling they were not where they were. Threngrin was walking close by him, whistling and kicking pebbles. If Threngrin was all relaxed, why was he so uptight, or was it because Threngrin hadn't even noticed the changed around them? The ground became really soft, it was almost like mud, but it wasn't. Basil hesitated if they should continue. He really had his doubts about this area. He has never seen anything like this. He stopped, and he slowly grabbed Threngrin's arm and motioned him to back up. Threngrin then noticed something glowing. It looked like a bright light up ahead of them, and it was near a tree.

Threngrin went to raise his feet to take one step forward, and then the ground opened. Thick black roots came up out of the ground, wrapping them around Threngrin's leg. Threngrin kicked, trying to break free, but he could not get them off him.

Basil stepped back as he watched Threngrin trying to break free. He could not believe what he was seeing. "Here we go again," he said, afraid to move.

Threngrin stopped moving when he saw this huge black tree moving toward him. The first thought that entered his mind was trees didn't move, but this one did. Then its tree limbs slowly reached out to him. The tips of the limbs had thorns that were very sharp. Basil remembered he had a pocketknife. He started cutting the roots that were wrapped around Threngrin's leg. The whole progress was very slow. Basil could only cut a little at a time. Basil soon realized he might not be able to free Threngrin. Not giving up, he continued to cut with the knife, cutting pieces off the limb. It was enough, causing the tree limb to back off a little. Basil realized as he studied the tree that he knew just what kind of tree this was. The kind you never get away from. He had never encountered one but had heard stories.

From what he had heard, you had to hit the center of the tree, destroying the living part inside. Basil knew he had to get close to the tree in order to do that. Basil slowly moved toward the tree, but the tree quickly took its limbs and started throwing thorns in every direction. Basil hit the ground. Many missed him, but some got Threngrin. Threngrin started to move rapidly. They were stinging him as if he was getting stung by millions of bees. Many of the thorns fell off, but some just broke off.

"Threngrin! Threngrin!" Basil cried out.

Threngrin couldn't answer. He started feeling dizzy, light-headed, and parts of his body were becoming numb. Basil watched as Threngrin slowly collapsed to the ground. The tree still had Threngrin in its grip, and Basil knew he had to do something fast. There wasn't much time.

Basil crawled as quickly as he could, and he got as close to the tree as he could. Being this close to the tree, it couldn't reach him. He took his knife, and as hard and as fast as he could, he stabbed the tree. He stabbed the tree in the same place over and over, taking out pieces. The tree tried to release another round of thorns, but it couldn't fight back. The tree was injured. It slowly released its grip of Threngrin. The roots gradually went back into the ground, and then the tree was motionless.

Basil picked up Threngrin, who was unable to move. "I-I—," was all Threngrin could say, and he passed out.

Basil wasn't sure how long Threngrin was going to be unconscious. He decided to carry him as far away from there as he could. Basil followed the trail, hoping it would lead them to the edge of the woods—at least this part of the woods. He carried Threngrin for what seemed like hours, and then he spotted a well-hidden area they could camp at for the night. He placed Threngrin on the ground and started a small fire. He was exhausted and could barely move. He lay down next to the fire, watching the stars in the sky. It didn't take long for him to fall asleep.

For Basil, morning came too quick. Rubbing his sleepy eyes, he noticed Threngrin was sitting up next to the small fire.

"Where are we?" Threngrin asked, rubbing his head.

"Not sure. I think we should be close to the mountains by the end of the day." Basil grinned."

"How did I get here?" Threngrin had a puzzled look on his face.

"Well, I picked you up and threw you over my shoulder like a sack of dry corn." Basil patted him on the back.

"What? Is that why I feel so sore?" Threngrin snapped.

"Well, I did carry ya, and no, you are sore from the thorns that were shot at you. So if you are ready, we need to be heading out," Basil hinted as he pointed toward the trail.

Threngrin slowly got to his feet, still feeling a little dazed, but he managed to put one foot in front of the other. Basil had figured the path they were on should take them north through the woods and into the mountains. There still might be a chance they would come to rough country and areas that would be hard to get through. They came to a crossing where the bridge they had to use looked worn down. Planks were missing, and it really didn't look sturdy or safe to cross. Basil went first, his eyes focused ahead of him, and all he could see were more trees. He put one foot on a plank, keeping it steady, and then he placed the other foot on the next plank, taking it slow. He finally made it across. Threngrin, not real sure about this place, placed one foot on the bridge, looking at the planks. He placed his foot on the plank, and the bridge started swinging back and forth.

"I am going to die!" he yelled out.

"No, ya not! Now move it!" Basil shouted back.

The wind started to pick up, and the bridge started to swing more. Threngrin could hear the planks cracking every time the bridge moved. He slowly placed his foot on the next plank. The bridge began to move more rapidly. Holding his breath, he reached for the next plank, trying not to look down for it was a long drop. He then reached out for the next plank. The wind picked up, and the bridge was swinging back and forth at great speed. Threngrin reached for the next plank, and he lost his balance and fell. Still on the bridge, he looked over at Basil. He shook his head and slowly got to his feet. He stood there for a minute, then reached for the next plank. The plank broke. His one leg fell through. Holding himself, he managed to pull himself back up. He looked at Basil with fear in his eyes. He slowly reached out for the next plank, and a gust of wind caught the bridge just right, causing it to swing in a circular motion, knocking Threngrin right off it. He quickly grabbed on to a plank.

"Help!" he yelled out.

Basil gasped for air as he saw Threngrin being tossed over the bridge. He quickly ran over to Threngrin, taking it slow as he crossed the bridge. He reached down for Threngrin's hand.

"Grab my hand!" he shouted.

Threngrin slowly reached up for Basil's hand. Holding on to Threngrin's hand, Basil slowly tried to lift him up. Threngrin's hand slipped, and he quickly grabbed the plank again.

"Grab my hand again!" Basil cried out.

The wind started to pick up more speed, and the bridge was swinging with great speed, causing it to be more difficult for Basil to hold on to Threngrin. Basil reached out for Threngrin again. Threngrin reached up with his one hand and grabbed on to Basil. Basil with all his strength pulled Threngrin up. They both lay on the bridge, feeling overwhelmed and filled with relief. The wind was becoming more and more intense. The planks were cracking one by one. They had to hurry to get across before it was too late. Basil took the lead, and Threngrin followed, and they slowly got across the bridge. His legs still shaking, Threngrin was so glad to see land. They collapsed to the ground and took a deep breath. The bridge soon made an awful cracking sound, and they watched as it crumbled and fell, landing below on the ravine.

"Well, at least we made it across," Basil said with a smile on his face.

Threngrin turned quickly toward him. "I could have died."

"Come on, let's go, you are safe." And Basil helped him up.

The morning sun was giving enough light through the trees, and they could feel the sunrays on their faces. Threngrin was enjoying the warmth from the sun, considering it had been a long time since he felt it on him. They moved along quickly through the trees and thick bushes. The path began to climb upward. This meant they were getting very close to their destination. Threngrin felt uneasy the farther they got. He felt as if someone or something was watching them. They did not speak, Threngrin's eyes searching for something as they continued forward.

It was late in the afternoon, and the path became more inclined. The trees were farther apart, and Threngrin could see the clear blue skies. Rocks were appearing, and they could see the tall peaks of the mountains—the mountains were now visible. They felt relieved to see them. They knew it was still going to be a rough journey ahead, but at least they were out of the forest and in open land.

Nightfall was soon going to be upon them, and they were losing daylight. They still had at least a day's journey before they would reach the mountains. Threngrin wanted to continue until they could no longer see. Threngrin could tell the air was getting cooler as they got closer. After a few more hours of traveling, they ran into a dense fog. It was coming from the mountains.

They decided it would be best to camp there for the night. With it being dark and the dense fog, they couldn't see no more than three feet in front of them. Basil gathered wood and started a small fire. After they ate their meal, Basil fell asleep quickly, but for Threngrin, it took him a little longer. All he could think about was Sirra, and he hoped he would find her. He closed his eyes and drifted off to sleep, dreaming of Sirra.

The ground underneath them began to vibrate, and rocks began to slide down the mountains surrounding them. Minutes later, the ground shook again. They were minutes apart, but each time they got harder and harder. Threngrin woke up quickly when a rock slid down the mountains and hit him in the back of his head. He jumped to his feet. "What the—," was all he got to say. The ground shook again and knocked him off his feet, landing him on his backside.

Basil couldn't get up quick enough. Rocks were slamming in too fast, making it difficult for him to gain his footing.

"I really don't like the sound of this!" Basil yelled, trying to free himself from the rocks.

Threngrin managed to get to the tree line to see if he could find out what was causing the rockslide. Every time he moved, there was another vibration, which caused more rocks to slide down the mountains. Basil stayed real close behind Threngrin as they slowly peeked around the trees.

The vibration continued, and more rocks slid down. They couldn't see anything as they were too far away. They both stood up, hovering over each other in hopes of getting a better look.

"What ya looking at?" a young man said, standing right behind them with his head on Threngrin's shoulder.

Threngrin jumped, turning around quickly, knocking Basil to the ground. "Where did you come from? Who are you?" Threngrin said with a puzzled look on his face.

"I come from all over the place—namely, I am from back that way." And he pointed to the north.

"And you are?" Basil asked, getting up off the ground, looking at Threngrin with a glare in his eyes.

"My name is Jack. They call me Jack-of-all-trades. Get it? Jack-of-all-trades," he said, patting Basil on the shoulder.

"What are you doing here?" Threngrin moved back away from him.

"I am—" He stopped in midsentence. Instead he glanced ahead of him to see what they were looking at. "You all planning to get over there mountains? I wouldn't do that."

Basil stared right into the young man's eyes. "And why not?"

"There are kobolds. There are lots of them running through all over these mountains." He chuckled.

"It don't matter. I am getting over those mountains," Threngrin snapped.

"It's your funeral." He grinned and walked away.

Threngrin and Basil stared at each other in complete silence. Threngrin had his mind made up. He was determined to make it over the mountains.

"You coming?" Threngrin asked, waving at Basil.

Basil looked at him, then the mountains, and back at him. "It's just my life." And he followed behind Threngrin.

They could feel the air getting cooler as they got closer to the mountains. The paths on both sides were covered with rocks and boulders. Trees were so close to the path, making it hard to travel. They started climbing up small cliffs, and they knew the closer they got, it was going to be nothing but rocks and huge boulders. They made it to the end of the path, but another path led the way up the mountains. It was more of an unstable path. Basil pointed up toward a ridge that ran along the mountains, which was more difficult to climb, but maybe they wouldn't run into any kobolds.

Threngrin wasn't going to debate. He just wanted to get on the other side of the mountains. Basil took the lead, and Threngrin followed behind. They weaved around big boulders. In some places, there were dead pine needles, muffling the sound of their footsteps as they walked. It had become a maze, climbing over rocks, dodging rocks that were coming down, and going around big boulders. Threngrin knew by the way this was going that it was going to be a long journey.

There was another huge vibration right where they were walking. It shook the ground so hard, Basil lost his balance and fell. The vibration was so strong, it caused a landslide of rocks and pebbles heading toward them. Threngrin dashed behind a huge boulder and immediately motioned Basil to follow.

They decided to take the trail that was ahead of them. It rose for the first fifty yards, and it was so narrow that only one person could pass at a time. They moved slowly, and some of the rocks were really razor-sharp to them. They walked really slowly to keep their balance as they made it around the bend. Basil peered ahead and saw there was an opening. The path was beginning to widen, and they soon would be safe from the kobolds. Just as they were close to the top of one of the mountains, they heard footsteps around them.

"We were spotted," Basil said in a low voice.

Threngrin looked around but couldn't see anything. "There is nothing around us."

"Trust me, they are around us," Basil said, looking at Threngrin.

There was no other way to go. They were already about a hundred feet up in the mountain, and it was a long drop back down. They had no choice but to try to keep going. They went another ten feet, and Threngrin felt like they had eyes on them from all directions, but he couldn't see anything. Soon they were surrounded by kobolds, and they were closing in. They had no place to run, no place to go, so they froze in their tracks. It wasn't long until they had twenty kobolds around them. They all had spears. There was no way they could escape. The kobolds captured and placed them in shackles.

One of the kobolds poked Threngrin in the back with its spear, forcing them to move forward. The mountain was covered with about four hundred kobolds. This was their tribe, their place of mining. Basil and Threngrin landed in a place they didn't want to be in.

They followed about fifteen kobolds. They were heading back down the mountain but only halfway down. The area was clear of rocks and boulders. It was mostly covered with trees and bushes. They were taken into a cave. The cave had so many paths, twists, and turns, they were having trouble keeping up where they were going. They were down one path, then turned down another until they were placed in a small dead-end cave. The kobolds' settlement did look like a small village. There were kobolds running all over the place in different directions, all doing different things. There were four kobolds outside the entrance.

The cave they were placed in had a horrible smell, the floor was covered with pine needle and leaves, and there was a lantern that was placed in the corner.

"We can't stay here. There has to be a way out," Threngrin whispered, pacing the floor.

"Well, at least we have a comfortable place to sleep in before we die." Basil chuckled.

Threngrin quickly turned. "Sleep!" he snapped.

"We have slept in worse places." Basil shrugged his shoulders.

Basil watched as Threngrin paced around the room. "Can't you just relax for one second?" Basil asked, comfortable on the floor. "Just think we are safe for now."

Threngrin stood in front of Basil. "What did you mean by that?"

"Do you think we are going to get out of this mess?" Basil laughed. "They are going to sell us to the highest bidder. Plus we are surrounded by four hundred or more kobolds."

"Sell!" Threngrin said, shaking his head.

"Sell, I mean—," Basil started to explain, looking up at Threngrin. "Never mind. I could be wrong."

Basil rubbed his eyes, turned onto his side, curled up into a ball, and closed his eyes.

"What are you doing? You going to sleep?" Threngrin said in a harsh tone.

Basil opened one eye with a slight grin. "I thought I might." He rolled over and closed his eyes again.

"How can you sleep with these things right out there?" Threngrin squealed.

Basil let out a small sigh, sat up, and looked at Threngrin with one eye open and one closed. "They are not going to do anything right now. I am exhausted. I need sleep." He covered a yawn with his hand and lay back down.

Threngrin kicked the pile of pine needles next to Basil. "I have to get out of here. I have to find Sirra. You hear me! You hear me!"

Basil blinked a few times, looking up at Threngrin. "I know, but for now we can't. Trying to escape will only get us killed, you hear me?" Basil fixed his pile of needles and dropped his head onto it. "Lie down and get some sleep."

Threngrin stopped in his tracks. "I can't rest, not here. I need out." He resumed pacing.

Basil yawned. "If you can't sleep, be quiet so I can."

Threngrin continued to pace, his mind racing, and then just outside their cave, he heard rocks clicking, barking, and some other unidentifiable noise. Threngrin stopped, and Basil shot straight up.

"What in the—?" was all Basil got to say, and he was interrupted.

"Sleep! You say sleep, nothing was going to happen. We are safe," Threngrin said, walking around the cave.

Threngrin started checking corners, examining everything, looking for something to use as a weapon. Basil raised his eyebrows. He had to break the silence.

"What are you doing?" Basil whispered.

"Finding something to use as a weapon, a way out. Start looking," Threngrin demanded.

"We got pine needles. We can needle them to death." Basil grinned, holding up a handful of pine needles.

Threngrin shot Basil an evil look.

Basil got to his feet as he continued watching Threngrin running around in circles. Basil then smashed his hand on the back of Threngrin's head. "There is no weapon. We are in a stone cave. No way out." Then Basil grabbed Threngrin by his arm. "And we are shackled." And Basil sat back down.

The footsteps were getting closer, and they could hear yipping sounds. Basil jumped to his feet, and he moved slowly toward Threngrin. They stood facing the entrance. They waited patiently as the steps got closer, and then there was a vibration. The ground shook, causing stones from the cave to fall on them. Threngrin got hit on the head with a rock, knocking him to the ground. Basil lost his balance and fell. They held their breaths until the air was clear from the dust and dirt.

"They are going to kill us," Threngrin whispered.

Within minutes, there was another vibration. Threngrin placed his hands over his head as more rocks fell on top of him. They lay there quietly as they listened to the sound from outside get closer and closer.

"We need to get out. There has to be a way to escape." Threngrin continued rubbing his head.

"Taking the risk—" Basil was cut off again.

"The risks of being captured? Well, that has already happened. Let's see the risks of being imprisoned. Well, here we are." Threngrin turned to look at him more clearly. "Perhaps sold or killed. That is sure going to happen if we stay."

Basil looked at him with his little bitty eyes. "I don't mind the risk, but it could be worse if we escape," Basil commented.

Threngrin shook his head as he took a step backward. "I am getting out." His mind was made up.

"You! You have a plan?" Basil whispered, hanging on to Threngrin's arm.

"Shhhh. Quiet," Threngrin whispered.

"You better have one that doesn't require us being shackled," Basil commented, holding up his arms.

Threngrin turned and looked at Basil, his eyes squinted. "You are hopeless," was all he could say.

The footsteps were really close, and the sounds were different in their steps but the same as before. They had no clue as to who was coming down the path. Some of the steps were light, and some were heavy. It was like two different creatures.

The footsteps ceased at the entry, and they both stood close to each other. Basil's heart started to pound really fast, fear and panic setting in. "Where is your plan now?" Basil whispered.

Not paying any attention to Basil, Threngrin closed his eyes. He didn't want to see his life ending right before him. One of the kobolds walked into the cave, then two, three, and four, till there were fifteen of them crowding the entryway.

Basil couldn't breathe as he stood face-to-face with them. His hands started to shake. Basil quickly tapped Threngrin on the shoulder. "When are we going to escape?"

Threngrin opened up one eye to take a quick peek. "We are going to die." He was surprised to see this many kobolds, and they were all of different sizes.

Four of the kobolds walked behind Basil and Threngrin, poking them in the back with their spears for them to move forward. Threngrin turned around, giving them an evil look, and the kobolds poked him again. Threngrin then walked ahead.

It was a day's journey, about ten miles from there to the town where the kobolds did their trading. There were at least fifteen kobolds that accompanied them on this journey. Their travel had been slow. The path at times widened and was clear. They were miles high up in the mountain, and it took time to get back down. Basil could feel the cool air on his face, which made traveling comfortable. There were trees all over the, separated from rocks and boulders. They were coming to an area that was forbidden. They only allowed kobolds for their trade.

Four kobolds took the lead. They watched out for any danger that might be ahead of them. They traveled through the forest, and the trees became thick. The branches covered the trail, blocking most of the sunlight. The sun began to sink, and it became too impossible to see the path, but kobolds didn't need to see. They knew where they were going. The moon was peeking, hanging above them, but it wasn't bright enough to see the path.

They continued to walk in silence Threngrin at times would stop, and the kobolds would poke him with their spears. Basil pondered what he knew was going to happen by the stories he had heard, and he could do nothing. He felt hopeless. His facial expression said it all. The kobolds would at times speak among themselves, but Threngrin had no idea what they were saying. All he knew was it wasn't good.

They came to boulders and fallen trees, and the path was beginning to fade. There was an odor that was getting stronger as they got closer to wherever they were going. Basil took in a deep breath, and the smell triggered a story he once heard. He knew now where they were going.

Basil leaned in closer to Threngrin. "We have to escape real soon. The place they are taking us is evil. There is no getting out once we are in."

"We will escape once we get there," Threngrin whispered.

"You don't get it. They will put us in a dungeon, and the only escape is by death." Basil has this fearful and panicky tone in his voice.

Threngrin thought really hard and long on what Basil said. He wasn't going to take the chance that Basil was wrong. He had to break away before it was too late.

Suddenly they came to a halt. Threngrin and Basil could see a small village ahead of them. Two of the kobolds took the shackles off them, and there were two kobolds standing next to them. Threngrin knew he had to do something fast. They were getting too close to the village. They started back, walking again. To Threngrin, there was no good time to break free. It was now or never.

"When I say run, follow me," Threngrin said, leaning over to Basil.

Basil had a puzzled look on his face, but without questioning, he nodded his head.

They were getting closer to the village. The smell was getting stronger. Basil and Threngrin looked at each other. "Run now!" Threngrin yelled. They knocked the kobolds down, and Threngrin picked up a bag the kobold dropped and dashed toward the forest. Spears went flying, and kobolds scattered quickly, going in all directions. The path looked like it was coming to an end. The thick forest made it hard to tell where the path started or ended. They were at the end of their road, with kobolds running directly behind them.

"We are not going to make it out alive!" Basil yelled.

In Threngrin's mind, there were no traps, or at least he hoped this was no trap. Basil then heard a cough or something like a cough. Basil slowly turned. There was no one on the trail. Then he heard it again.

"Threngrin, don't move. Did you hear that?"

Threngrin stopped for a second. "Nope." And he bent down to pick up the bag.

In that moment, Threngrin realized it was a trap. Threngrin then heard a rumbling sound, and he quickly grabbed the bag and ran back to Basil. It was so dark, they couldn't tell which way it was coming from.

"The kobolds have caught up to us," Threngrin whispered.

"I don't think so. I think it's something else," Basil replied. Although he could be wrong. This was the kobolds' territory.

Then just off to their left, they could barely see it, they couldn't believe what they were looking at. As it got closer to them, Basil realized what it was. It was a huge boulder rolling down the mountainside, heading right toward them.

"Jump!" Basil shouted. Threngrin quickly dashed toward the bushes. The boulder just missed him by inches.

"I told you this was a trap. Now we will be lucky if we get out of this alive!" Basil yelled from the top of his lungs.

Threngrin couldn't help it. He grinned, looking at Basil. "There might be some good stuff in here," he said, holding up the bag.

140

First it was a stone, then a spear, coming from the bushes behind them. Basil quickly ducked and turned, but the stone got him in the shoulder. Soon another boulder came rolling down the mountain, and it went right between them. Then another came right down the path. It was rolling so fast and it appeared so quickly, they didn't have time to move. Threngrin fell onto the boulder. He flung himself around and managed to push himself off and landed in a mud puddle.

Threngrin struggled to get to his feet. Something grabbed his leg, knocking him down back into the mud. Then something grabbed his other leg. Threngrin knew whatever it was, it was going to drag him into the forest. Threngrin managed to twist and turn to break free from one of the grips, but he had to kick and fight hard to break free from the other grip. He slipped, slid, and rolled himself out of the mud and landed at Basil's feet.

Basil grinned from ear to ear as he helped Threngrin up off the ground and back on his feet. "I told you, but you had to have the bag. Now look at ya."

Threngrin, dripping with mud from head to toe, was so proud of himself, he held the bag really high up. "I got the bag and have not lost it."

Chapter Eighteen

Sirra sat on the edge of the cave. They were up in some mountain, and it looked to be a hundred-foot drop. As she could tell, she was unconscious for two days and had little memory of what happened. The dragon, whom she called Goldie, had been really quiet. It had made no attempt to leave. Was this her new home now? She couldn't help but think about Threngrin. He was out there somewhere, either alive or dead. It's something she would never know. From time to time the dragon would come to the entrance, look out toward the horizon, and walk back in. It's like it was waiting for something or someone. Sirra just wished she knew what was going on.

Sirra could feel the wind coming from the north. There were clouds that were forming a solid dark gray covering overhead. From the distance, she could see the mist rolling in, covering one side of the mountain. She watched as lightning struck across the sky. A storm was heading her way. The wind picked up very quickly, and she felt a drop of rain on her arm. The storm was closing in. Although she was safe, she didn't feel safe.

Sirra walked backed into the cave and sat down on the cold ground, her back up against the wall. The dragon looked at her, walked toward the entrance, and turned to look at her once again as it nodded its head. In the blink of an eye, it flew toward the sky. Sirra jumped up and ran toward the entrance. She placed her hand over her mouth as she watched it disappear in the sky. She was now completely alone. Did the dragon leave her here for good, forever? Sirra sat back down on the ground, bringing her knees up to her chest. She brought her head down to her knees and closed her eyes.

The dragon had been gone for hours. She got up and started pacing around the cave. The cave wasn't very big. It was about the size of a large bear cave. She began to worry that the dragon was never coming back and she would be stuck here for the rest of her life. Then she heard a sound coming from outside the entrance of the cave. She dashed as quickly as she could, hoping the dragon had returned. It did. The dragon returned with its claws full—with berries in one claw and twigs in the other. It then flew back out, heading down the mountain. A few minutes later, it returned with a squirrel.

Sirra was so stunned and surprised. The dragon not only went to get food for her but also went hunting. Sirra took the twigs and made a small fire. She finally got to have a real hot meal. After Sirra got done with her meal, she sat on the ledge of the cave and watched as the sun set. Tears ran down her face, and she started missing home.

Sirra felt very exhausted, although she hadn't done anything to feel so tired. She finished her meal and curled up on the floor and fell asleep. She started dreaming of home and the people there, the journey she had been on, and Threngrin. The dream she had was so upsetting, she woke up with tears in her eyes. She felt her body was so tense. In her mind she was still sleeping. Then she saw the lightning, then heard the rain hitting the ledge of the cave. She knew then she was awake. She rolled over and closed her eyes and drifted off back to sleep.

That morning, she woke feeling sluggish. It felt like she hadn't slept. She felt drugged and exhausted. There were parts of her dream she remembered, nightmares of Threngrin being lost and she couldn't find him. Her mind was so exhausted, it felt like she never slept. She rubbed her eyes, breathed in the cool air that was coming from outside, and realized she was still there.

"Are you asleep?" she asked the dragon.

The dragon lifted its head and glanced at her.

"Are we going to stay here forever?"

The dragon tilted its head to its side and laid its head back on the ground.

She could feel a knot forming in the pit of her stomach. The dragon was not saying anything to her. Without saying a word, she sat there, staring outside the cave. It was still raining. Sirra could smell the fresh rain in the air.

Her mind wandered back to Threngrin. She could feel him tugging at her, his voice echoing in her head. Sirra shook her head to clear her mind. She glanced at the dragon again. She had to remind herself this was not the time and she needed to remain calm.

In her mind, she felt Threngrin was gone, although she could hear his voice, and she was latching on that. Still she had complete doubt that he was alive.

She looked at her hands, they were shaking, and she had to force them to stop shaking. She looked at the dragon again and shook her head.

"You are going to tell me what we are doing here!" she yelled.

The dragon looked at her again but didn't say a word.

Threngrin's voice started to haunt her mind like a ghost. She started to panic. It was controlling her thoughts. All the memories of Threngrin sat there in her mind, and the worst part was not knowing if he was alive or not.

Sirra sat there on the floor, she rolled her eyes, and she let out a small scream. She clenched her teeth together. She couldn't handle it anymore, she rose up, and her eyes filled with tears, but her hands were no longer shaking.

The sense she was feeling now was the feeling of isolation, being so cold. It sent a chill through her spine, and the thought hit her like a brick. She started to panic more. The thought of her being here forever filled her head, and she ran to the entrance of the cave. She threw back her head and started to cry.

Her cry echoed in the room. She felt cold, and her teeth began to chatter. Was she really cold, or was it fear? Looking out the cave, she wasn't able to run. The cave was so high up, there was no path she could follow, and where would she go? All she really could do was to give the dragon what it wanted, and that was to stay here and wait. She tightened her fists, not liking that idea, but really, what choices did she have?

The dragon glanced up to her, its head tilted. "It will be all right."

Sirra walked over to the dragon and got on her hands and knees on the cold floor of the cave. She was still shaking, the cool air coming from the outside. She took in a deep breath. "Why won't you tell me what I am doing here? My friend is out there, lost somewhere."

The dragon placed its head next to her shoulder. "It will be all right."

"What do you mean everything will be all right!" she yelled.

The dragon just stared at her, not saying a word.

"I know you know something, but what?" she stated.

Sirra had a real hard time believing it. She threw her arms up and got up and walked to the entrance of the cave. She sat down, and the dragon sat down beside her. Instantly she turned to look at the dragon. It looked at her, and their eyes met. It had a soft, gentle look on its face—such a pure, innocent look. She opened her mouth to say something, but she could not say a word. She turned to look outside, listening to the gentle rain that was hitting the ledge of the cave, and she tightened her teeth again to keep from crying.

The sun was going down, and the temperature was dropping, so Sirra walked back inside and started a small fire. She used up the last bit of wood she had. She even ate the last bit of berries. Sirra felt exhausted, drained. She lay down next to the fire to get warm. She wasn't getting anywhere with the dragon. She hoped in the morning she would. She closed her eyes and drifted off to sleep.

- -

As fast as their legs could go, they continued running, never looking back. They wanted to get as far as they could. The forest was so thick of trees that at times they had to duck the branches that were hanging low. They ran around trees that had grown on the path. The path itself was not the best. There were twigs, loose pebbles, and even fallen tree branches. Keeping their balance while running was very difficult for them. The sun had gone down, and it was completely dark. Neither one could see where they were going.

"I can't go any farther," Threngrin cried out.

Basil stopped and turned around. "We must," he said, placing his hand on Threngrin's shoulder. "This is still kobolds' territory. We have to continue on."

Then off in the distance, Threngrin saw something on the ground next to a tree. There was just enough light coming from the moon for Threngrin to spot it.

"Look!" He pointed to the tree. Threngrin started walking toward it.

"No!" Basil yelled. "It's a trap!"

In Threngrin's mind, there were no traps, or at least he hoped this wasn't a trap. Basil then heard a cough, or something like a cough, coming from behind him. Basil slowly turned around, there was no one on the trail behind him, and then he heard it again.

"Threngrin, don't move. Did you hear that?"

Threngrin stopped for a second. "Nope." And he bent down the pick up the bag.

In that moment, Threngrin realized it was a trap. Threngrin then heard a rumbling sound, and he quickly grabbed the bag and ran back to Basil. It was so dark, they couldn't tell which way it was coming from.

"The kobolds have caught up to us," Threngrin whispered.

"I don't think so. I think it is something else," Basil replied. Although he could be wrong. This was the kobolds' territory.

Then just off to their left, they could barely see it, and they couldn't believe what they were looking at. A huge boulder rolling down the mountainside was heading right toward them.

"Jump!" Basil shouted. Threngrin quickly dashed toward the bushes. The boulder just missed him by an inch.

"I told you this was a trap. Now we will be lucky if we get out of this alive!" Basil yelled from the top of his lungs.

Threngrin couldn't help it. He grinned, looking at Basil. "There might be some good stuff in here," he said, holding up the bag.

First it was a stone, then a spear, coming from the bushes directly in front of them. Basil quickly ducked and turned, but the stone got him in the shoulder. Soon after, another boulder came rolling down the mountain, and it went right between them. Then another came right down the path toward them. It was rolling so fast and it appeared so quickly, they didn't have time to move. Threngrin fell onto the top of the boulder. He flung himself around and managed to push himself off and landed in a puddle of mud.

Threngrin struggled to get to his feet. Something grabbed his legs, knocking him down back into the mud. Then something grabbed his other leg. Threngrin knew whatever it was, it was going to drag him into the forest. Threngrin managed to twist and turn to break free from one of its grip, but he had to kick and wiggle to break free from the other grip. He slipped and slid and rolled himself out of the mud and landed at Basil's feet.

Basil grinned from ear to ear as he helped Threngrin up off the ground and back on his feet. "Told you, but you had to have the bag. Now look at ya."

Threngrin, dripping with mud from head to toe, was so proud of himself. "I got the bag and haven't lost it," he said, holding the bag up in the air.

They continued down the path, and everything was real quiet. Threngrin didn't tell Basil about the incident in the forest. He figured it was best he didn't know. Basil led the way. He had better eyesight than Threngrin. Threngrin then saw Basil duck as a spear went flying past him. He lost his footing and went down to the ground. Without thinking, Threngrin ran to Basil's side. Basil had this sick certainty that it was the kobolds and they were outnumbered.

Something from the forest grabbed Basil by the arm. Basil picked up a rock to smash the creature in the head but dropped it, which then turned into a slap. The creature tried to gain control of Basil by grabbing his other arm. Threngrin tried to kick at the creature but lost his balance and fell to the ground. Basil, struggling with the creature, managed to free his one arm, and he went to punch it. Then he, too, lost his balance, falling on top of Threngrin. Basil heard Threngrin laughing as they watched the creature disappear.

Threngrin pushed Basil off him. They got up and brushed the dirt off them. They stood there looking at each other in complete silence, and then Threngrin couldn't hold back any longer, and he broke out in complete laughter.

"Laugh, go ahead and laugh." Basil looked at Threngrin. There was nothing more he could say.

"We are alive." Threngrin chuckled.

It was too dark to tell what it was, and it happened so fast. Basil had this feeling this wasn't the end and there were more to come. Basil stared out into the forest. He thought he had seen something pass between two trees. Within seconds, a spear went passing by right between them and struck a tree that was behind them. Staring at each other, not saying a word, they took off running blindly down the path. They paused for only a few minutes, breathing heavily, listening for any sounds of danger.

Minutes later, Threngrin spotted a glowing copper ring that appeared to be near a tree. Then it vanished just as quickly as it appeared. Threngrin watched for a few seconds, and then it reappeared again. Something about it was drawing Threngrin's attention, and he had to go and check it out. He grabbed Basil by the arm and started walking toward the tree. Threngrin took the lead. He trampled through mud, tripping and stepping on twigs, and pushed away branches to get close enough to the glowing copper ring. They were just a foot away when something moved. They didn't back away fast enough, and mud and twigs splattered them. As they wiped the mud off their faces and removed some of the twigs from their hair, the glowing copper ring disappeared. They heard branches snapping behind them, and spears flew in all directions.

The look in Basil's eyes showed anger and rage. Without saying a word, Basil slapped Threngrin on the back of his head, grabbed him by the back of his shirt, and took off running. They didn't speak a single word, but their exchanges of glares said it all. Threngrin had trouble keeping up with Basil as he was dragging him out of the forest and back onto the trail. Then without saying a word, Basil started walking south on the path.

They continued on their journey without pausing. Basil wanted to be clear of this territory. Then they would be safe, and then they can rest. Basil started to walk slowly. Everything had been really quiet, but something caught his attention, a feeling that reared up inside him. It was like a warning that this was not over yet. Basil was getting tired, and Threngrin was already in a state of sleepwalking. They couldn't go on any farther no matter what he was feeling inside. Basil cleared away some bushes and decided they would hide there for the remainder of the night. It didn't take long for them to fall asleep.

The morning sun was just barely over the top of the trees, and Basil and Threngrin started the day early. They made their way to the edge of the forest, and they could see the mountain right in front of them. Even though they hadn't heard anything from the kobolds, it didn't mean they were not surrounding them. Basil spotted a small trail that led up the mountain. It was a little bit out of their way, but this way they should be safe from the kobolds. They continued to follow the rugged step trail up the mountain. Basil, standing on the path, pointed upward to a sandstone ridge that climbed high up toward the sky. They were finally close enough that they could see the top of the stone pointing to the west, and Basil knew then that they were on the right path.

Basil was in front of Threngrin, climbing up on the rocks. They followed the line of rocks and boulders, and the path was barely wide enough for them to fit through. They must have traveled about two hundred feet up the mountain, when Basil found a good spot to go where the kobolds wouldn't find them.

Nervously they inched upward, clinging on to rocks as they pulled themselves up toward the next rocks. Neither one of them had any experience in mountain climbing. This was a whole new experience to them.

Basil could feel the temperature getting cooler, and a gust of wind was hitting their backs. Threngrin was getting weak. The wind gust got him just right, and he slipped. Basil quickly grabbed his arm, breaking his fall. Threngrin managed to grab the rock in front of him and pull himself up. Waving his hand, he motioned for Basil to continue.

They had been climbing now for three hours. They sat down on a huge boulder. Out of breath, looking ahead of them, they could not believe what they were seeing. The path just got smaller. There were twists and turns. Threngrin paused for a moment. He looked down just to see how far they were. He saw rocks along the edge, and one slip meant a plunge down. It was toward a certain death.

Threngrin stood still, his legs very wobbly. A gust of wind coming from the west made them move as far away from the ledge as they could. Threngrin slipped, and a loose rock slid over the side. They listened as the rock bounced off other rocks, till there were no longer any sounds.

"Is this the only way?" Threngrin yelled.

"Yes, this way is the only way to get to the other side of the mountain!" Basil yelled back.

They continued on, fighting the strong wind. The wind was so strong, it was ripping through their hair, making it hard for them to breathe. With every step they took, it was hard for them to maintain their balance, to keep from being blown off the mountain. They finally reached the last bend, and they had to go around. Basil slowly went around it, but a gust of wind caught him just as he turned the corner. Basil slipped and fell over the ledge. Threngrin quickly got down on his knees and looked over.

Basil was holding on to one of the rocks with both hands, not letting go. The wind was strong, causing Basil to swing back and forth, making it hard for him to hang on. Threngrin looked around to see if there was a way down to him. Basil was out of his reach where he was. Threngrin saw a small path just down below him, and if he could go down there, he might be able to reach Basil.

"Hold on!" Threngrin yelled.

"Hurry! I can't hold on much longer!" Basil cried out.

Threngrin slowly placed one foot on a rock and put his hand on another, making his way down toward the path. Threngrin finally landed on the path. He took a deep breath and got on his hands and knees, and from there he crawled. The path was very narrow. He had to take it slow, or he would be over the edge too.

"Hurry! I am slipping!" Basil cried again.

"Don't rush me!" Threngrin yelled back.

Within minutes, Threngrin was right above Basil. He looked down and saw Basil. He slowly reached out his hand toward him. "Grab my hand!" Threngrin yelled.

Basil stretched out as far as he could, but Threngrin was still too far away. "I can't," Basil said with fear in his voice.

Threngrin moved a little closer to the edge. "Try again!"

Basil placed his right foot on a rock, trying to push himself up closer to Threngrin, but the rock gave way. Basil quickly grabbed on to a rock in front of him.

The wind was getting stronger, and Threngrin was having trouble keeping his balance.

"Come on, reach for my hand!" Threngrin yelled out again.

"I can't do this! I can't hold on much longer!" Basil cried out.

"You can do it," Threngrin said, waving his hand at Basil.

Basil slowly reached up to Threngrin, and Threngrin quickly grabbed Basil's hand. A strong gust of wind caught Basil, causing him to swing more rapidly. He looked into Threngrin's eyes with fear. Threngrin could feel Basil slipping out of his hands. Slowly, inch by inch, Basil slipped away.

"No! Basil!" Threngrin cried out as he watched Basil fall down below.

Threngrin moved back away from the ledge with tears in his eyes, and he curled himself up into a ball. He couldn't believe Basil was gone.

Threngrin sat there listening to the wind howl. He had no idea where to go from there. He didn't even know where he was at. Threngrin sat there staring off the edge of the mountain, trying to find the strength to carry on, but all hope for him to survive was gone. Two hours had gone by, and Threngrin still couldn't move. He was still in disbelief that Basil was gone. It was a chilling thought, remembering as he watched his friend fall to his death. Threngrin then thought to himself, *Maybe if I—*

"Lost something over the edge? It's a long way down there," a voice said, coming from behind him.

Threngrin turned and jumped quickly to his feet. "You! You!" were the only words he could think of.

Basil was standing there covered with scrapes and cuts from hitting the rocks during his fall. "You thought you could get rid of me that easy?" Basil said with a grin.

"You're alive, but how?" Threngrin said, hugging him so tight.

"When I lost my grip, I landed on a huge boulder. I was shocked to find myself still alive. When I looked up, I realized I only fell about forty feet down. I managed to get back onto the path, and here I am," he said, waving his hands again.

"I am so happy you are alive. I thought—" His voiced cracked.

"I know. Now let's get off this mountain before it gets dark," Basil said, leading the way.

They finally made their way down the mountainside. It was a very slow process, seeing how injured Basil was from his fall. The temperature had changed, and they could feel the warm air hitting their faces. Within a short distance, they got really warm. The sun was dropping behind them, and they were at the edge of the forest. No trail nor path did they find. They were somewhere but completely nowhere. They continued on a little longer, but Basil had reached his limit. Threngrin decided to rest under an old oak tree, and Basil collapsed to the ground. They were exhausted, their bodies covered with perspiration from the heat of the sun. They were used to the cool temperature, and the heat drained them.

Soon the sun had disappeared, and they were in complete darkness. The only light they had was the light from the moon and the bright stars above them. Threngrin found some berries along some trees, and he made a small fire for the night. Basil ate a few berries, and soon after, he fell asleep.

Threngrin couldn't sleep right away. The thought had entered his mind—what if they don't survive and he would never see Sirra again. The thought haunted him. He tried closing his eyes, but Sirra's face kept him from falling asleep. He lay there staring up at the sky, counting the stars that shone above him, and soon his mind drifted off to sleep.

The sun started to heat up the forest, and Basil tapped Threngrin on the shoulder. He slowly moved around, and with one eye open, he glanced up at Basil. Threngrin could already feel the sun, not realizing they had slept most of the day away. Threngrin jumped to his feet.

"The day is almost gone!" Threngrin shouted.

"I am doing fine, thanks for asking." Basil grinned.

"Oh, oh, how are you doing?" Threngrin said, grabbing his things.

"We are almost there. Relax, everything will be fine," Basil said, tapping him on the shoulder.

They soon headed out, looking for the trail that might just lead them to the village. Basil was looking for any signs that would show them the way. They had reached the center of the forest, and they continued without pausing. The forest had thick moss that covered the ground, along with heavy tree limbs. Many were tangled together from being so close. Basil got this strange feeling they were closer than he thought. Just ahead of them, there appeared to be an opening, a clearing in the forest. Traveling became slow once they hit an uneven ground. Tree roots were breaking up through the ground, making ruts and cracks on the ground's surface.

After several hours of walking, Basil came to a complete stop. He just realized that up ahead of them was clear land, which would lead them to the trail that would take them to the village.

Basil turned to Threngrin. "Straight ahead is where we need to go."

Threngrin nodded. "Shall we?" He smiled.

They continued to travel, and it seemed like they had been traveling for hours when they finally found the trail. Threngrin collapsed to the ground. His feet hurt, and he needed a rest. Basil sat down on the ground next to him.

"It is not far now. We should be there by nightfall." Basil placed his hand on Threngrin's shoulder.

They slowly got to their feet and started walking, trying to pick up the pace a little more. The sun was beaming on them directly now that they had few trees to cover them.

"I can't wait till we get there. Food, bath, real water—it all sounds so good," Threngrin said.

"Stop!" Basil said, turning toward Threngrin.

"What is it?" Threngrin asked, looking around.

"Shhhh." Basil said as he was trying to listen.

Threngrin looking around but couldn't see or hear anything.

Then Basil's hand got cold. He felt the fear inside of him. He could hear in the distance the sound of trumpets going off—the village was under attack.

"We are not far, the village is up ahead, and it's under attack. We must go now," Basil stated as he took off running.

Threngrin looked at Basil and took off running behind him. They ran as fast as they could in hopes of getting to the village before it's too late.

The dragon smelled something in the air. It was a strange faint smell. It grabbed Sirra by the waist with its claws, and quickly they flew off toward the sunset. Sirra could barely see where they were going. The sun was so bright, and with the wind, it was hard for her to keep her eyes open.

They were flying for about four hours when the dragon landed in the clearing of the forest. The dragon pushed her to move forward, and Sirra looked at it with a puzzled look on her face, but she paid it no mind and started walking. Soon they reached a village. She turned back toward the dragon, and it nodded its head and flew away.

The village had stone walls surrounding it. The village appeared to be friendly and very welcoming to all travelers. She passed through the gate without any hesitation and went to the street. The village was very busy, people shoving and pushing just to get to the shops and markets that were lined up down the street.

She continued on her way, and she found herself standing in front of a tavern, which brought back memories of Threngrin. She slowly walked up to the swinging doors and stood there. Everything about the place was very much the same as she remembered, yet so different.

"Come on, lass, getcha something to eat," a young voice said, walking into the tavern.

Sirra walked through the swinging doors. The tavern was crowded with people. Not one person paid any attention that she was there. A young gnome walked up to her.

"You gonna eat, or just stand there," he said with a grin.

"I have no silver or gold. I can't afford anything," she said.

The food did smell really good, and it had been a very long time since she had eaten real hot food.

"Come, let's get you some food. You look like you need some," the young gnome said, taking her hand.

They walked over to a round table that was near a window. She looked at the gnome, nodded her head, and sat down. She glanced out the window, and she watched the people running up and down the street. Many were laughing and whistling.

"I will be back with some food for you." He nodded and walked away.

Inside the tavern, she saw many people, of different sizes. Many were at the bar drinking, laughing. Some were sitting at the tables, eating or playing some kind of game she'd never seen before.

"Here you are, my lass, eat up," he said, putting the plate down in front of her.

"What is this place?" Sirra asked quietly.

"You a traveler? Many people are travelers. They stop by to sell, trade, to eat, and then move on. Many live here. They stopped by here, but they never left." He giggled. "This crowd, well, they live nearby. You look like you are lost, my dear lass, if I may say."

"I am—" She paused for a moment. "I got attacked and lost everything, and I am lost."

"You need a room? No worries." He waved his hand to a young dwarf. He whispered something in his ear and nodded. The young dwarf soon walked away. "Now eat, and we'll get you to a room." He patted her on the back, nodded, and walked away.

Sirra sat there looking at her plate of stew. She had no clue what it was, and it just smelled really good. She slowly took a bite, it melted in her mouth, and it was like nothing she had ever tasted before. It didn't take her long to finish her plate. She pushed her plate back and finished the mug of ale.

She sat close enough to the bar. She heard many tell tales of fights they had encountered. She listened to an old gnome telling his story of a battle he had in Belgian, how he barely escaped from a creature and how he had to fight to get to safety. Another jumped into the conversation and told his story, and she sat there listening to the four gnomes go on and on with their stories. Then she felt a hand on her shoulder, and she turned around quickly.

"You ready for your room?" he said softly.

Sirra nodded, and she pushed the chair away from the table.

She followed the young gnome down the street. She passed by shops, a blacksmith, a food market, gems—there were so many, she couldn't keep up with them all. She even saw a clothing shop. They finally paused in front of an inn, and he turned toward her.

"Come on in," he said with a smile.

Something caught Sirra's eye, and she looked up and saw the dragon flying above her. It never left her side, and she grinned from ear to ear.

She walked inside. The inn had a few tables in the center and a countertop in the corner. A young halfling came walking up to her.

"You need a room? I show you."

The halfling showed Sirra to her room, where there was a bath waiting for her and clean clothes lying on the bed. Sirra turned, and the halfling nodded and walked away.

A warm bath and a warm bed to sleep in—Sirra couldn't believe she was here. How she had been waiting so long to bathe and to sleep on something soft. Sirra took her time bathing, enjoying the warm water on her skin. When she finished, she put on the clean clothes that were there for her.

Sirra couldn't sleep. Something about this place was really strange to her. She walked outside and stood there in the street. Two guards passed her, and they were wearing clothes that she had never seen before. The material covered their heads and their faces. Across from her was a park, and children were running through the pond, laughing, chasing each other. It was midday, the air was warm, and she watched as people pass by her to meet with friends, or maybe they were heading home for a quick meal.

Then she spotted a building. The building was so impressive, but only parts of the building remained standing. There were huge granite rocks that surrounded it, and overgrown weeds had taken over the building. From what she could see, the building had a beautiful structure to it. She wondered what happened to the place. She walked over to the place and sat down on the bench that was in front of it.

Sirra then heard people yelling, screaming. Sirra quickly jumped to her feet and headed toward the center of the village. People grew in number quickly, running in all directions. Some of the villagers had formed a circle. Sirra moved her way in to hear what was being said. From the corner of her eye, she saw a gnome that was short. He had dark hair, and he was stocky and wore a beard, stumbling through the village. His clothes were torn, and he had slash marks on his face and hands. People were running, gathering what they could to defend themselves. Many stood talking to each other, waiting for someone to take action.

"There is a rabid bear outside the village. Gather the children! Run for your life!" the gnome yelled as he tried to stay standing. "Run!"

Sirra ran to the blacksmith and asked to borrow a weapon. The halfling gladly gave her a short sword. She ran through town, holding her sword, heading for the main gate. Many people watched as she ran past them, and out the gate, she went. The guards and the people were afraid of the bear from stories they had heard. No one wanted to tackle a bear, especially this one.

Sirra made it out the gate. She searched the area carefully and saw no bear. Everything seemed to be quiet and normal. After a few minutes of walking around, she decided to go back to the village. She turned and ran directly into the bear, knocking her to the ground.

The bear stood on its two back legs. It stood six feet tall, and it let out a loud roar. The people in the village heard it. Sirra quickly got back to her feet, and the bear lashed at her with its claws. Sirra quickly jumped back, and then it lashed out at her again. This time it got her in the side. Sirra swung at the bear with her sword, slashing it in the chest. She swung again and got it in its side. The bear got down on all fours, roaring again really loud, and charged after her. She didn't move quickly enough, and she hit the ground. The bear moved slowly on top of her, and she could feel its breath hitting her face. She saw its stained teeth, and the smell from its breath was making her sick. The bear let out another loud roar as it opened its mouth wider. Sirra quickly reached for her sword lying on the ground, and just as the bear was moving in for the, kill Sirra stabbed it in its chest. The bear collapsed on the ground next to her. Sirra gradually got up off the ground and headed back to the village.

A crowd of people stood there at the gate and greeted her with great gratitude. They were shaking her hand, and some even offered her gold. Sirra made her way through the crowd to the center of the village, and a young gnome stood there looking at her.

"Thank you!" he said as he reached his hand to hers. He shook her hand and gave her a hundred pieces of gold. He slowly turned and walked away.

"It's coming. It's coming!" someone yelled.

Then the sound of trumpets went off. People scattered. Sirra was so confused. She killed the bear, and it couldn't be coming. Sirra finally stopped someone. "Who is coming?"

"The red dragon! Run if you can." And the old halfling ran off.

Sirra turned toward the sky, and she saw Goldie flying in all directions. She quickly ran outside the gate, and there she saw Goldie above her, hovering. It was there for only a second, and it was gone. Sirra ran back into the village, and people had scattered everywhere. Then from the west, a red dragon flew down with fire coming from its mouth. It hit a house on the far side of the village. Sirra watched as flames shot up, and the house was gone.

Sirra ran to every building, every house, trying to help people out, to get them to a safe place.

Threngrin and Basil just reached the village when the red dragon made its first attack. Threngrin was about to take off running, but Basil grabbed his arm.

"I have to go help," Threngrin said, looking into Basil's eyes.

"If this is what you want, I won't stop you," Basil said with a soft voice.

Threngrin nodded his head. "I have to." And he took off running.

The sound of the trumpets went off again. The guards parted and headed for the gate. Threngrin saw the village people outside their homes. Many were panicking, not knowing where to go or what to do. Threngrin started directing people to head outside the village, where they would be safe. He ran into one home, gathered the people by the hand, and told them where to go. Threngrin stood outside a villager's home. He could see the red dragon in the sky, and it was flying in circles, its wings wide open as it flew overhead. The dragon circled again and swooped down very low, making another pass over the village. The people started to panic more. People started to fear that they were all going to die. There was no way they were going to escape. The red dragon then circled around again.

Then from the sky, its fiery breath hit home after home with flames. The fire soon spread to other homes.

Sirra saw the red dragon was making another round. As she was yelling at people to get out of their homes, she saw Goldie. Goldie slammed into the red dragon's side, knocking it off course. She knew for now they were safe.

Smoke soon filled the street, and ashes poured down, covering the building, the street, and the people. It became really hard to see. Screams of fear turned to screams of pain as some people died in their homes from the fire.

People started to scream out, telling others to head toward the forest. People started trampling over each other, pushing as they made their way to the gate. The red dragon made another pass. It dropped another fiery breath with flame onto a few more homes. The dense smoke choked people. It stung their eyes, and tears blinded them as they watched their homes being destroyed. The heat was so great that the building Threngrin was next to blew apart. Threngrin could feel the blast with great force.

Sirra froze as she watched Goldie making another attempt to knock the red dragon out of the sky. Sirra watched as the red dragon quickly turned around and headed right toward Goldie. With its fiery breath, it shot out flames, hitting Goldie in its side. Sirra could hear Goldie letting out a roaring sound. She quickly turned her attention to the village.

"Head for the forest! Head for the forest!" Sirra yelled out.

She saw a building in flames, and there were people inside. She quickly ran to save them. A dark shadow covered the village as the red dragon drove down on them. Sirra could hear men, women, and children screaming as another home got hit. For a moment Sirra felt helpless. There was nothing she could do to help the villagers.

Then she saw Goldie flying straight toward the red dragon. It hit the red dragon so hard, the red dragon tumbled in midair. She knew then that if Goldie wasn't giving up, neither should she. Sirra helped the people out of their homes and told them to head for the gate.

She stood in the street, and she noticed a crowd of people standing outside near the inn. The inn was in flames, and there appeared to be people inside. As Sirra got closer, she could hear people screaming, then a voice she thought she knew too well.

"Listen!" Threngrin yelled, trying to overcome the noise of people screaming. "I am going in to help these people. The inn is in flames only on the back side."

"You don't have much time," Basil stated.

"Just get them to the gate!" Threngrin yelled.

Threngrin got real quiet as he listened. He could hear the wings of the dragon getting closer and closer.

"Get them to the gate!" he yelled and ran back into the inn.

Sirra thought she saw Threngrin running back inside the inn, but she wasn't sure. As she was trying to get through, Basil was pushing the crowd to head for the gate.

"Head for the gate now!" he yelled.

But for Threngrin, it was too late. There was a whistling sound and a big boom. The inn, which was made of stones and wood, shook really hard. Sirra could hear wood splitting and breaking and a thud as boards began to fall, and soon the building started to collapse. Sirra watched, feeling paralyzed at the sight of beams one by one giving way.

"Get out!" a voice yelled.

Sirra took one more glance, and to her, it was Threngrin. The beam right under Threngrin gave a cracking sound, then split. Sirra tried to run, but Basil grabbed her by the arm and pulled her back. The beam soon gave way. The inn was now on top of Threngrin. Then Sirra heard a screeching, roaring sound. It could only mean one thing.

"The red dragon is dead! The red dragon is dead!" someone yelled.

Goldie, she thought. *Where is Goldie?* Her worst fear was that she lost not only Threngrin but Goldie too.

Sirra then screamed as loud as she could, and she broke away from Basil. She got on her knees, lifting away stone and wood.

"Threngrin!" she cried out.

The stones were heavy, and the beams, she could only move them inch by inch.

"Don't just stand there! Help me!" she yelled.

Basil and a few others pitched in to help, and within a few minutes, she found Threngrin, barely alive. They dragged him out of the rubble and onto the street. She placed his head in her lap.

She placed her hand on his chest. She could feel his heart fading, and tears rolled down her face. She felt something nudging her in the shoulder. She turned and saw it was Goldie. Its body was completely covered in burns, but it managed its way to her. It placed its head next to her, as it took its last breath, and then it closed its eyes. Sirra felt its breath leaving its body. A dragon she did not like, a dragon that became her best friend.

Basil walked up to Sirra and placed his hand on her shoulder. "Close your eyes, and count to three."

Sirra looked up at this strange man. "What?"

"Go on, close your eyes, and count to three," he said, waving his hand.

Sirra slowly closed her eyes, and as she was counting, the man quickly made a few circles around them. And in the blink of an eye, everything changed once again.

"What I am doing here? What just happened?" Threngrin said, looking up at Sirra.

"You are okay."

Sirra and Threngrin then looked around them. The village was back to normal, and people where rushing to the market, pushing through the crowd to meet up with friends. It took Sirra and Threngrin a few minutes to realize that they were back in their own hometown. Being a little confused, they both looked up and saw that Basil was no longer there.

"What?" Threngrin yelled at the old gnome standing there. "It was you. Pilwinkle, you made this whole illusion, and you were Basil?"

Pilwinkle was the oldest gnome in town. He could make illusions happen without anyone realizing they're illusions. Pilwinkle had been around for over ninety years and had seen a lot, but one thing he was good at was illusions, which got him into trouble at times.

"Wait, you mean, this whole thing was never real, and it was all an illusion? And Goldie?" Sirra stated.

"Well, yes, none of it is real. It was an illusion. You said you wanted an adventure. I gave you one." Threngrin took one step toward him.

"You even made Goldie up? I can't believe you. Why!" Sirra yelled.

"Well, just think of the adventure you both had." Pilwinkle chuckled

"And all the things we found?" Threngrin asked.

"It's gone," Pilwinkle stated, shrugging his shoulders. "Sorry, you can't keep what you never really found."

"Oh, I can't believe you did this, and Goldie, you—," she said, holding her fist up at him.

Pilwinkle walked over to Sirra and placed his hand on her shoulder. "I can make things that are so true, but—"

Sirra slapped Pilwinkle's hand away from her before he could finish his sentence. "I don't want to hear it," Sirra snapped.

"But wait, Sirra. Look up," Pilwinkle said, pointing to the sky.

And there was Goldie, flying down toward her. "He is yours to keep," Pilwinkle said.

Sirra ran up to Goldie with tears in her eyes. She couldn't believe it was here. She couldn't believe it was alive and it was hers to keep. She was still upset at Pilwinkle, but overall, she was happy to have Goldie.

"But I am still going to kill you," Threngrin said as he walked toward Pilwinkle.

"Threngrin, come on, you have to admit it was a good, fun adventure," Pilwinkle said, holding his hand up to Threngrin as he was backing up.

"Fun? It was no adventure. You made the whole thing up, you old goat. That was a dirty old trick!" Threngrin yelled.

"Watch it. I can make a door, and you'd never know what's on the other side." Pilwinkle chuckled.

"You—" Pilwinkle quickly put his hand over Threngrin's mouth.

"Now, now, Threngrin, just wait for your next adventure." Pilwinkle smirked as he ran off.

"I am going to kill you, Pilwinkle." And Threngrin ran after him. "I am going to kill you!"

Sirra gave Goldie another hug. The dragon looked at her with great happiness and joy. But one thing did lie on her heart, and she had to ask, "So you knew this whole time?"

The dragon smiled, leaned over, and it whispered in her ear, "I love you too."

Sirra and the dragon laughed as they watched Threngrin chase Pilwinkle. Sirra was glad to be back home. What an adventure—one they will never forget.

CPSIA information can be obtained
at www.ICGtesting.com
Printed in the USA
BVHW030941060219
539540BV00014B/11/P

9 781796 013610